More Wild Westerns

MORE WILD WESTERNS

Edited by Bill Pronzini

Walker and Company
New York

First published in the United States of America in 1989 by Walker Publishing Company, Inc.

Published simultaneously in Canada by Thomas Allen & Son Canada, Limited, Markham, Ontario.

Library of Congress Cataloging-in-Publication Data

More wild westerns / edited by Bill Pronzini.
    p. cm.
  ISBN 0-8027-4097-9
  1. Western stories. I. Pronzini, Bill.
  PS648.W4M67   1989
  813'.0874'08—dc19   89-5616
                                            CIP

Printed in the United States of America

10 8 6 4 2 1 3 5 7 9

CONTENTS

ACKNOWLEDGMENTS

"The West's Number One Problem," by Ryerson Johnson. Copyright © 1945 by Short Stories, Inc. First published in *Short Stories*. Reprinted by permission of the author.

"Gamblin' Man," by Dwight V. Swain. Copyright © 1947 by Popular Publications, Inc. First published in *Dime Western* under the title "Sentimental Gentleman of Death." Reprinted by permission of the author.

"The Mestenos," by H. A. DeRosso. Copyright © 1955 by Stadium Publishing Corp. First published in *Western Novel and Short Stories* under the title " 'I Will Kill Even You.' " Reprinted by permission of Scott Meredith Literary Agency, Inc., 845 Third Avenue, New York, N.Y. 10022.

"Long Guns and Scalp Knives," by William R. Cox. Copyright © 1942 by Popular Publications, Inc. First published in *Dime Western*. Reprinted by permission of the author.

"Dig My Grave Deep," by Talmage Powell. Copyright © 1949 by Popular Publications, Inc. First published in *Fifteen Western Tales*. Reprinted by permission of the author.

"The Big Hunt," by Elmore Leonard. Copyright © 1953 by Popular Publications, Inc. First published in *Western Story Magazine*. Reprinted by permission of the author and H. N. Swanson, Inc.

"Plague Boat," by Frank Bonham. Copyright © 1942 by Short Stories, Inc. First published in *Short Stories*. Reprinted by permission of the author.

"The Last Pelt," by Bryce Walton. Copyright © 1954 by Popular Publications, Inc. First published in *Western Rangers*. Reprinted by permission of Mrs. Ruth Walton.

"Comanche Passport," by Will Henry. Copyright © 1951 by The

INTRODUCTION

Knighthood's still in flower. For, riding the crest of popularity at the present time . . . is the Western story.

On that grim dark day when romantic literature perishes, the soul of man shall perish, too. But as long as ideals are cherished; as long as stark courage engenders shining admiration in the heart; as long as men have splendid creeds to which their lives are pledged, Romance, a Joan of Arc in glittering armor, shall roam the earth.

The savage satire of Don Quixote failed to slay her, and the modern realists whose pens are held in far unsteadier fingers than those of Cervantes cannot prevail . . . For the Western story is America's saga of chivalry. It is Uncle Sam's contribution to high adventure. The vast rolling prairies of the new continent gave up its gold, its grain, and yielded a literature as well.

These words, perhaps better than any other, capture the spirit of pulp Western fiction. And well they should, for they were written more than fifty years ago to introduce the very first anthology of pulp Western stories, *Western Thrillers* (1935); and they were penned by "The Little Giant of the Pulps," Leo Margulies, editorial director of the Thrilling Group, who was responsible in the 1930s, 40s, and early 50s for buying millions of words of frontier fiction annually for *West, Thrilling Western, Popular Western, Rio Kid Western, Range Riders Western,* and many other magazines. If anyone knew and understood Western pulp, it was Leo Margulies.

He says further in his *Western Thrillers* introduction that stories of the West "remain the modern 'Idylls of the King.' They are the essence of that glamour, that romance which is America's own heritage, which will live as long as men are taught to read and to write. [And] I'm sure that if you've ever dreamed of the Old West, if you've ever thrilled to the jongleur's tales of derring-do, if you've ever sighed to ride a charging bronc over an endless plain with the clean smell of sage in your nostrils, there's something in this book which will cause your heart to pick up a beat."

This was true of the stories in *Western Thrillers,* and just as true fifty-one years later of the entries in *Wild Westerns* (Walker, 1986), and is equally true fifty-four years later of the selections in *More Wild Westerns.* The thirteen tales in these pages—which originally appeared in such now-brittle and crumbling pulp-paper periodicals as *Dime Western, Western Story, Short Stories, Fifteen Western Tales, Western Rangers, Zane Grey's Western Magazine, West, Western Novel and Short Stories,* and *Northwest Romances*—are more of the best of what the Western and adventure pulps offered their readers. And that is entertainment of the first order.

One might even say, as Leo Margulies did about his *Western Thrillers,* that what awaits you here is a veritable "fiction feast."

—Bill Pronzini
Sonoma, California
August 1988

More Wild Westerns

THE HORSE THIEF

Charles Alden Seltzer

STORIES of cowboys and cattlemen, of cattle drives and ranch and range life on the frontier, have been the most popular of all Western fiction throughout this century. Owen Wister's Virginian *was the first great cowboy hero; others who have stood the test of time include Clarence E. Mulford's Hopalong Cassidy and B. M. Bower's Chip of the Flying U. The cowboy hero was likewise king of the Western pulps, where he could be found in every issue of every title from 1920 into the 1950s. Writers such as Walt Coburn and Charles Martin built entire careers writing little else but cattle-baron and range-rider tales for the pulps—with such success on Coburn's part that in the early fifties, a short-lived periodical was launched by Popular Publications in his honor:* Walt Coburn's Western Magazine.

Another successful practitioner of the cowboy story was Charles Alden Seltzer (1875–1942). In a career that lasted more than forty years, beginning in 1900 with the publication of his first novel, The Council of Three, *Seltzer wrote highly romanticized—and highly popular—yarns about the rangelands of Arizona and other parts of the Southwest. Not all of his novels feature cowboys and cattlemen, but the best ones do:* The Trail to Yesterday *(1913),* "Drag" Harlan *(1921),* A Son of Arizona *(1931),* Silverspurs *(1935), and* Treasure Ranch *(1940). His most accomplished short stories are likewise cowboy adventures: those in his two collections,* The Range Riders *(1911) and* The Triangle Cupid *(1912), and "The Horse Thief," an early tale first published in* Outing Magazine *in 1912 (and reprinted in slightly altered form in the pulp* West *in 1950, the version which appears here).*

It was an opportunity too good to be missed. By sheer accident, Ben Ferris had seen Dave Rankin loping his pony over the trail towards Dry Bottom.

Ferris leaned forward to watch Rankin's sturdy shoulders bobbing along the trail far below. A little grin lighted his pleasing features. That meant the Circle Y ranch would be relieved of Dave Rankin's somewhat baleful presence for quite some time. And likewise it meant that Rankin's daughter Martha would be temporarily accessible to one Ben Ferris. For there was no denying that Dave Rankin looked upon Ben Ferris and his attentions to his daughter with a noticeable lack of enthusiasm.

"To be downright blunt about it," Ferris admitted, "I'd say the old boy hates my—uh—insides."

There was something more to it than that. Rankin had been missing horses for some time and had reached the boiling point about it.

"There's no room in this country for horse thieves!" he had loudly and publicly declared. "And danged little room for nesters, which is sometimes simultaneous with horse thieves. I'm serving fair warning—I'm putting my man Hubbell on the job to get these rustlers and I ain't particular whether he brings them in dead or alive!"

Hubbell was a gunman of repute in that country, and Rankin's stand was therefore not to be underestimated. Moreover, Ferris had the uncomfortable feeling that whenever Rankin talked about horse thieves, he meant none other than Ben Ferris.

"But shucks," he shrugged it off, "any fool would think a man didn't have the right to run a little ranch."

He watched Rankin disappear among the cottonwoods and whirled his pony to line it out in a dead run for the Circle Y.

* * *

Ferris struck the washout back of the ranchhouse and came upon a girl of eighteen, hanging the family wash upon a sagging line between two trees. His heart leaped, as for a moment he thought it was Martha, but then he recognized her as the younger sister, Mary.

"Hello," he said.

The girl looked up and saw him, and her lips parted in an unmistakable flash of pleasure at seeing him.

"Why, hello, Ben!" she cried, and made an attempt to force back the windblown, golden hair which rippled forward over her eyes. "It's been ages since you've visited us."

"No secret about that," Ferris said candidly. "Martha home?"

The animation died on the girl's face. Abruptly she turned back to her wash. Ferris observed the change, and though he was not a conceited man, he would have been obtuse if he had failed to understand it. She liked him, admired him. He was flattered, but there was no room in his mind or emotions for her and her problems. His whole being was focused to a blinding point upon her sister Martha. He felt a nudge of pity for her and even a certain comradeship, for he realized that he was treating her much as her sister Martha treated him.

"I'm sure glad to see you, Mary," he said.

"Yes, you are," she said, her voice muffled because of her turned face. "You asked about her before you said a word about me. She's where she usually is—in the hammock. Reading, I reckon. She's done nothing else since she's been home from the East."

With which vindictive words she gave herself to the flapping wash, ignoring Ferris completely.

The cowboy's face puckered, but the situation was beyond him. Without further words he spurred his pony to the corral gate where he dismounted, took down the bars, removed the saddle and bridle, and turned the horse loose.

Then he walked briskly around the corner of the ranch-house.

Left alone, the girl stood stiffly, staring straight ahead at a sheet which threatened to flap in her face. After a moment her hands rose to cover her face and she stood that way, with head downbent and the sun making a tangled glory of her hair.

Ben Ferris found Martha in the hammock with a book. She looked up languidly and made a sound which he interpreted as a greeting and then went back to her book.

Ferris's sombrero had come up, and it waggled loosely in his hand. Martha's welcome had certainly been less cordial than her sister's. Did it mean his presence was undesirable? Or merely that Martha, with her Eastern ways and reserve was less effusive? He was both irresolute and resentful. Yet the resentment disappeared immediately when the girl looked up from her book again and gave him a bewitching smile.

"Sit by me," she said. "Fetch that chair and set it here where I can get a good look at you. You haven't been to see me in ever so long."

She was beautiful, there was no denying it. Her figure was slender and lithe, yet full, with a suggestion of plumpness that was most attractive and that showed to good advantage in the hammock. She was, though Ferris had never chanced upon the word, glamour itself.

He felt her charm, the romance surrounding her, and felt the terrible craving to be with her all the time which so deviled him. Yet he was not blind—he might have resented the blunt statement that she was fickle—but felt and saw in her actions a certain insincerity that troubled him mightily.

"It wasn't all my fault, being away so long," he said. "I wouldn't say you treated me right smart when I was over here last time."

"No? You're really very entertaining, Mr. Ferris. Just how did I treat you?"

He shrugged. "I've forgot most of it. But you called me 'original' and it don't tickle me to be insulted."

Martha bit her lip. "I like men who can give as good as they take," she said.

It was not the first time she had flicked him with the quirt of sarcasm. Ferris shrugged.

"Reckon I'm not a top hand at ray-par-tee," he said. "Mebbe you do better with that gunman, Hubbell."

"Mr. Hubbell is a gentleman," Martha said.

"How would you know?" Ferris inquired mildly.

Her eyes suddenly brightened. "Why, here's Mr. Hubbell now!"

She raised herself and sat on the edge of the hammock to watch the man approaching.

Hubbell was not big. But he was as compact and muscular as a cat and he walked with the ease and grace of one. Ferris, grudgingly, could not but admit his attractiveness and could see how Martha might be interested in him.

Yet there was something about him which stirred doubt in the young rancher's mind. Some suspicion, some feeling that when it came to the pinch Hubbell might not be there—an idea that way down there might be some yellow in the man's makeup.

He knew of Hubbell's speed with a six-gun. Rankin had not been bluffing when he made his brag. Yet Hubbell had been on his search for two months and no horse thieves had been caught. Ferris had his own ideas about that, too.

Hubbell came up to throw Ferris a look of insolent dislike.

"Not working today?" he inquired.

Ferris returned the look. "You reckoning to be my boss?" he replied.

"No, thanks," Hubbell returned with heavy irony. He looked at the girl. "You must find reading more interesting than talking to some men," he observed.

"Why, yes, I do," said Martha, smiling up into his eyes. "But Mr. Ferris is so original he would never bore me."

There it was again, that highly suspect word "original." What did she mean by it, anyway?

"You're both very interesting," Martha went on. She caught the glare of dislike which was fairly crackling in the air between the two of them, and her voice rose in delight. "Why, I do believe you'd actually fight right this instant. And over me!"

The voice and the tone jarred Ferris unpleasantly. She sounded positively delighted at the prospect.

"No, I won't have it," Martha said. "But I do love to see a man who can shoot—who can use a gun when it is really needed."

Ferris saw the smug superiority on Hubbell's face. The gunman, he knew, would be fully half a second faster than he in getting his pistol out and was considered a dead shot. That took him out of Ferris's class completely so far as hostilities were concerned.

He became aware that Mary was standing nearby and realized she must have heard some of the conversation. There was something in her eyes which might have been mockery, but it changed as she glanced from him to her sister.

"What would you like for dinner, Miss Martha?" she asked in the tone of a servant addressing her mistress.

Martha appeared not to notice the heavy sarcasm. "Couldn't we have chicken?" she asked.

"If you'll kill them," Mary replied.

"Oh, very well," Martha said, with irritating mildness. "If you won't, I'm sure Mr. Hubbell will oblige."

Hubbell grinned with relish. "There's some chickens," he said, pointing to some scratching near the pasture fence. "Mebbe Ferris would like to shoot them?"

Ferris reddened. He knew he couldn't shoot the heads off

chickens at fifty feet, and he hated Hubbell bitterly for making a fool of him.

"No thanks," he replied stiffly. "I'm no chicken executioner."

He caught Martha's eyes upon him, filled with scorn, and thought he detected pity in Mary's eyes.

Hubbell sneered. His gun flashed. Three reports rolled as one as three chickens, headless, flopped in the dust.

Ferris looked away, lips tight. After a while he became aware of movement, glanced up to see Martha and the gunman walking casually toward the riverbank. Mary was still near him and there was something different from pity in her eyes.

"I'm sorry, Ben," she said. "Everybody can't shoot chickens like Hubbell. But you might help me pluck them."

It was two weeks later that Ben Ferris met Dave Rankin on the river trail, almost within sight of Ferris's little ranch. Unlike his usual custom, Rankin halted and grinned insolently at Ferris.

"I hear Martha's developing some finicky appetites," he commented.

"Meaning?" asked Ferris warily.

"Why, lately she's sorta stuck on chicken dinners. Providing," he added, "she can get someone to shoot their heads off."

The young man flushed and held his peace.

"That gunman of mine," went on Rankin, "can shoot other things besides chickens. Was I you I wouldn't monkey around with him."

"Dave," said Ferris, "I reckon I'm not just imagining things when I suspect you're trying to sic Hubbell onto me. Do you think I stole your horses?"

"What I think and what I can prove is two different things," Rankin said. "And I'm not saying before I can back up my words. But I'll tell you this: there's too many nesters in this country. A man-sized ranch ain't got a chance to feed its stock. That ranch of yours—"

Ferris laughed coldly. "I know what you're driving at, Dave," he said. "My quarter section is proved up and neither you nor your gunman are scaring me out. Hear?"

"I'm not in the mood for arguing with you now," Rankin said. "I got business in Las Vegas. But I've told Hubbell to keep his eyes open. You might remember that."

He urged his pony forward and did not look back.

For a time Ferris sat his horse, thinking. "Sounds like Rankin expects some horses stole while he's away," he muttered. Then a grin stole across his face. "Be a pity to disappoint him." His teeth flashed. "So it would!" He wheeled his pony and spurred hard for the ranch. . . .

Just at dusk, Hubbell unsaddled his mount at the corral, having come in from a ride with Martha. A clatter of hoofs advertised the presence of a rider. A stranger rode up and stopped at the gates. "Know a fellow named Hubbell here?" he asked.

"I'm Hubbell."

"Yeah? Got a letter for you."

"A letter for me?"

"Yep. Was riding along the Dry Bottom trail, going to Lazette, when I met a feller hitting the breeze the other way. Said his name was Dave Rankin of the Circle Y and asked me to bring this letter along to Hubbell. So if you're him, here's your letter and I'm on my way to Lazette. So long!"

Hubbell turned the letter over several times wonderingly, then tore it open.

Hubbell:

I'm sending you this by a man I met near Dry Bottom. I picked up some information that there's a deal on tonight to steal some of our horses. Can't turn back to help you, but you can handle this all right yourself. Hide in the brush near the firs alongside Yellow Horse crossing and bore the fellow who is stealing the broncs. Go alone—a

*crowd might scare him off. He's sure to be at Yellow Horse. I'd come
myself, but I got to be at Las Vegas. Good luck. Burn this note.*

Dave Rankin

Hubbell resaddled his pony. He tied it to the corral rail
and proceeded to the bunkhouse where he ate lightly, saying
nothing to any of the men. After his meal he returned to his
pony, mounted, and departed up the river trail.

＊

Yellow Horse Crossing drowsed in the moonlight. Where the
red buttes broke abruptly off and sank to the level of the
river bottom, there was a dim trail that led to the grove of
firs about which Rankin had written. Hubbell knew the trail
well.

He reconnoitered first, dismounting and scouting the
shadows of the rock promontory that overhung the trail. He
was a long time gaining the shadows, but when he did was
surprised to find two horses tied there. With a triumphant
grin, he sank further back into the brush to await the coming
of the men who had stolen these animals.

His only emotion was scorn for the ease with which the
whole business was coming off. A sound penetrated his
consciousness. He wheeled swiftly, hands dropping to his
holsters, to see half a dozen men ringing him, guns drawn.

"Hands up!" came the command, and Hubbell did not risk
drawing his own guns against such odds.

"We've got him, boys," said one of the men. He came
forward into the moonlight and Hubbell recognized Ferris.
At about the same moment, Ferris recognized him.

"Shucks!" he said. "It's Hubbell."

Grim-faced punchers advanced to surround the gunman
and disarm him. With a start Hubbell recognized the man
who had brought him the note that evening.

"I reckon you boys are making a mistake," he said to
Ferris.

The latter did not smile.

"Mebbe you think it's a mistake," he retorted coldly. "But I reckon you won't deny you was pretty close to them horses." He laughed ironically. "We've been expecting you. I reckon when Rankin hears about this he'll know why you haven't catched that horse thief you've claimed to be looking for."

"What are you talking about?" Hubbell demanded. "You don't think I was stealing these horses?"

"No?" jeered Ferris. "Ask the boys what they think?"

The grim silence told Hubbell what they thought.

"It'll tickle Rankin a heap to learn how you been playing him for a sucker," Ferris went on. "Pretending to be looking for his horse thief when you were the thief yourself all the time."

"You fellows are just funning," Hubbell said, "but you don't scare me, so call it off. I came here to catch the thief. Got a note from Rankin telling me." He pointed a finger at the man who had brought the note. "Ask him—he brought it to me."

Ferris turned. "Did you give him a note from Rankin?"

"I ain't seen Dave Rankin in a month." Literally he was telling the truth—he hadn't seen Rankin in a month. He had told Hubbell merely that he had met a man who gave his name as Dave Rankin, but hadn't said it was Dave Rankin. A very technical point.

"Where is this note?" Ferris demanded of Hubbell.

"I burned it, like Rankin said!" Hubbell cried. Grins appeared on the faces of the men.

"Yeah," Ferris said coldly. "A man brought you a note, only he don't seem to know anything about it. And you had a note, only you burned it. And we found two of my horses here and caught you sneaking around in the brush. I reckon that's enough, Hubbell."

Two of the punchers seized the gunman's arms. A third tossed the end of a rope over a tree branch. A fourth somberly cocked his six-shooter.

Hubbell's fortitude suddenly deserted him. His knees

melted, he sagged and began to plead and to babble. Some of the men smiled derisively, others turned their backs. Then all withdrew, leaving Ferris and the captive alone.

A little later they heard Ferris calling them. They returned, again ranging themselves about Hubbell. The once arrogant gunman was crushed, a drooping figure of a man who could meet no one's eye. Ferris spoke.

"I want you boys to witness that this here man has promised to hit the breeze out of the country. I'm letting him off and he's getting out and ain't never coming back. That right, Hubbell?"

The gunman nodded without speaking. His horse was brought. He was boosted into the saddle. Grimly and silently, the little ring of men watched him depart down the river trail.

Dave Rankin heard the news at Dry Bottom on his way back from Las Vegas. When he found Ben Ferris sitting beside the hammock where his daughter Martha reposed, Dave put the best face possible on the matter and came forward with a smile.

"I'm sorry I got you wrong, Ben," he said, extending his hand. "Who'd ever think it would be Hubbell that'd turn out to be the thief? How'd you get on to him?"

Ferris met his eye calmly. "Dave," he said, "if you want the truth, I didn't have a smidge of proof. I was like you—I had heaps of suspicions, but no evidence. Fact, I didn't think I could get the deadwood on Mr. Hubbell. I set a trap for him, hoping, mebbe, to scare him out of the country. Nobody was more surprised than me when I scared a full confession out of him! He was your thief all right, but Dave, it was just plumb luck that turned him in."

Rankin laughed. "I like a man that's lucky," he said, and cast a significant eye at his daughter Martha. "Stay for dinner, Ben. Mebbe Mary'll have chicken."

"Hubbell a horse thief," Martha said. "Who would ever have believed it?"

"Me," said Ferris.

"Well, I'm glad he's gone," Martha said. "I never quite liked him, anyway."

At which remarkable statement, Ben Ferris's eyebrows climbed up and threatened to become lost in his hair.

"Now you," said Martha demurely, "you are—you are—"

"Original," supplied Ferris. He sighed. "I ain't forgotten what happened the day Hubbell shot the chickens."

"You mean my walking off with him? Oh, I just wanted to humor him. Wouldn't pay to antagonize a man who could shoot like that, would it?"

"Reckon not," Ferris said dryly. "You don't think I antagonized him by chasing him out of the country, do you?"

"Oh, you!" said Martha. "We did have chicken for dinner that day. And a little while ago I saw Mary killing some chickens for dinner. Isn't that odd?"

"Very odd," said Ferris. His usual fluster at merely being in her presence was strangely missing. He felt cool, detached, curiously relieved. He stood up and stretched languidly.

Martha surveyed his tall figure with admiration. "Would you like to walk down to the river with me?" she asked.

"Reckon not," said Ferris. "Hubbell did that and look what happened to him." He started off, then glanced back over his shoulder. "You take your walk," he said. "I'm going to help Mary pull the feathers off them chickens."

THE WEST'S NUMBER-ONE PROBLEM

Ryerson Johnson

IT is a popular misconception that pulp editors were only interested in violent action stories with hard-boiled heroes, stereotypical villains, familiar settings, and conventional plotlines. In truth, pulp editors wanted what any good editor wants: originality in plot, character, theme, and writing. And when they got a story such as "The West's Number-One Problem," as Dorothy McIlwraith did at Short Stories in 1945, they not only bought it with all dispatch, they featured it prominently on the cover of the issue in which it was published.

Just what was the West's number-one problem? Fencing, of course. "It was so real in the years just after the Civil War," Ryerson Johnson wrote to the readers of Short Stories, "that questions pertaining to fencing occupied more space in the public prints in the prairie and plains states than any other issue—political, military, or economic. . . . What I set out to do in this story was to come at the barb-wire revolution from a new angle—way back when it was only an idea in the minds of a few dreamers. . . . Before the barb-wire men, were the hedge men—professional hedge growers, traveling salesmen, brokers, wholesalers. Every one of them stood to have his means of livelihood cut from under him by the introduction of wire for fencing. [So] it was pretty much every man for himself, dog eat dog, and the devil take the hindmost. It makes good dramatic material for fiction."

It does, indeed.

A former coal miner, and a constant traveler, Ryerson

Johnson was a prolific contributor to the Western and adventure pulps during the thirties and forties. Among his output were numerous stories set on the Far Northern frontier, and a series of action novelettes for Star Western *about the famous "gunman of freedom," Len Siringo. Two of his pulp serials were published as novels,* South to Sonora *(1946) and* Barb Wire *(1947); the latter tells the whole barb-wire story, from its invention on through its sometimes bloody, westward sweep. Johnson is still actively writing today, some sixty years since his first published story, selling fiction and articles to a wide variety of adult and young-adult publications.*

A man with a nickeled law badge on his leather vest watched incuriously from the ferryman's tar-paper shack while Hally's wagon came off the landing apron. The wagon rocked with sodden creakings as Hally led the mules to the tie-rail askew between muddy snags of willows.

He had some time to kill. He had to wait for the ferry to go butting back across the Mississippi for Jake and the other wagon. Excitement needled him softly as his eyes traced out the road that wound off across the Illinois flood bottoms to the bluffs, blue in the miasmic autumn haze.

Lincoln's country!

That was how Hally Harper, of Texas, had always thought of it up north here—Abe Lincoln's country. In Texas the War Between the States had never really touched them closely. No invading army had raked them up and down. Some blood had been spilled, but it hadn't wet down Texas land; and no barns had been burned. Hally had been much too young for the war anyway, so that now, ten years afterwards, standing on Lincoln's land, there was no bitterness in his heart—just this excitement as he breathed in the alien air of the great gray river, air so thick with earthy essence that to a dry-land man it was like inhaling frogs and fish and mud.

His lank body bent, and his hand scooped up some of the caked river loess. He examined the dirt with critical interest, held it to his nose to smell, let it dribble away between rolling fingers. While his hand dusted itself against travel-worn jeans, his hungry eyes kept looking. So this was the black dirt country, where corn grew tall and hogs grew round with fat, the place which—according to Little Bit Ewing's father, who should know—was destined to become the market feeder for all the cows in Texas.

Thinking of Little Bit's father, of course, made him think of Little Bit. And thinking of Little Bit pulled at him inside somewhere, made him feel sad and lonesome and very far from home. Little Bit was only seventeen, three years younger than himself, but the way she talked at him, with that grown-up woman seriousness, made him feel younger than *she* was sometimes. Little Bit had blond hair that was natural-curly, and the same tawny-smooth color, he'd bet, as this Illinois corn when it was silking out.

It was because of her that he was here, so he could prove to her good and plenty that he had reformed, and become the kind of man a girl could depend on, a good provider. Money had never interested him a nickel's worth. Not till now. He just liked to be figuring on things, new things, and working to make things grow.

But Little Bit had shown him how wrong that was. It was downright scan'lous, she averred, the way he went around all the time with his head in the clouds and let people take advantage of him. It wasn't as if he wasn't smart. She'd point out that he had been almost the first one to foresee that fencing was going to be the West's number-one problem. He hadn't let her tough-hided father or anyone else talk him out of that notion.

"The open range is doomed," he had indelicately informed Little Bit's father, who was one of the real old-time cowmen. "With these new railroads reachin' out onto the plains, bringin' in more and more settlers, dry-land farmin's the order of the day. And farmin' and ranchin' can't abide side by each—not without proper fences—"

"Proper fences, there's the catch," Little Bit's father had pounced upon him. "Here on the plains there ain't no proper fences. Too expensive to haul in plank and rail all the way from timber country. Government statistics show that fences out here cost more'n the stuff they inclose—"

"Sure," Hally pounced back. "That's why the West's been so slow to grow. No proper fences. But now there is one. Hedge—"

"Hedge!" The vast contempt of the open-range man was in the word. "Hedge! I've seen it all. Shanghai, bloomer, mesquite, Cherokee rose. . . . I've even heard 'em advocate, serious, prickly pear. But there's somethin' the matter with all of 'em. Either it costs out of sight to grow, or takes too long, or it spreads all over creation, or the stock butts through it, or *eats* it—"

"I didn't say just any kind of hedge, Mr. Ewing. One special hedge. Osage orange."

"You meanin' bois d'arc, young Harper, like grows wild all up and down the cricks? What the Indians used to make their bows from?"

"The same, Mr. Ewing. Full grown, it won't cost hardly fifty cents a rod. Four years after planting it'll make a thorny wall, as a fella says, that's pig-tight, horse-high, bull-strong. Yes sir, Mr. Ewing, osage orange is the answer to the fencin' problem."

Mr. Ewing disposed of the argument by saying flatly, "I haven't got any fencin' problem, young Harper."

But Hally hadn't let him get away with that. "Time's quick coming when you will, sir," he had sounded dire warning.

It certainly wasn't very bright of Hally, Little Bit had pointed out severely, for him to cross her father this way—not when Hally pretended to love her father's daughter so much.

Pretended! When it was making him sick, he loved her so much! But she'd fall in love with him all over again. She'd drop Jake like a hot pancake when they got back to Texas again, and flashed the profits of this wagon trip on her. Four thousand and eight hundred dollars! That's the way this boom Illinois market was going to pay off on what he was wheeling in the two wagons. Little Bit would see then what kind of a provider he'd be.

Oh, this *pasear* into the corn country was going to fix everything fine for everybody! Even Jake, one way of looking at it. Because Little Bit had never been Jake's girl anyway, not rightly speaking. So he wouldn't miss her for very long. It might even be a relief to him, because the main thing Jake liked to do was make money, and with Little Bit out of his life he'd have more time for making it, because Little Bit was the kind of girl who took an awful lot of a man's time—

"You hard o' hearin', bub?"

It wasn't so much the voice that snapped Hally out of his daydreaming, as the sun glinting in his eyes from the nickeled law badge. The man himself was the one who had been standing in the doorway of the ferryman's shack when Hally drove off the ferry. Little and mild looking, he carried a day's growth of gray stubble on his leathery face. From under a shapeless felt hat his blue eyes looked out, mild too, but somehow sharp at the same time, not missing anything.

Hally stirred, blinked. "I can hear all right."

The lips warped into a slow grin, showing tobacco-stained teeth. "I spoke twice and you never budged. I dunno what, exceptin' a woman, could put a man out of the world thataway."

Hally's face turned a brick red. He clamped his lean jaws tight and looked away, trying to think of something man-of-the-world to answer. His glance was held by the hedge straggling back over the bottom land from river's edge. Leafless now, its thorny branches were limned against the autumn sky. Cornstalks and other flood debris clogged the hedge on the up-current side, and where the water had undercut, the orange-yellow roots, like exotic snakes, were tangled.

Hally's head jerked to indicate the hedge. "Always heard as how this was uncommon good country for osage."

The marshal nodded. "That what you wheellin'? Seed?"

"Yeah. Osage orange seed. Sixty bushel. Thirty on this wagon, and thirty comin' across on the next ferry." In his mind he made some more arithmetic. At $80 a bushel on the Illinois market, or thereabouts—eighty times sixty: $4,800! And that was enough for a Texas boy to get married on.

The lawman was watching him, and now with the same elaborate casualness a man down home might have shown in questioning a stranger, he said, "Texas, I'm guessin', judgin' from the down-country hat."

"Texas, yeah."

"Think o' that. All the way from Texas with seed."

"The close corner of Texas. Fannin County on Bois D'Arc crick."

The lawman's next words seemed to Hally to be framed with a casualness wholly unneedful.

"What's seed sellin' at down there?"

"Twenty dollars when I left." Hally felt suddenly uneasy before the other's mild stare, and he didn't know why.

The marshal busied himself rolling a cigarette. When the pause began to be awkward, Hally said, "With a boom market like what you've got here, I reckon she fluctuates a little every day." He paused as he realized that unconsciously he was matching the other's over-casualness of tone. He made himself ask the question directly.

"What's it sellin' at here?"

The marshal put a match flame to his brown paper cigarette, and looked away over the drab bottomlands.

"Twenty dollars," he said.

Out on the river the crawling ferryboat exchanged toots

with a St. Louis packet. Overhead a crow flapped lazily, cawing.

Hally blurted, "Reckon I didn't hear you right."

"You heard me, bub. Twenty dollars."

Hally tried to tell himself that he had sensed what was building up from the second the marshal got so careful in his talk. But he hadn't sensed it, and the shock was on his face.

"Twenty dollars," he made dazed talk. "I could have got that much back home. From eighty to twenty—I don't see how, even in a runaway market—Why, I read it in the paper myself. The Galveston *News*. Eighty dollars on the Peoria, Illinois, market—"

The marshal was shaking his head. "I been takin' little fliers in seed myself, same as everybody else around here. Couple years ago we went osage-orange crazy. Seed nosed up to eighty dollars a bushel. It ain't been anywheres near that since. Here the last couple months it's been up and down from twenty."

"Mister, I'm tellin' you I read it in the papers myself—"

The marshal let smoke seep, thin and blue, from between his lips. "Somebody bring you the paper maybe to read, bub?"

"Why yeah—my friend that's comin' across on the next trip of the ferry with our other load."

"You see the date plain?"

"Plain as the nose on your face."

"Was it on the outside of the paper, or on the inside where the market reports was?"

"Why, on the outside—and the inside too, I reckon—"

"You reckon. But you ain't sure? Think hard."

"No, I ain't sure. Not exactly. But I saw the date on the outside, and my friend brought me the paper. Why, we're in this together—In a way, we are. Why, you're not meanin'—"

"You been bounced, bub," the marshal said dryly.

Hally stared helplessly.

"It's a trick I heard tell of before," the marshal said. "Somebody shows you the paper. The date's all right on the outside where you see it big and it makes an impression. But on the inside where it counts, it's smudged or tore off, or even doctored if the bunco man is sharp enough."

"But this was my friend!"

"Sure. They always are."

Hally was fumbling in the pocket of his blanket-lined jacket. He yanked out a folded legal document. "I—there must be some mistake somewhere. I've got a contract—"

The marshal looked it over. "Humm," he said. "Humm. This friend of yours, this party of the second part, this Jake Cole, he furnishes the teams and wagons, huh, his time and labor, at the fixed charge mentioned here?"

Hally nodded. "That's Jake's main business—freightin'."

"But the equity to the entire sixty bushels remains with you?"

"That's right. I'm a professional hedge grower. It's my seed—"

The marshal handed back the contract. "Bub, you don't own one solitary seed of that sixty bushels. Time it's sold off at twenty dollars and you pay your freightin' bill to this party of the second part you won't have a red cent left. You might even be owin' a little. You could likely save yourself money by abandoning the wagons here and now, turnin' around and headin' for home."

Hally just stared, his throat dry and tight. And they started coming back to him now—the damning little details of their wagon trip across the wild humped hills of Arkansas and the tail of Missouri, that put the guilt squarely to Jake Cole.

That lawyer friend of Jake's in Paris, Lamar County, next to Fannin—Jake had insisted on making everything legal on paper. For Hally's own protection, Jake had explained. But after that first stop they'd stayed on the back roads and never rested over at any towns. Jake had made the trip before, and he would always know a shortcut that took them around the towns. And twice when it looked as though they'd inevitably be spending the night at a town, Jake had had something go the matter with his wagon, so that they'd stopped to fix it, and then driven through the towns at night to make up for lost time.

All this just so Hally wouldn't get a chance to talk to anybody who might have some honest quotations on the osage orange market. There was even the time they found the Kansas City newspaper. But Jake made sure he had the first look at it—and by the time Hally got it, the market sheet was missing.

Oh, Jake had been slick all right. Starting from the very first when he had come fawning with his proposition.

"Sure set you up pretty with Little Bit, now wouldn't it, if you rolled home with a hat full of money that you got by shrewd dealin' up North—"

"What's Little Bit got to do with it?" Hally had flared. "You and her—"

"Not anymore." Jake's voice sounded real sad. Everybody, when they first met Jake, thought he looked a little funny. He was big, with a red beefy face, but his eyes and mouth were little. The face looked too big for the eyes and mouth, or the eyes and mouth looked too little for the face. Something anyway. Everybody noticed it. But that was only at first. After you got to know him he looked all right, the same as anyone else.

"What you meanin', not anymore?"

Jake shook his head, looking dolefully sincere, with his little eyes and little mouth screwed up so tight they were almost buried in his chunky face. "Be honest with you, Hally," he said confidentially. "I figured I could make the grade for a while. But Little Bit, she's got you in the bottom her heart. Only thing is, she says you never could make enough money to head up a family, that you're goin' to be all your life wastin' your time experimentin'—"

"Yeah, I know," Hally cut him off.

His experimenting had been a particularly sore point with Little Bit. She took the position that he was always trying to find a new way of doing something, when the old way was perfectly all right. Like about trying to improve on osage orange fence.

Hally had taken over Lafe Clendenning's droopy nursery stock, worked and fussed with it until he had the finest glossy green grove, with the closest growing branches and the most thorns of any in Fannin County. He even figured out a way of separating the seed from the sticky pulp of the hedge oranges, by forcing the milled pulp through a kind of sluice box with holes bored in the bottom. His seed came out so clean he only had to wash it through two waters, and he got better than a bushel of seed from a thousand hedge oranges.

But after he had a good thing in osage orange, was he satisfied with that? Oh no, not Hally. He had to start experimenting then about a different kind of fence, a brand-new kind with wire, that hadn't even been invented yet. Hally was trying to invent it. *Invent something to put him out of his own business!*

"But, Bitty, osage orange ain't as perfect as I thought. Hedge just ain't the answer to the West's number-one problem. Shades too much ground for one thing. And there ought to be a fence, cheap like hedge, but that you could put up in the twinklin' of an eye almost, instead of waitin' four years for it to grow."

"And while you putter," she said bitterly, "we wait *twenty* years before we can get married, is that it? You keep saying when are we going to—but how can we, ever, Hally? You won't come down to earth long enough to even make a decent living for one, let alone two. It's not as though you couldn't. You—you're the smartest man I know—in a way. You predicted about the doom of the open range and about fencing being the West's number-one problem, and all, and—I love you, I love you! But you just don't care."

This last was said with tears and it made Hally feel awful. He felt still more awful when Little Bit went to the next schoolhouse dance with Jake Cole, who, whatever else they said about him, was a shrewd dealer and was putting his money by.

Hally didn't do anything about it except sulk, and the upshot was that Little Bit started going to *all* the dances with Jake Cole, and inviting him out to her father's ranchhouse for dinner Sundays.

Now on the bank of the river, Hally became aware of the marshal's intent look, and of his own hand involuntarily balled into a fist, smoothing itself against the palm of his other hand. "I am looking forward," he said gently, and more to himself than to the marshal, "to seeing Jake lead his mules off the ferryboat."

The marshal's troubled eyes held on him. "Now don't you be gettin' ideas too big for your Texas hat, bub. You been buncoed—but legal. This ain't cow country you're in now. We got law here."

"What kind of law is it," Hally wondered bleakly, "that helps a bunco?"

"Right or wrong, it's the kind we got. You'd be surprised how most of my trouble nowadays comes from you plains fellas makin' the river crossin' here. Gettin' so's I might's well set up office in Homer's ferryboat shack." He paused, frowned. "You packin' a gun?"

"No," Hally told him. "I won't need no gun. I whaled the daylights out of him when we were kids. Reckon I can do it again."

Hally went and sat down in the dirt by the river where the ferryboat would land, and by the minute as he sat waiting he got less dazed, less hurt, more purposefully angry. His eyes stared hard and bright as the steam ferry came hammering closer and closer, smudging its yellow smoke across the back trail made by the stern wheel spanking the muddy water. When the boat touched shore he didn't even wait for the wooden landing apron to be let down. His boots sloshed water and he climbed aboard, confronting Jake Cole there at the head of the mule team.

With Jake shying back, alarm in his round little eyes, quick knowledge and defiance in the set of his little mouth, Hally lambasted him:

"I know why you done it, Jake. You made money on me. But that wasn't all. You lied to me too—about Little Bit. You ain't through with her, like you said. You figured by this deal to discredit me more in her eyes than what I already am. You didn't aim to tell her about the two-year-old Galveston paper you sprung on me, did you? No. You'd just make out like it was my lame-brained idea to come up here and gamble on the seed market. You knew that without my seed money I'd have a hard time to carry over till next crop. You knew I'd have to sell somethin'—maybe my whole grove—"

Jake was still backing away, his big shoulders hunched, the little mouth working. "I don't know what you're talkin' about—"

"Seed," Hally enlightened him. "Twenty dollar seed! Been sellin' for twenty all along, the same here as at home. And good and well you knew it—"

"You locoed or what?"

"Jake, here it comes!"

Hally moved in with a Sunday punch calculated to knock Jake, big and beefy though he was, backwards off the ferry. But Jake had time to hunch his shoulders more. Hally's fist skidded from the blocky muscles and struck an indecisive glancing blow on Jake's cheek.

Jake covered up, backing against the mules, then clinched when Hally came tearing in again. Jake was bawling all the time. Things like: "Quit it, Hally! For Gawd's sake. What's gone the matter with you? I don't want to fight you. I ain't mad at nothin'. Quit it now—cut it out—"

Hally, mad all the way through, saved his breath for his punches. In the clinch he strained and bucked, trying to break clear of Jake's bear hug, ramming at Jake—short-traveling blows that he knew, maddeningly, weren't hurting much because Jake was holding in too close.

Out of the tail of his eye he could see the ferryboat man and the marshal, interested spectators, edging closer. Jake started directing his pleading at the marshal: "Haul him offa me. I don't want to hurt him. He's my friend, but he's gone locoed. He don't know what he's doin'—"

Hally got in a shoving blow against the face that seemed to loosen Jake's hold. Hally could feel Jake's binding arms going lower, working down around the midriff, and hope bit Hally hard that there would be elbowroom pretty quick now for a haymaker, though in that same high moment of hope there was vague wonderment that Jake should be weakening so fast.

All at once there was a new quality about Jake's pleading voice, a panic-stricken note, and that was odd too because there was nothing about any of this to make Jake *that* much afraid. Hally glimpsed the little eyes under their sun-bleached brows popping with what seemed like stark terror. He still didn't get it, but the next moment he did, as Jake appealed pitiously to the marshal:

"Help me—the gun! He's going to kill! He's got a gun! In his pocket. He's tryin' to pull it out. I'm holdin' agin' it—but I can't—much longer. The gun—in his pocket—help me—"

From underneath the flapping leather vest the marshal drew his own gun from its snug hip holster and moved in fast. There was a gun in Hally's side coat pocket all right, just as Jake had said—a small derringer, a weapon vicious as a stub-tailed rattler.

The marshal in his way was merciful. When Hally wouldn't quiet down, when he persisted like a wild man in going for

Jake even in the face of the marshal's drawn gun, the marshal didn't strike with the heavy six-shooter barrel. He stepped in and dropped Hally with a single chopping blow of his fist— the fist weighted with the derringer he had lifted from Hally's own pocket.

Illinois jails, Hally took dismal note, were not much improvement on Texas ones. Though in Texas it was easier to stay on the outside of them. Maybe it was true, after all, what they said about the North—those diehards back home who were still fighting the Civil War ten years after it was over.

They said a southerner didn't have a chance in the North, that it was bossed by scallywag politicians who would throw you in jail just on general principles. *And keep you there!*

Jake Cole was anyhow halfway to blame for it though. Lower'n a snake in a wagon track—why, he hadn't known a Texas man had it in him to be so deceitful. And Little Bit— well, any girl who would go and take up with a man the stripe of Jake Cole—well. Jake could have her, and good riddance.

But there would come one fateful day when he rode back to Texas when he would stomp into Little Bit's no-account house that Jake would have built for her, and he would shove Little Bit to one side if she got in the way, and her children too—her red-faced, bug-eyed, fish-mouthed children—and then he would put his fist to Jake Cole the way he had meant to do today. Man, he would knock him clean through the plaster into the yard outside.

"Ain't he some pretty," he would say to Little Bit, and then he would stomp out again.

Maybe the next day he would go back and do the same thing again, because in Texas they didn't put he-men in jail for troddin' varmints.

He felt something nudging him. He stirred on the edge of the built-in wooden bunk, and lifted his head from cupped hands, looking up wearily. His frowsy cell mate, an old man, stubbled and shag-haired, drunk or crazy, maybe both, was staring at him with rheumy-eyed intensity.

"You hard o' hearin', younker? I been talkin' and you don't answer me none. Jus' rockin' and groanin'. You got the miseries?"

"I got 'em bad," Hally confided.

The oldster nodded sympathetically. "I dunno which is worst, miseries or stomach ache."

"Miseries is worst."

The old man pressed so close that Hally had to turn his head to miss the alcoholic breath. "Goin' to show you somethin' to cheer you up, younker." The old fellow's eyes took on a crafty look. "They think I'm crazy in this town, and every time I take a drink and get to feelin' my oats, like, they puttin' me in here. They're ignorant. They's destiny overshadowin' 'em and they don't know it. But you, younker, you got sense enough to recognize genius when you see it—and overshadowin' destiny. Ain't it the truth?"

Hally let him rant.

"You won't tell nobody, will you, what I'm about to show you?"

"I won't tell," Hally humored him.

Secretively, the old man stumped to the other bunk, lifted the corn-husk tick, and from beneath it took out something wrapped in a grimy flour sack. He brought it back to Hally.

"Always carry it with me," he said. He unwrapped it with slow and blundering hands, held it close for Hally to see. There was a new light in the oldster's eyes, a kind of slow fire; it might have been pride reflected there.

Hally looked at the strip of one-by-one board with nails driven through it every three inches so that the points protruded on the far side.

"What is it?" he asked helplessly.

"Overshadowin' destiny." The old man leaned close, whispered confidentially, "Folks comes and goes in this river town. Keelboats and packets. I talk to everybody. And what do I learn? I'll tell you. Since civilization has crept out from under the benevolent shade of forest trees and ventured out on the trackless plain, they is a problem overshadowin' the land. It is the West's number-one problem. It is the fencin' problem—"

Hally groaned, and rubbed his face with his hands, and looked at the old man through his fingers.

"The doom is on the open range," the old man went on. "Fences are the thing. But what kind of fences? You may well ask, younker, on account I am the prophet of the fences, unhonored here in Grand Tower. Now I will tell you what kind of fence. Not board, which is too expensive. Not hedge, which is pretty, and also useful for birds to build nests in, but which is slow to grow and troublesome to maintain. Not wire, which is too smooth, carryin' no authority with range critters. None of these things. But this!" He shoved close the board with the nails driven through it. "Wood married to wire. The answer to our number-one problem. Destiny—here in my hands."

"How does it work?" Hally asked politely.

"I'm glad you asked. I'll tell you. You take a smooth wire fence, see? And you hang this board on the fence." He made exaggerated motions of hanging the wood on the fence. It didn't seem funny to Hally. But it didn't make any sense either.

His hand waved weakly out. "You just—hang it on the fence."

"All along wherever the fence goes. And whenever a beef critter takes a notion to leave for more greener pastures, and he starts to push through the fence, he feels the nails stickin' him and they determine him to stay at home. Wood and nails married to wire. The West needs a fence before it can grow. Here's the fence. Destiny!"

From the old man's trembling fingers Hally took the absurd piece of wood with the nails driven through it. Reflecting on some of the half-baked theories that he had spouted back home on the fencing question, he wondered, wryly, if he had sounded as crazy as this old codger. Maybe, he speculated, but for the grace of two-score years and a river of Monongahela whiskey, there stand I.

&

He couldn't help but think of the time Little Bit's father had brought in some wire to use for a corral fence. Johnny-on-the-spot with his sage predictions when the spools of wire were rolled down from the wagon at the Ewing ranch, Hally had said:

"Won't work."

Mr. Ewing took a tug on his cow-prong mustache and wanted to know why the hell not.

"Cows'll push right through it," Hally said. "Give 'em a few days to find out the wire won't hurt 'em—they'll push right through it. Needs somethin' they'll respect—like thorns."

"You would say that—you bein' in the hedge business," Mr. Ewing remarked dryly, and he went right ahead and strung his wire.

The next morning, early, Mr. Ewing came out and found Hally bending suspiciously over the new fence.

"What in the name o' Satan you doin', young Harper? If you're cuttin' my wire, I'll—"

"You know I wouldn't cut your wire, Mr. Ewing." Hally looked pained. "I'm tryin' to make an improvement on it, is all. When I got home last night I got me an idea—"

Mr. Ewing could see now that Hally had a bundle of osage orange switches on the ground beside him. There were some more switches that he had woven in and out between the wire of the fence.

"You call that an improvement?" Mr. Ewing kicked vigorously at the pattern of thorny switches between the wires.

Hally stood a little back, his long face maybe a little sad, his gray eyes certainly dreamy. "It seemed like a good idea when I got it. You see, Mr. Ewing, wire might be all right to send telegrams on, but it ain't the answer to the fencin' problem in the West. Wire's too smooth and delicate. The critters'll push right through it."

"I remember," Mr. Ewing said, "you were explainin' it to me yesterday."

The sarcasm didn't bother Hally. He said, still in his dream, "If I could think of somethin' to make the hedge switches stay in place better—some way to fasten 'em quick and cheap—But shucks, cut from the branch, them switches would weather too fast anyhow. Everything considered, Mr. Ewing, I don't think that hedge married to wire is the answer to the fencin' problem."

Mr. Ewing said, "Huh," in a very satisfied manner. "For once in my life, young Harper, I am findin' myself plumb in agreement with you."

But Mr. Ewing wasn't feeling so satisfied the next day. His new white-face bull that he had imported to build up his native stock, leaned against the smooth wire of the fence a couple of times, tentatively—then went through it as though it wasn't there.

Even Little Bit, by some kind of obscure feminine logic, seemed to hold Hally responsible for the bull going through the fence.

"If you'd just stick to your hedge," she said, "instead of dissipating your—your fine talents on trying to invent something to put you out of business even more than you already are—Really honey—"

All at once Little Bit, Texas, osage orange hedge, even this Grand Tower jail, disappeared from Hally's awareness as though he had never heard of any of them. He had been staring at the dinky piece of wood with the nails in it, almost without seeing it. Now suddenly his hands started shaking worse than those of the old man, and he felt the flesh under his clothes prickling hot and cold.

There is a kind of thought that comes in a flash of lightning brilliance, whole-born and clean, and comes rarely in the lives of men. It is apt to be simple—and tremendous in its potentialities for changing the world as we know it. Such a thought, Hally dimly sensed, was this.

Like a man sleepwalking, he got up and moved across the splintery planks to the cell door. "Marshal!" he yelled. "Marshal!" He shook the bars of the door.

His voice was hoarse, and the old man looked after him strangely. "You feelin' a mite teched, younker?"

Hally kept up his racket until the marshal came from his office down the corridor from the jail cell.

"That won't get you nowhere, bub."

"Look, all I'm wantin' is some thin nails and a piece of wire, and a pair of pliers."

"What in the hell for?"

"I got an idea. I got to make somethin'."

The marshal of Grand Tower looked at Hally's knuckles showing white from the force with which he gripped the bars, he noted the way the sweat seeped out on his forehead, and he saw the light that was in his eyes, a kind of slow fire.

"Why sure, kid," he said quietly. "Sure. I guess it won't hurt none."

While the marshal looked on from beyond the barred door, and the old man squatted close with excited rubbering eyes, Hally worked feverishly with the pliers, bending the nails almost double and wedging them on the wire.

He held up his creation and talked, not to the marshal, but to the old man who would understand. "Not wood married to wire. But metal married to metal, see?"

"Aye, younker," the old man said. "But metal on metal won't hold in place." His grimy fingers poked out to move a bent nail on its wire axis. "Slips around no matter how you bend it. I tried it myself, long ago. It takes the wood to hold the metal prickler in place."

Hally's head nodded slowly. "You're right—the idea's no

good." He could feel the life seep out of him, right out of his fingertips.

Then there it was again, unasked, unbidden—a brain nudge from the gods.

"Wait a minute!"

Hally took the pliers and commenced cutting the wire in foot lengths. He stopped with half a dozen and fastened the lengths together in a kind of chain, but putting a half-inch crimp in the end of each length and coupling one to another.

"Now we'll turn the crimped ends out a little to each side." He made the adjustment with the pliers, and held up his wire chain. "Now what have we got? Thorn-wire—but without the wood!"

He stretched the wire chain tighter and tighter between his two hands. It broke at its weakest link—and Hally's spirits broke with it.

The old man wagged his head sympathetically. "It ain't practical. It'd be always breakin' somewheres. You need the wood. Like I showed you. I've tried every other way. And I ain't the only one. Up the north part the state, De Kalb and Hinckley and Kankakee and them places, everybody's workin' on it. They trot 'em out at their county fairs, the fandanglest things, and none of 'em works like my wood an' wire."

Hally's hands lay limply before him where he squatted on the floor. "Thought sure I had it that time," he muttered. "But I reckon wire just ain't the answer."

He didn't realize what he was doing at first. Unwilled, unnoticed, his hands were moving, twisting one of the soft lengths of wire around and around another one. Then he saw what he had, and he felt the first faint nudging of that power that was maybe clear outside of himself, outside of his mind at least, his conscious mind—and then it was there again, that lightning of the gods, striking a third time in almost the same place, consuming him in a flash of clairvoyance that left his fingers nerveless, his body hot and cold.

His lips moved. "Wire," he murmured, "*is* the answer. Only not just *one* wire. It takes two. Two wires twisted, for strength, and to hold the prickers in place. Here's what I mean; I'll show you."

He grabbed up the remaining long length of wire and looped it around one of the jail bars. Then he took an end in each hand and started twisting one wire around another until he had a double-strand wire.

"And we'll use, not bent nails," he said excitedly, "but other little pieces of wire for the thorns or prickers. Cut 'em on an angle to get the points." He demonstrated with the cutting pliers. "Later I'll figure on a machine to do it quicker. . . . Now we force the prickers in between the twists on the doubled wire, see, and bend 'em north and south so they don't slip out. The twists in the main wires will keep the prickers from turning. We got it! The fence the plains country needed! Smooth wire wasn't enough. But smooth wire doubled, twisted, and armed with wire thorns—"

"Destiny!" the old man's awed mutter sounded. "Like I propheted all my long life—only without the wood."

Hally went to the door, gripped the bars and talked through them to the marshal. "I got to get out of here—sudden."

The lawman shook his head, frowning. "She's out of my hands, bub. Your partner's swore out a warrant agin' you, legal, chargin' intent to kill and attack with a deadly weapon. That's serious. You got to be bound over for the grand jury, to stand trial—"

"But I got work to do!" Hally said furiously.

"That's never no mind to me, bub. Your partner said you get kill-crazy sometimes, that there's bad blood in you, that you was packin' that derringer and threatenin' him with it all the way up from Texas—"

"He lied! I never even knowed that gun was in my pocket. When he was clinched with me in the fight he put it in my pocket a'purpose so's he could get you to arrest me—"

"That's what you told me before. In the law business you find out nearly everybody's got his alibi for everything." The marshal started moving away. "Anyhow, I don't make the laws; I'm only paid to enforce 'em."

Hally fumed and shook the door—then quieted down and went back to his creating, perfecting the crude idea which he knew with surety was the answer to all his fence experimenting. He decided it would be most efficient to bend up a batch of the double-pronged wire thorns separately. He could even figure out halfway how to do it. Use something with a moving shaft, something—well, like a coffee grinder. Put a couple of pins in the end of the shaft, turn the handle and feed the wire between the moving pins. The wire would coil around the pins, and some kind of cutting attachment could be rigged up to cut off the completed wire thorns. It could be a continuous process. Sure. Then string the coiled thorns on a long piece of wire and twist another wire around it, leaving a wire thorn every few inches between the twists. Nothing to it!

But first he had to get out of this damn' jail! It was very depressing. Here he could solve the West's number-one problem and he couldn't figure out a simple thing like how to get out of a locked room. He brooded on that until nightfall when the marshal came bringing their supper: fried young rabbit and mashed potatoes with rabbit gravy, big slabs of white bread with butter and sorghum, pickled peaches, and coffee with rich cream and sugar in it, all prepared by the marshal's wife.

The marshal stuck around and watched them eat. Afterwards he unlocked the cell door and jerked his head at the old man. "All right, Wood'n-wire; I guess you're pretty near sober."

Before the old man went out, he paused in the yellow light that sifted down from the wall lamp in the corridor and gripped Hally's hand with both his own. "Here," he said. He presented Hally with the dirt-glazed flour sack containing the strip of wood with the nails driven through it. "I want you to have it, younker. Makes me feel kind of clean some-how—like when you give up idols and false gods when you get the true religion. You've showed me the gospel way about fencin'. It ain't wood married to wire. It's smooth wire twisted double and pronged with more wire."

After the old man had stumped out, the marshal said quietly, "It's dark enough now. Give me five minutes or so to get to the other end of town, then try the door. Should you find it unlocked, bub, leave your conscience guide you. And if I was from Texas and lookin' for a man with sixty bushels of osage, I wouldn't go to Peoria. I'd take the North Pike out from town and head for Murphysboro. Leastways there was a lad in this town hired today to drive a Texas wagon there. And it sounds reasonable to me on account Murphysboro's a sight closer to here than Peoria, with the seed market about the same."

Hally blinked incredulously in the yellow light. "You mean you—you'd do that for me—"

"I don't guess there's any local taxpayers as would object—"

"But the law—"

"Maybe it ain't so much different here than in Texas, bub. The law gets to workin' an injustice, and straight-away a man starts figurin' how to get around it. I wasn't sure about you this mornin', but now I made up my mind."

"Gee—why, well, thanks, Marshal—shucks—"

"That wire you twisted up today—you think you really got somethin' there?"

"Marshal," Hally said warmly, "that hank of wire sounds the death knell of the open range. Likewise the hedge business. I predict that two short years from now, there won't be another professional hedge grower in the United States."

The marshal grinned. "A fella'd better start tradin' short then on osage orange seed, hadn't he?"

"I reckon," Hally said, but with less enthusiasm, recalling all of a sudden that hedge growing was his business.

❦

Hally stayed on the road all night, and with the help of a lift part way in a doctor's buggy, he was in Murphysboro the next morning. He scouted around, and at Shivley and Neeson's Livery Stable he located Jake's mules and the two wagons still loaded with osage orange seed. He washed up and got breakfast at the Little Gem Cafe on the Court House Square. He still looked pretty grubby in his travel-worn clothes. But there was no help for that. He inquired around and went to see a lawyer.

J. Worthington Plunket at his rolltop desk, in his wing collar and black string tie and black coat; and with his white fingers that kept lacing while the thumbs twirled, was not so much different, Hally observed, from Texas lawyers. Hally explained about the osage orange seed.

J. Plunket, attorney at law, looked at the contract and gave his dry and measured opinion. The party of the second part, he opined, could indubitably secure a court attachment on the seed and prevent Hally from selling until the freighting bill was paid. Hally would be indeed fortunate, he said, if he had enough money left with which to pay his lawyer for this consultation.

"All right," Hally said, "that's how I thought it was anyhow. It don't matter. The hedge business is doomed anyhow. Here's the main thing I wanted to see you about." From out of the old man's flour sack he lifted a sample length of pronged and twisted wire. He waited expectantly for the glow of interest to show in the lawyer's eyes.

J. Worthington Plunket merely looked bored, even a little annoyed.

"It's a new kind of fence," Hally enlightened.

J. Plunket's thumbs twirled. "So?"

"I invented it—me and an old man in jail—I mean in—in

another town. I want the papers drawn so he gets his share of the profits."

The lawyer continued to stare. And now there was no doubt of it; the expression on his pursed lips was one of annoyance.

"I want to get it patented," Hally persisted.

The lawyer tilted forward in his swivel chair. "Young man," he said severely, "we have jails in this state for those who infringe upon patent rights."

Hally looked a little dazed.

The lawyer further elucidated. "The whole top half of this state has been racing for the patent office this summer. There must be by this time fifty patents issued or pending for this"—his white hand waved out—"barbed wire. Why there is even a man in this very township manufacturing some of it under a royalty arrangement with a patent holder from De Kalb. And now, young man, if you will excuse me"— the swivel chair turned back to face the rolltop—"my time is valuable."

Still dazed, Hally found himself outside the door. He almost bumped into Jake Cole without seeing him as Jake turned the corner on the square-brick sidewalk and approached J. Worthington Plunket's office. Jake was the first to get his voice. His little eyes bulged like peeled grapes, and his little mouth kept opening and shutting.

"Hey," he blurted, "I thought—How'd you get—"

"I shot the marshal and burned the jail down," Hally told him. "And it ain't half what I'm goin' to do to you."

He would have swung then, regardless of Illinois law, its jails, and its lawyers. But the door behind him creaked open. A suave voice said, "Ah, the party of the second part, I believe. Come in—come in—"

Jake went in right now, and the door snap-locked behind him. Hally moped away down the street. The autumn sun filtering through the bare branches of the maples did not warm him. Even the squat houses built of Bellville brick seemed to glare with hostile intent through their windowed eyes. Fannin County and Little Bit were a million miles away and this was the moon or somewhere. And he was sure sunk. He'd thrown a wide loop, and no chance now for another toss.

He did remember after a while about the lawyer mentioning a man in the township who was manufacturing what he had quaintly called barbed wire. There couldn't any good come of it, but now that he was here it wouldn't hurt to take a look. He inquired around and walked north from town on a rutted road bordered on both sides by osage orange hedge. Tall prairie grass, cured on the stem, swaddled the road clear to the wagon ruts. The wind made a mournful rustling in it.

Hally stopped at the first farmhouse with a white picket fence around the front yard. He turned in at the gate and followed the board walk around to the back. A young man, bareheaded and sun-kilned, and maybe a few years older than Hally, had his sleeves rolled up and was washing in a tin pan near the pump. He looked up and smiled, gray eyes frankly curious, as Hally came around the corner of the house.

"Thought I heard the gate squeak. Been meanin' to oil it. . . . Howdy, stranger."

Hally said howdy, and introduced himself as Hally Harper from Texas. "Was lookin' for Joe Trihey," he said, "who runs a—a barb-wire factory." He looked expressively around at the house and the cluster of farm buildings: summer kitchen, henhouse, plow shed, barns. "Reckon I've stove up against the wrong place."

The farmer reached for a towel, plunged his hands in the unbleached muslin, and rubbed vigorously. He hung the towel back on its wooden peg. "Nope, this is the right place, all right." He stuck out his damp brown hand. Hally took the hand and they shook. "Just sittin' down to dinner." He clapped Hally on the back. "You come on in and join us."

After the grief he'd been through, this was so much like the neighborly "light an' set" welcome he was used to at home that Hally felt a lump rising in his throat, and he turned and started pumping water strenuously to splash some water on his face before any tears might show.

Dinner was hearty and friendly, with the Mrs. in her blue print housedress continually jumping up to bring on hot, covered dishes from the kitchen, and hovering around them while they ate; and the three children kicking the legs of their chairs while they ogled the guest and giggled over their secret knowledge.

After dinner Joe took Hally out in back to the milk shed. He lifted the whittled peg on its leather strap and let the flimsy plank door swing wide. He waved Hally proudly inside.

"My fence factory," he said.

Hally looked about bewilderedly. Then, eyes focusing to the dimness, excitement prickled him as he saw what was stacked in the corner: finished fencing wire wound loosely on big wooden spools—six spools of it, ferocious stuff with inch-long steel thorns, or barbs as they called them up here, daubed with red lead to keep them from rusting.

Hally caught his breath again as he saw the doctored-up coffee mill with the casing cut away and the two pins driven into the end of the shaft so that the barbs could be given the desired bend when the handle turned—just about the way he had pictured it back in the Grand Tower jail.

"Now come out in the yard," Joe invited, "and I'll show you how I twist the wire."

They stopped in front of the grindstone.

"That?"

"Sure. I grease the wire and carry one end of it to the top of the windmill. The kids climb up with a bucket full of barbs and string 'em on the wire, let 'em gravity-feed down. They think it's fun. Next we take two fifty-foot lengths of wire and hook 'em up on one end with the grindstone. The kids turn the crank and I space the barbs between the wires as they start twinin' together. Result: a fence that shades no land, that's better'n hedge or boards—"

"You don't have to sell me!" Hally exclaimed. He stood looking, his expression rapt. "A coffee mill and a grindstone—destiny in our hands."

"Course, the way I'm goin' at it," Joe apologized, "it ain't much more'n a hobby. I can't turn out the wire much faster'n I can use it here on my own place. But I think a mint of money could be made if a fella was to go after it serious-fashion. Folks around here think I'm cracked on the subject. But I claim barb-wire is the comin' fence in the West. I think the demand is goin' to exceed the supply for a while." His voice warmed with his enthusiasm. "What makes it so practical—it's a natural for machine production. There's patents already pendin' on machines the same principles as these of mine, only operated by steam, fast and cheap. You buy the smooth wire from Washburn and Moen in Massachusetts. Then make it into barbed wire and sell it. A man could make a mint of money. But shucks, it takes money to start a thing like that—money that I haven't got."

"How much money?" Hally asked tensely.

"I've figgered till I'm black in the face. I can't get it down below three thousand."

Hally took a long breath. "Joe, could you use a partner?"

"With three thousand dollars? You joshin'?"

"No, I'm not joshin'."

Their eyes caught, hung.

"You mean *you* got three thousand? Cash?"

"No, but I know where I can get it."

Hally's jaws set, grim as death, and Joe, watching him uncertainly, laughed shortly.

"You goin' to rob a bank? You know we got laws up here—"

"Oh, I've found out all about your laws, Joe. No, I'm not goin' to rob a bank. But I'll go get the money—right now."

Hally didn't go looking for Jake Cole. He just went to the livery stable and sat on a stool and leaned back against the end post of a box stall, and waited for Jake to come to him. It was along the middle of the afternoon when Jake showed up. When he saw Hally sitting there, whittling, apprehension—and calculation—chased themselves all over his beefsteak face again, with his little eyes narrowed, his little mouth pressed tightly.

"Now listen, I don't want to have any trouble with you—"

"You aint' calculated to—much," Hally said. He got up and came toward Jake slowly, the knife still in his hand. He kept his voice low, not to scare Jake so much that he'd turn and run. "I just want one thing from you, Jake. Three thousand six-hundred dollars—that bein' the sum I would of netted up here on the osage orange seed, accordin' to the way you represented it to me."

Jake kept backing away, his eyes on Hally's whittling knife. "You'll get what's comin' to you, Hally," he said shrilly. "You know you will. After you've paid me my rightful freightin' bill."

"Freightin' bill will swallow the whole thing, and good and well you know it. But it ain't just the seed of the osage oranges I'm talkin' about now. It's my whole grove. I'm sellin' it to you unencumbered for $3,600 cash in hand."

Jake stopped backing away. His eyes blinked in quick speculation. "How come you're wantin' to sell all of a sudden?"

"Why you think?" Hally flared. "You reckon I want to go back and be the laughin' stock of Fannin County? After the way you played me—"

"You mean you ain't aimin' to go back?"

"Not if I can sell that grove."

"What about Little Bit?"

"Little Bit Ewing," Hally said bitterly, "is out of my life just like osage orange."

Jake tried not to look too satisfied. "You'd want cash, huh?"

"Cash."

Jake appeared to consider. He said carefully. "I have got pretty friendly with J. Worthington Plunket. We could go to him now and he could fix up the papers. Yes, I think he would do it. We could sell the sixty bushel of seed and I could arrange for a transfer of additional money from my Kansas City account. Lawyer Plunket can introduce us at his bank here in town. There is just about time before closing."

"Let's go," Hally said.

J. Plunket handled the details. He was very efficient about it. The pink-cheeked cashier at the Murphysboro bank pushed the money under the bronzed grille, and Jake Cole took it and counted it out to Hally. It was all there—minus the lawyer's fee, which Jake explained it was the universal custom for the one who got the money to pay. If the fee seemed unduly large, that was because the transactions had been put through with undue haste, lawyers everywhere commanding extra remuneration for transactions performed unduly.

It never entered Hally's head that Jake and the lawyer planned to split the fee between them. It didn't even occur to Hally that the fee was exorbitant. He had only two thoughts at the moment. One was of Little Bit Ewing who was now out of his life forever, and it was nostalgic and sad. The other was of Jake Cole, and it was immediate and pleasant.

Hally tucked his money in an inside pocket and carefully buttoned his jacket. Then he treated them all to a display of Texas individuality; he rubbed his hands, and somewhat like a great humped cat he started stalking Jake Cole.

"I been waitin' too long for this," he said.

The shocked cashier and the lawyer stared helplessly, horrified not so much by what was obviously about to happen to Jake Cole as by the impropriety of it happening inside the cherrywood-finished and marble-slabbed Murphysboro bank.

Jake Cole was horrified too. But not about the improprieties. Just about what was going to happen to Jake Cole. He started backing away, making ineffectual fending motions with his big hands.

"Now look here, Hally; there's law up here—"

In the end he must have adjusted to the inevitable because he stopped, and then lunged forward, beating Hally to the punch with a fist swung like a scythe, wide and low, at the stomach.

Hally had just time to heel sideways and suck his middle in and let Jake's fist scrape past—and practically let Jake knock himself out against a hungrily awaiting fist. Hard on the chin where he had intentioned it—a mule-kick punch that Hally felt clear to his elbow.

Jake didn't strike his head against the Ozark marble floor. That was because, heeling back, he rammed into J. Worthington Plunket. That worthy went down first, flaying the air with outreaching hands. He landed most undignifiedly, spread out on his own coattails, inadvertently cradling Jake's collapsing body in his lap.

It was all very satisfying. Hally straightened his jacket at the collar and strode out the door. The first thing he saw out there was a girl who looked almost more like Little Bit than Little Bit herself.

She was struggling down the street from the direction of the railroad depot, with a useless parasol, a hat box, and a vast carpetbag banging against her knees. Even her clothes were amazingly like Little Bit's, from the perky little piece of black velvet with Christmas-tree-looking ornaments sewed on one side of it, and which she wore for a hat, to the blue and orange tweed traveling suit pinching her almost in two in the middle, but making her look wonderful above and below.

"Little Bit!" Hally shouted, with all the restraint of a bawling Texas longhorn.

His heels broke echoes from the square bricks of the sidewalk as he ran. And then she was in his arms, her bags and boxes plumping about her, while Murphysboro business men and shoppers, startled and grinning, looked on from the doorways.

Little Bit was crying and talking all at the same time, and Hally, ecstatically piecing things together, learned that:

She never could stand that Jake Cole anyway, and only went with him to make Hally jealous, and to try to get him to have a little more sense of responsibility, but she was afraid she had laid it on too thick about him not making any money, and she didn't care if he ever made any money or not; she loved him just the way he was and wouldn't change him for the world—well, not much anyway; he was a precious, precious thing, and to prove it she had come all the way up here by stage and the Cairo and Fulton Railroad and some other railroads to tell him so, because she was afraid he might get discouraged and maybe never come back to Fannin County and to her, after the way Jake, the horrid, slippery, crawling thing, had tricked him about the price of osage orange seed in Illinois—

That was where Hally got his first dazed word in. "But how could you be knowin' about that, Bitty?"

"Well, I know Jake, don't I? And I could put two and two together. I could read in the paper what osage orange seed was selling for up here—about the same as at home. Jake made you think it was a lot more, didn't he? But I don't care, honey. I've brought enough money for us both to get home on—"

"Why, Bitty; I don't need any money." Hally raked the currency from his pocket. "I sold my grove to Jake. There's thirty-six hundred dollars here—minus the lawyer's fee. Look!"

Hally himself was doing some double-distilled looking, but not at the money. From the tail of his eye he could see Jake Cole, standing disheveled and groggy, in front of the bank. He was flanked by two men. One was the lawyer, likewise disheveled. The other was a hard-bitten individual who wore a law badge. The lawyer and Jake were doing the talking, and all three men were looking at Hally in a manner hostile.

Little Bit had eyes only for the wad of money. "Oh, oh," she wailed, "it's worse than I thought! Thirty-six hundred! Your place is worth twice—"

"It won't be—not for long. Why, honey, I'd of been cheatin' Jake if I'd charged him more. The way it was, I only charged him what he'd guaranteed I'd make on the seed deal. You see, what Jake don't know is: osage orange is goin' plumb out, honey. Barb-wire's comin' in. I'm goin' to stay up north here and come in with it—"

She tugged at his arm. "Look, there's Jake now! Coming this way. He looks mad, kind of. He's got two men with him. They all look mad, and one of 'em's wearin' a law badge—"

"This is the law-riddenest country!" Hally sighed, and moving his lanky body to conceal his actions from the approaching three, he crammed the money into Little Bit's two hands. He talked swiftly. "Put it out of sight quick, honey. Then I tell you what to do: take the money and give it to Joe Trihey—the first farmhouse on the road north from town with a white picket fence around it—"

"But Hally," she gasped, "I—I don't understand. Where— will you be?"

"Me? I'll be in jail again, honey. But you're not to worry, hear? I reckon with all the law they got up here, there ain't one that a man can't be married in jail. Anyhow, they don't anywhere keep manufacturers long in jail—"

"Hally Harper, are you going crazy—"

"Could be." He grinned down at her. "Crazy in love anyhow. And crazy rich maybe. Leastways we will be if barb-wire takes the place of hedge—"

"Honey, I don't understand anything," she broke in, "and I'm scared, and I—I don't like it up here. Let's go home, Hally—right now." Through wet lashes she smiled her persuasive best. "Why honey, you've got the—the West's number-one problem to solve, don't you remember?"

"I've plumb solved it," he told her, and pulled her close. "From now on you're my number-one problem."

He had just time for a quick sample of how he proposed to solve that one before he felt the hand of the law on his shoulder.

THE DRIFTER

W. C. Tuttle

THE drifter—a stranger who arrives unannounced in a particular town or place, and who may or may not be "just passing through"—took many forms in Western pulp fiction: an outlaw on the dodge or intent on mischief, a man fleeing his past, a cowhand looking for work, a bounty hunter or gunfighter after quarry, a fiddlefoot seeking adventure or a place to put down roots. Drifter heroes were so common that it took a clever writer to come up with a new wrinkle in utilizing one, and an even cleverer writer to do so in that rarest of pulp fare, the short-short story. W. C. Tuttle was one such clever writer, and "The Drifter" is his wryly ironic variation on the theme.

Beginning during World War I, and for more than thirty years, W. C. Tuttle (1883–1969) was a tireless contributor to the Western and adventure pulps, in particular such magazines as Short Stories, Blue Book, Adventure, West, *and* Western Story. *His first novel,* Reddy Brant, His Adventures, *appeared in 1920; his 84th and last novel,* Medicine Maker, *was published in 1967. In the heyday of the pulps, his series about roving cowboys-cum-detectives, Hashknife Hartley and Sleepy Stevens, was especially well received. Tuttle's life, chronicled in his 1966 autobiography,* Montana Man, *was every bit as unusual and interesting as his Western stories; among other things he was president of the Pacific Coast Baseball League from 1935 to 1943.*

Old Baldy McGrew brought him to Canyon City, tied on a pack-saddled mule, as inert a mass of humanity as I have ever seen. Baldy said that apparently this feller was riding over the high-water trail, when some of it broke loose and dropped him and his horse down into the canyon where Baldy was working on his placer mine. The horse died immediately.

Doc Machin took over the case, if you could call it that. Some of us packed the man down to Doc's place. He wouldn't weight over a hundred pounds, soaking wet and in the full bloom of health. Doc was what we called a professional half-breed—half M.D., half horse doctor.

A miner said, "Doc, he sure as hell don't look like much."

"He's a human being," Doc said, and went to work on the wreck of human flesh and bones.

Things were booming in Canyon City, and we went back to our work, letting Doc do his darndest. New mines were opening up most every day, and new people coming in all the time. We're so far away from civilization that we have to read a weekly paper from Gateway, sixty miles away, in order to occasionally remember that we're still part of the U.S.A.

My folks christened me Eustace Hollingsworth Smith, but everybody calls me Silent Smith. Well, I suppose it's for the same reason that they call a tall man Shorty, or a fat man Skinny. I'm a barber in Canyon City.

Our town is kinda famous due to the fact that we have only one street, and you can't get lost. If you're in town, you're somewhere on Main Street, or you're an expert mountain climber. For a tight little community of gun-packers, where the law is administered by a city marshal and a self-made magistrate, we don't have much blood-and-thunder to cope with. Part of the reason is because there's only one way out of town—the stage road to Gateway.

Our biggest headache was when the notorious Piegan Kid and his gang took over Canyon City. This Piegan Kid's past was papered with reward notices, and his four men were probably wanted everywhere, except in decent society. The Kid had always worked alone, but now he had a gang.

No one paid any attention to their arrival. They took over

the marshal's office, confiscated all his guns, and then proceeded to take guns away from everybody they met, until Canyon City was practically gunless. They cleaned out the bank, the Alhambra Saloon and Gambling Palace, along with the stores and post office and some individuals. I locked the door of my shop and made my exit through a smashed window. Before they got through, I don't believe there was a whole window on Main Street, and everybody was under cover.

This lasted for a half-day. Then a cowboy managed to pile onto a horse and head for Gateway. The Piegan Kid, realizing that the party was over, decided to pull out. He was the last to get mounted. The others, loaded with loot, were riding fast when somebody who still had a gun took a last shot at the Kid as he whirled away from the Alhambra hitch-rack. He stung the Kid's horse, and the horse sun-fished into the hitch-rack, dumping the Kid on his head.

So we tied him up tight, dumped him into the seat of a springwagon, and took him to Gateway. The law and twelve honest men decided to hang him as soon as they could build a gallows. The Kid laughed at the law, even if he didn't have a visible chance to last a week.

But it seems that the Piegan Kid was sort of a masonry expert. With probably some outside assistance, he removed a few square-feet of that old brick jail wall, and faded out in the night. The real discouraging part of it was, as far as we were concerned, a note he left in the jail, which read:

Tell Canyon City I'll be back.

Our doughty marshal, Sam Hughes, said, "I wonder what he meant."

I say he's doughty because he doubts everything he hears. But he's always been a mighty man in times of peace. That Piegan Kid affair kind of made a lot of us doubt each other.

Pop Lester, who runs the best cafe on the street, summed it up pretty good when he said:

"Let's face the truth for once. The Piegan Kid and his gang scared hell out of all of us."

And to cap that, our sky-pilot, Testament Thompson, made the shortest prayer of his life. All he said was, "Amen."

I don't know how he did it, but Doc Machin put that skinny specimen back on his feet. He didn't look like much, but he could walk on his hind legs again. Doc brought him to me, and I cut off about a bale of hair and whiskers, which slimmed him down a lot. He was just a skinny-faced kid, about five feet, seven inches tall, with a pair of awful sad eyes. He didn't have any money and he didn't have a gun. He said he lost it when his horse fell into the canyon. His kind would look funny with a gun anyway.

Doc couldn't charge him for medical attention, and he's had to feed the little feller all this time. After a time he told Doc to call him Shorty. It was funny, but you couldn't dislike the little devil, and you couldn't like him either.

Slim Barry, boss of the Alhambra, looked Shorty over, trying to figure out if he'd be worth trying out as a swamper, but all he said was: "He's just like a cipher with the sum rubbed out."

But big-hearted old Pop Lester gave Shorty a job washing dishes in the cafe. The pay wasn't very big, but it gave Shorty a place to sleep and three meals a day. Shorty never complained. It took him quite a while to learn the job, but Pop was patient. Della Finley, the top waitress, thought Shorty was sweet. Maybe that wasn't the right word but it was the best thing anybody said about him.

Shorty still wasn't entirely cured. He had a limp in his left leg, his right arm troubled him, and he said he still had headaches. Someone remarked that when Doc sewed up the twenty-seven stitches in Shorty's scalp, he went too deep with some of 'em.

I gave Shorty a free shave every couple days, and once I asked him if he aimed to stay in Canyon City.

"Maybe," he answered.

"Just waiting to get well, huh?" I said.

"Just waiting," he said.

A couple times a month a bunch of us old-timers meet in a back room of the Alhambra and kind of map out things for the good of the Community. One time Shorty's name was mentioned, and someone said he was getting along pretty good now. Nobody complained about him, we just talked.

Shorty wasn't very old, and it was sort of a shame for him to keep on washing dishes and all that. We thought he had no ambition at all. Pop said that Shorty would make a real good dishwasher, if he'd learn how to do things and keep his mind on the job.

"I've seen him stand there, a dirty plate in one hand and a rag in the other, and just stare at the wall for five minutes while everybody is yelling for plates. I dunno, maybe that fall kinked him up pretty bad. What do you think, Doc?" said Pop.

Doc Machin took his time answering, as he always did.

"I don't rightly know," confessed Doc. "He's a queer, quiet, little washed-out devil. You know, one day he said to me, 'Doc, what's a man's name worth?' Just like that. He had me stumped and all I could say was, 'Shorty, in this country a name don't mean a thing—they're so easy to alter.' He seemed to know what I meant. So then I said, 'It ain't so much the name as what you do with it.' "

"Well," said Pop, "there's one thing sure—Shorty won't ever hurt anybody. If he knows more than six words, I've never heard 'em. The only thing is, I can't afford to pay him much; not enough for him to ever get stage-fare to Gateway, even if he wanted to get out."

Well, the upshot of the meeting was that eleven of us agreed to pay Pop a dollar apiece a week, so he could pay it to Shorty. Pop said it would have to be that way, 'cause Shorty wouldn't take charity. I thought of all those shaves and Doc Machin thought of what he had done free—but we dug up the money.

I asked Pop the next day if he gave Shorty his raise, and Pop wasn't too happy. I asked Pop what Shorty said.

"I asked him if he didn't think he'd soon have enough money to move to a better place, and he said, 'It's nice here. Maybe I can save enough money to buy a horse.'" Pop answered.

I asked Pop if he knew why Shorty ever came to Canyon City, and he said he asked Shorty that same question.

"Well?" I asked.

"He just stared at the wall—a plate in one hand and a dishrag in the other," said Pop. "Maybe he don't remember."

The next day, along about noon, I was in Pop's place eating at the counter. Pop was there, leaning against the counter talking with me. I could look through a service window and see Shorty back there, washing dishes. Sam Hughes, the marshal, was over at a table, talking with Henry Justine, the banker. Several other folks were in there, eating and talking.

Then it sounded like a handful of firecrackers were going off down the street, and it was still two months short of Fourth of July. A couple more went off, closer this time, and a window of the cafe went out in a shower of busted glass. The door was flung open, and a man sprawled across the floor.

"The Piegan Kid and his gang!" he yelled, and started crawling into the kitchen on his hands and knees.

The scene in there changed awful fast. Sam Hughes and Henry Justine went to the floor, and it looked as though both of them were trying to get behind the same chair-leg. Another bullet came through the broken window and smashed the glass on a framed picture behind the counter.

I don't want anybody to think that I'm so brave I could sit there and tell what happened. The fact is, I was paralyzed from the knees down. Loose horses were running around the street, a runaway wagon team took the porch-posts from under the porch at the Alhambra, and the air was full of dust. I remember looking back through the service window, and I saw Shorty wiping his hands on his dirty-white apron. It just struck me that he wanted to go out clean.

Somebody yelled that a fire was starting at the south end of the street, but nobody made a move to try and put it out. Then Shorty came from the kitchen, still wearing his old apron, sleeves rolled up. As he started for the door, I wanted to yell to him to get down, but my voice sounded like a little whistle. Then he opened the door and walked out.

The Piegan Kid gang was out in the middle of the street, shooting the windows out of the two-story hotel, when Shorty came out, and turned to the left. I managed to get to the busted window on my hands and knees, and I peered out. I couldn't see Shorty, but I could see them five outlaws, smoking guns in their hands, their eyes following Shorty, as he went up the sidewalk.

It seemed as though every sound died out suddenly. Them five men just stood there, paying no attention to anything else.

I figured that Shorty had gone into the marshal's office, from the way the five outlaws acted.

Maybe I'm just a nosy old devil or maybe I forgot to be careful—but I *had* to see what was going on out there. I stuck my head and shoulders through the smashed window, where I could look straight up the street. Just then Shorty stepped out of the marshal's office, with a .30-30 carbine in his hands. He stopped short, feet braced, with the butt of the gun against his right thigh.

If any man ever contemplated suicide it was Shorty. All five outlaws were looking at him, probably too amazed to shoot him. Then the Piegan Kid came to life and swung up his gun. It seemed as though all the windows of the marshal's office faded out in a blast of gunfire, but the Piegan Kid was spinning on one high heel, his gun flying over his head.

One man began turning around like a tired pup, and ran into another one who was doing a soft-shoe dance, looking down at his own feet, arms outspread. Another one tossed his gun aside, backed up, hit the calves of his legs against the sidewalk, and fell flat on his back. I dunno what happened to the fifth one. When I saw him, his nose was in the dirt.

It was all over in split seconds. Shorty, during all that fusillade, never even moved his braced feet. He levered out the last empty shell, turned back into the office.

We all suddenly got real brave, and went out there. Not one of the five was worth Doc's attention.

A short time later Shorty went back to the cafe to his job.

I don't believe Shorty wanted to leave Canyon City, but the bank bought him a horse and the rest of us bought him a saddle. Sam Hughes gave him a belt and a Colt .45.

Somebody had to notify the sheriff and the coroner at Gateway, so I took the job. Shorty said good-bye, and we pulled out.

While the sheriff and the coroner were getting ready for the trip to Canyon City, the sheriff talked to Shorty.

"So you got the notorious Piegan Kid," he said. "You're a mighty big little feller. Dozens of rewards, big money rewards. I'll see that you get the money."

"Don't bother, mister," said Shorty quietly. "You'll find out he wasn't the Piegan Kid—just a name-rustler."

Shorty rode away then in the dark. Don't ask me what he meant.

GAMBLIN' MAN

Dwight V. Swain

GAMBLERS, like cowboys and drifters, were also a staple of pulp writers. Most often these "knights of the green cloth," as they were later known, were portrayed as either villainous rogues, bent on cheating every man they played with, or heroic champions of justice who would not have turned a dishonest card if their lives depended on it—and with very little shading in between. Mr. Devereaux, the protagonist of "Gamblin' Man," is therefore something of a fictional rarity: a gambler who has both good and bad qualities, and who has a curious sentimental streak besides. His adventures in the town of Crooked Lance are most entertaining as a result.

*Trained as a journalist, Dwight V. Swain supplemented his income in the forties and early fifties by selling short stories, novelettes, and novellas to the pulps. In addition to Westerns, he wrote science fiction, mysteries, and adventure yarns, and was a frequent contributor to the magazines in the Ziff-Davis chain (*Mammoth Western, Mammoth Detective, Fantastic Adventures, Amazing Stories*). Two of his long pulp science fiction tales were published in paperback in the fifties—* Cry Chaos! *and* The Transposed Man. *In recent years he has lectured widely and published a number of nonfiction books on the art of successful writing.*

Stiff-lipped and grim, Mr. Devereaux fingered the double eagle and wondered bleakly if all hulking, loudmouthed men were scoundrels; or was it merely that Fate chose only uncommon blackguards to send his way? Even worse, why did he not discover their connivings before they'd stripped him down to twenty dollars? He had one double eagle left. His last.

Across the table the man called Alonzo Park scooped up the cards, squared the deck, and riffled it in an expert shuffle. In the process he also managed an incredibly deft bit of palming that ended with six cards missing, just as in previous games.

Almost without thinking, Mr. Devereaux left off fingering the gold piece and instead caressed his sleeve-rigged double derringer.

This table around which they played was jammed in a corner at one end of the El Dorado's bar. It was out of the way, yet close to the source of supply of the red-eye of which Park, who owned the place, seemed so fond. It was a good twenty feet to the door, twenty feet past cold-eyed, gun-slung loungers who wandered about the saloon.

Park's voice cut in, a reverberant, bull-throated bellow. The man's meaty features glistened red as his own raw forty-rod whiskey.

"Lafe! Drinks all around!"

In silent, studied apathy, Mr. Devereaux allowed the cross-eyed barkeep to refill his glass and continued his appraisal.

A sheepherder sat to his left, no gun showing. Beyond him, a rat-visaged nondescript from the livery stable, toting a rusted .45. Then Park, ostensibly unarmed; probably he favored a hideout gun. And finally, to Mr. Devereaux's right, completing the circuit, a brawny, freckle-faced young fellow, Charlie Adams, who swayed drunkenly in his chair and held solemn, incongruous converse with a long-skirted, china-headed doll over a foot tall which he kept propped on the table before him.

Mr. Devereaux's hand turned out a mediocre pair, augmented by another—equally mediocre—on the draw.

Again he weighed that last remaining gold piece and studied Park. Finally he shoved the double eagle forward.

The sheepherder and the nondescript threw in their cards.

Charlie Adams hesitated, ogling Mr. Devereaux owlishly from behind the doll, then followed suit. For a moment Park, too, hung back. But only for a moment.

"Raise you, Devereaux! I'll call your bluff!"

Mr. Devereaux could feel his own blood quicken, the hackles rise along his neck. Imperceptibly, he hunched his left shoulder forward, just enough for the black frock coat to clear his armpit-holstered Colt. The sleeve-rigged derringer held an old friend's reassurance.

"And raise you back, Park," he said softly. He reached into the pot, removed his double eagle as if to replace it with something larger.

A harsh, raw note crept into Alonzo Park's bull voice. He thrust his chin belligerently forward. "Put in your money, Devereaux. Put up or shut up."

Mr. Devereaux allowed himself the luxury of a thin, wry smile. He breathed deep—and savored the fact that this very breath might be his last. He pushed the thought back down and brought out the Colt in one swift, sure gesture.

He let his voice ring, then.

"Misdeal, Park. I'm betting my gun against your stack that there are less than fifty-two cards on this table—and that we'll find the others in a holdout on your side!"

Silence. Echoing eternities of silence, spreading out across the room. The sheepherder and the nondescript sat stiff and shriveled. Adams stared stupidly, jaw hanging, the big doll clasped to his chest.

Gun poised, feet flat against the floor, Mr. Devereaux waited. He watched the muscles in Park's bull neck knot, the hairy hands contract. "God help you, you dirty son!" Park rasped thickly. "I'll have your hide for this!"

"No doubt," Mr. Devereaux agreed. He gestured with his Colt to the livery groom. "Look under the table-edge for a holdout."

The man flicked one nervous glance at the gun, then bent to obey. He came up with two aces and three assorted spades.

Mr. Devereaux let his thin smile broaden. "I win." He rose, started to reach for Alonzo Park's stack. And he realized, even in that moment, the magnitude of his error.

The cross-eyed bartender whipped up a sawed-off shotgun with a bore that loomed big as twin water buckets. It seemed to Mr. Devereaux in that moment that he could hear the faint, sweet song of angel voices.

A gun's roar cut them short.

Sheer reflex sent Mr. Devereaux floorward, wrapped in vast disbelief at finding himself alive. He glimpsed the scattergun, flying off across the room. He stared at the cross-eyed bartender, while that worthy swore and clutched at a bleeding hand.

Big Adams, drunk no longer, came to his feet. He still gripped the doll, but now the china head was gone. The muzzle of a .45 protruded from its shredded, smoldering neck. Left-handed, he reached a nickeled star from his pocket and pinned it on. His freckled, good-natured face had gone suddenly cold, his voice hard and level.

"You're under arrest, Park. The town council held a private confab last night. They decided Crooked Lance needed a marshal an' gave me the job. The first chore on the list was to clean up the El Dorado."

❧

The day dragged drowsily, even for Crooked Lance town. September's shimmering, brazen sun hung at two o'clock, the straggled clumps of cholla and Spanish bayonet a-ripple in its heat. The choked, close scent of sun on stone, and dust and dirt and baking 'dobe, rose faint yet all-pervasive. Even the thrumming flies droned lethargy, and the tail of breeze from distant, cloud-capped mountains alone kept the sparse shade tolerable.

Peace came to Mr. Devereaux. He loved such sleepy days as this, days for dreams and smiles and reveries. Relaxed and tranquil, he contemplated the padlocked El Dorado from his chair on the hotel porch. He wondered, in turn, how Alonzo

Park liked his cell in the feedstore that served Crooked Lance as a makeshift jail.

The man was a fool, Mr. Devereaux decided soberly. Else why would he stay here, insisting on trial, instead of thankfully accepting Adams's offer to let him ride out of town unfettered, on his own agreement never to return? What possible defense could he offer? Did he actually believe he could salvage his fortunes?

The thought brought Mr. Devereaux's own financial state to mind. Adams was holding last night's poker pots as evidence till after the trial this afternoon. It left Mr. Devereaux with only the one twenty-dollar gold piece. He contemplated the coin wryly. He flipped it. His last double eagle, still.

The scuff of feet and the acrid breath of rising dust cut short his reveries. He looked around to see Crooked Lance's new marshal and a chubby, fresh-scrubbed cherub in pigtails and starched gingham round the corner hand in hand, the cherub wobbling ludicrously as she vainly tried to make her short legs match the lawman's long strides.

Adams nodded greetings, dropped into a chair beside Mr. Devereaux on the porch. He grinned boyishly.

"This here's my gal Alice, Devereaux. You better be nice to her, too. That was her doll I was totin' last night."

The cherub giggled and hid her face in her father's lap.

"You said you'd get me another dolly, Daddy. You promised." A tremor of excitement ran through her and she raised her head, eyes shining. "I know just the kind I want, Daddy. Missus Lauck's got one in her window. Blue eyes that close, and real gold hair."

Adams grinned again. He dandled her, gleeful and squealing, on one knee.

"Don't push me too fast, honey. Wait'll I draw at least one pay." Then, to Mr. Devereaux: "Guess we better mosey on over to the schoolhouse for court. Trial's set for two thirty. Soon's it's over I can give you back your money."

Mr. Devereaux nodded, rose. Flat-crowned Stetson in

hand, he stared off across the desert miles. An indefinable weariness washed over him, as if some queer, invisible shadow had crept across the turquoise sky. He caught himself wondering how it would feel to bounce a pigtailed daughter on one's knee. . . .

It being Crooked Lance's first trial, the town council had voted in the mayor as judge. He sat behind the teacher's desk in the little adobe schoolhouse now, a thin, stooped, balding man, gavel in hand, gnawing his lips. He served as a barber, ordinarily, and these new responsibilities rode heavily upon him.

Mr. Devereaux chuckled benignly and let his gaze travel on. The little room was a babble of voices, the bare wood benches already filled. Whole families were out: fathers, mothers, children. Others, too—and over these he did not chuckle. Silent, too-casual men with guns lounging along the back wall. Last night they'd been lounging the same way at the El Dorado.

Adams brought in the prisoner.

Park had recovered his poise. Jaw outthrust, red face bright with what might pass for righteous indignation, he strode aggressively to his place. When, for the fraction of a second, his gaze met Mr. Devereaux's, his eyes were venomous, mocking, strangely mirthful.

Mr. Devereaux frowned despite himself. Almost without thinking, he touched his derringer's butt.

His Honor rapped for order, peered hesitantly down at the prisoner. "You want someone to help you, Park? You got a right, you know."

Park glowered. "I don't need help for what I've got to say."

Adams took the stand, told how he'd set in on the game at Park's own table, feigning drunkenness. He'd picked that particular game, he explained, because he wanted to find out whether the El Dorado's owner, personally, was doing the cheating the council had ordered him to investigate. Further, he'd figured that table as most likely for action, Mr.

Devereaux being a man who "looked like he knew his way around a deck of cards without no Injun guide, an' hard to buffalo, too!"

Park's only comment was a contempt-laden snort.

As before, Mr. Devereaux frowned. Instinctively, he shrugged the black frock coat smooth about his shoulders. The Colt's weight stood out sharp in his consciousness. Then the judge was calling him forward to take the stand.

In an instant Alonzo Park was on his feet. "Your Honor!" he bellowed.

His Honor started, cringed. Finally he made a feeble pass at pounding with his gavel. "Now, Park—"

"Don't 'Now Park' me!" the prisoner roared, his face the hue of a too-ripe plum. "Now's the time I speak my piece." He glowered and his eyes swept the room. Yet somehow, to Mr. Devereaux, there seemed to be a certain theatrical note about it all, as if the man were carefully building up a part.

Park went on. "You've called me a crooked tinhorn on the say of that jackass Charlie Adams, and I've kept quiet. But I'm damned if I'll let you ring in this gun-wolf, too!"

The judge chewed his lips, looked uneasily from Park to Adams to Mr. Devereaux and back again. "What you got agin' him, Lon?" he queried uneasily.

Mr. Devereaux saw the triumph in Park's eyes, then—the murderous glee the front of indignation veiled. He stared in dismay as the man whipped out a flimsy, too-familiar pamphlet.

"This is the 'wanted' list of the Adjutant General of Texas!" Park bellowed. "You've brought me up for crooked gambling, but your chief witness is a card shark and a killer, on the dodge from a murderous charge!"

Mr. Devereaux could feel the tension leap within the room. His own breath came too fast. As from afar he heard the El Dorado's owner shout on, work himself into a frenzy.

"Your haywire marshal gave me a chance to run out if I wanted to, but I stayed. I guess that shows whether I'm guilty or not! This tinhorn planted that holdout under the table. He figured to chase me out of town so he could take over the El Dorado—"

Somewhere at the back of the room a man yelled, "Park's right! Turn him loose! That Devereaux's the one should be in jail!"

The schoolroom exploded to a screaming madhouse. A tribute, Mr. Devereaux thought dourly as he maneuvered himself against the nearest wall, to Alonzo Park and his carefully-stationed loungers.

The judge brought down his gavel with a bang. It was the first time since the beginning of the trial that he had showed such force and vigor.

"Case dismissed!"

"What about Devereaux?" somebody yelled.

As if in answer, Charlie Adams shoved forward, gun out. His good-natured face had gone worried and grim.

"I got no choice, Devereaux. You're under arrest!"

6

A cloud had swept down during that stormy schoolhouse session, Mr. Devereaux discovered. Already it impinged on the sun's bright sphere, a scudding wall of night stretched off to the distant mountains. The wind had quickened, too; freshened. Now it came whipping through Crooked Lance in gusts and buffets, sucking up little geysers of sand that swirled and rustled like dry leaves.

"Let's go, Devereaux," Adams said. His voice was flat.

Carefully, Mr. Devereaux adjusted his flat-crowned Stetson, shrugged smooth the black frock coat. It was a useless gesture, really, now that the heavy Colt was gone. Its absence gave him a queer, off-balance feeling. The sleeve-rigged derringer alone remained to comfort. That, and the gold piece. One double eagle. He laughed without mirth and flipped it in a glittering arc. Together, Devereaux and Adams moved out into the street.

The storm came faster now, blotting out light, racing

hungrily on across the desert. The wind increased with it, drove tiny stones into Mr. Devereaux's face. Dust choked him. Sand gritted between his teeth.

Voiceless, he strode on. The thing was inevitable, he supposed, a peril that went with notoriety. Periodically he was bound to be recognized. The only marvel was that any lobo vindictive as Park had been content to leave an enemy to the law.

They passed the shuttered, padlocked El Dorado. The Silver Lady, too. Grant's Drygoods. Lettie Lauck's millinery.

Lettie Lauck. Mr. Devereaux pondered the name, remembered Alice and her doll. Alice, the fresh-scrubbed cherub in her pigtails and starched gingham. He wondered, a bit wistful, if he would ever see her again.

"Turn here," Adams said.

The feedstore that served as jail had an inner storage room—zinc-lined against rats—for a cell. The marshal prodded Mr. Devereaux toward it.

Mr. Devereaux sighed. It was coming now. It had to come. He touched the derringer's butt.

Marshal Adams swung open the storeroom's heavy door. "In there."

Mr. Devereaux studied him, caressed the derringer. "You believe it, then, Charlie?" He made his voice very gentle.

"Believe what?"

"The things Alonzo Park said."

Adams laughed. It had a harsh, unhappy sound. "What does it matter? Your name was in that book. You're on the owlhoot."

"A packed jury might call things murder that you wouldn't, Charlie."

He could see the sweat come to Adams's broad forehead. Then the jaw tightened.

"Sorry, Devereaux. That's twixt you an' the Adjutant Gen'ral of Texas. Folks here just hired me to hold up the law, not judge it."

Again Mr. Devereaux sighed. Nodded. The loose-hol-
stered years went into his draw. "I'm sorry, too, Marshal. I
can't take that chance." Cat-footed, he backed towards the
open outer door.

Behind him, a gun roared.

Mr. Devereaux leaped sidewise—swiveling; firing. He
glimpsed only a blur of motion as the gunman jumped away.
That, and Adams pitching to the floor.

The minutes that followed never came quite clear to Mr.
Devereaux. He acted by instinct, rather than logic, reloading
the derringer as he ran. No need to ask himself what would
happen if Crooked Lance's shouting citizenry should find
him here by the fallen marshal, gun in hand.

But the townsmen were out already, a dozen or more of
them, headed across the street towards him at a dead run
even as he broke cover. Mr. Devereaux turned hastily, to the
tune of oaths and bullets. He ducked between two buildings,
to come out seconds later in an alley.

The jail-and-feedstore combination was of frame construc-
tion set on low, stone corner posts close to the ground. Mr.
Devereaux dropped, rolled into the shallow space beneath
the building.

There followed an eternity of dust and rocks and cobwebs,
lasting well over an hour. When his pursuers finally gave up
and silence once more reigned, he wriggled forth and stumbled stiffly to his feet.

The storm had brought with it an early dusk. Wind
whipped the black frock coat tight about his legs as he tried
to dust away the worst of the debris from beneath the
building. Aching, irritable—and infinitely cautious—he gave
it up, headed for the livery barn on down the alley.

The nondescript groom sprawled asleep in the haymow.
Ever wary, Mr. Devereaux prodded him awake.

Grumbling, bleary-eyed, the man rose, peered at Mr.

Devereaux through the stable's gloom. His lantern jaw dropped. "You!"

Mr. Devereaux favored him with one curt nod, brought up the derringer. "At your service. And now, if you'll saddle my black stallion . . ."

The nondescript swayed, still staring. His words came out a half-coherent mumble. "I thought you was over there at Park's."

"Park's?"

"Sure. The El Dorado. One o' Park's boys got scared about you bein' holed up there. He come round huntin' Adams."

Mr. Devereaux compressed his lips to a thin, straight line. "Adams is dead."

"Dead?" The groom eyed him queerly. "Who says he's dead? He come in here lookin' for you not half a hour ago. Doc Brand patched up that hole in his shoulder."

"He . . . wasn't killed?"

"Uh-uh. Not even crippled bad."

'One o' Park's boys come huntin'. . . .'

Mr. Devereaux stood very still. Discovered, with a strange abstraction, that he was hanging on the beats of his own heart. Of a sudden his mouth grew dry.

The nondescript was speaking again now, eyeing the derringer as he rubbed his lantern jaw. "You carry that thing in a sleeve-rig, don't you? Adams was tellin' 'bout it while Doc Brand fixed him up."

"Indeed?" Mr. Devereaux stiffened. "In that case, perhaps you'll favor me with the loan of your Colt." He stepped close, reached the rusting gun from its holster.

"Yeah, sure." The nondescript shifted uneasily, licked his lips. "I'll get your horse up, too."

As in a dream, Mr. Devereaux followed, patted the nickering stallion's sleek jet neck. "This is a time for travel, boy," he heard himself say. "We'll give this groom our double eagle for his gun and be on our way."

'One o' Park's boys come huntin'. . . .'

One of Park's men had come hunting, to tell an honest marshal where a wanted man was hiding. Only it wasn't true. He, the hunted, hadn't been there.

In his mind's eye he pictured Alonzo Park with his bull neck and meaty, flushed face. Yes, Park would use a fugitive's name to bait a trap for an honest marshal.

"Did Park's man find Adams?" he asked, and in spite of all his efforts he could not make it sound quite casual.

"Uh-uh. He'd already left."

For a long, wordless moment Mr. Devereaux stood there. Slowly drew in a deep, full breath. His lips felt stiff, unreal.

The groom shuffled his feet. "If you'll just lemme get there . . ."

Ever so faintly, Mr. Devereaux smiled. Again he patted the stallion's neck. He replaced the gold piece in his pocket.

"That won't be necessary now. I've had a change of plans." And then, after a second: "If the marshal asks for me again, you can tell him I'm at the El Dorado."

⊙

Alonzo Park sprawled in the selfsame chair he'd occupied the night before, back to the bar, red-eye whiskey at his elbow.

"You scared me, Devereaux. I was beginning to be afraid you wouldn't come."

Mr. Devereaux raised his brows, allowed his curiosity to show. "You expected me, then?"

"Expected you? Of course I expected you." Park laughed. "You've got a rep for being a sentimental fool, Devereaux. They tell stories about it all the way to Montana. Last night Adams backed your play, so I knew you'd come when you heard he'd bought himself some trouble."

"And so?"

"So now we wait till Adams shows up to pinch you. Both of you'll turn up dead. Then I'll tell it that you forced me to hide you out at gunpoint. You killed Adams, and I killed you. The town will give me a vote of thanks." Again he leered. "Nice, eh?"

Wordless, Mr. Devereaux shrugged. It had seemed such a good idea, this check on Park. Interception by the cross-eyed, shotgun-toting barkeep was another story. They'd nailed him cold, overlooked nothing save the derringer in their search. They'd have found it, too, except that he'd transferred it to a new hideout within his flat-crowned Stetson after the stable groom's comment on the sleeve-rig.

So, now he stood here before Alonzo Park in the echoing, dimlit El Dorado. The scatter-gunner still covered him from behind the bar—grim, incongruous against the background of mirrors and pyramided bottles. Two other Park gunmen crouched by the street-front windows at the far end of the room, eyes glued to cracks in the shutters.

One of the men by the windows sang out, low, tense. "It's Adams! Here he comes!"

Park grinned wolfishly. "Well, Devereaux?"

A chill rippled through Mr. Devereaux in spite of his control. He had to fight to keep his tremor from his face. "I bow to superior talent, sir!" He took off the Stetson, mopped his brow. His sweating fingers closed round the derringer's butt. His knuckles showed white.

"He'll be here in ten seconds, Lon!" the gunman said.

Mr. Devereaux turned a trifle, stared straight into the bartender's crossed eyes. The shotgun's barrels loomed like cannon. Desperately, he tried to give his voice the right inflection.

"These maneuverings raise a thirst. Make mine Mill's Blue-grass, please."

For the fraction of a second the bartender's gaze wavered toward the bottles stacked behind him.

Mr. Devereaux brought the derringer up past the Stetson's brim, fired once. A black spot the size of a dime appeared just above the man's left cheekbone.

Chill, rock-steady now, Mr. Devereaux swiveled.

Park snarled, clawed a pistol from beneath his coat.

Mr. Devereaux fired the other barrel. He watched two of Park's bared teeth disappear, the man himself totter over backwards.

Behind him, the street end of the room reverberated gunfire. He swung. Park's gunmen were already down, Charlie Adams coming forward stiff-legged, a smoking .45 in his hand. The marshal bent, twisted the pistol away from the dead Park.

"A .31. That's what Doc Brand said shot me," Adams said.

Other men were crowding through the door now, bug-eyed, excited men with loud voices. Mr. Devereaux ignored them, held his own tone steady. He even managed to inject a faint, ironic note. "You were looking for me, Marshal?"

The other's freckled face froze. "I still am. You're wanted back in Texas."

"And duty's duty?" Mr. Devereaux sighed. Of a sudden he felt very old, very weary. "So be it, Marshal. A man must play it as he sees it." Then: "Dry work, Marshal. If you don't mind, I'll have a drink."

Very carefully, he rounded the end of the bar, stared down at the fallen, cross-eyed barkeep.

"Dead." He bent, as if to move the man away. Then, instead, he snatched up the scattergun and straightened fast. "Buckshot means burying, gentlemen. Do I have any takers?"

No one moved. Then Adams let out his breath, scowled.

"Damn you, Devereaux!"

Somehow, to Mr. Devereaux, it sounded like a benediction.

Wordless, he backed through the El Dorado's open doorway, whipped loose the reins of a big, snake-eyed bay at the rail, and led the beast out of view beside the building. He fired the scattergun into the air as he booted the bay across the rump, hard.

The horse let out a snort second cousin to a Comanche war whoop and took off with a thunder of hoofs. Mr.

Devereaux ducked back into the shadows and stood stock still.

The rush of feet in the El Dorado came like an echo to the big bay's thunder. Shouting, cursing, the marshal and his men boiled out the door, forked saddles and raced off in wild pursuit.

Mr. Devereaux waited till they were out of sight. He'd pick up the black stallion at the livery barn according to plan and head off south. There'd be plenty of time. Yes, plenty of time . . .

Again Lettie Lauck's shop caught his eye. It was lighted. He could see a tall young woman moving about inside.

The doll was still there, a big one, even bigger than the one Charlie Adams had carried. The eyes were wide and blue, the hair shimmering gold, the gown of silk. It was a beautiful doll.

The price tag was there, too: twenty dollars.

Almost without thinking, Mr. Devereaux reached into his pocket, fingered the double eagle. His last double eagle, still.

With a start, it came to him that the sky had cleared. The stars were out and the wind no longer blew. For an instant he almost thought he could hear Charlie Adams's shouts as he spurred his riders on. He smiled. . . .

Still smiling, he stepped inside the shop. He doffed the flat-crowned Stetson politely as the tall young woman came forward.

"The doll in the window, please," said Mr. Devereaux.

THE MESTENOS

H. A. DeRosso

ANIMALS were prominently featured in many pulp stories. In some they were the viewpoint characters, with humans relegated to minor (and sometimes nonexistent) roles; such writers as Jim Kjelgaard and Paul Annixter were particularly adept at this type of story. Horses, of course, were the animals most often used, with dogs the second favorite. But good pulp stories were published about all sorts of other creatures, among them bulls, wolves, moose, bears, cougars, beavers, and even walrus.

Horses—or rather mestenos, or mustangs—*are the featured animals in the story which follows, in particular a "great and wise" stallion called Roano. A peculiar, symbiotic relationship between Roano and a horse rancher named Feliz is the focal point of the tale. "The Mestenos" is also notable for the haunting element of mysticism introduced at its climax—an element that was usually frowned upon by pulp Western editors.*

H. A. DeRosso (1917–1962) began writing while in high school in the mid thirties, and made his first sale to Western Story *in 1941. For the next fifteen years he contributed more than two hundred short stories, novelettes, and novellas to most of the Western pulp and digest magazines (and occasional stories to a smattering of mystery and science fiction magazines as well). His five published novels are all Westerns:* Tracks in the Sand *(1951),* .44 *(1953),* The Gun Trail *(1953),* End of the Gun *(1955), and* The Dark Brand *(1963, published posthumously). Almost all of his frontier fiction is offbeat, character-oriented, with more depth and feeling, and more substance, than standard pulp fare.*

"Try to understand, Feliz," Eastland said. "We don't like to harm the mestenos but we have no choice. Can't you understand?"

Feliz looked at the men in front of him, sitting in their saddles. Cobardes, he thought. I understand. I understand so well I could kill you, Eastland, and you were once my friend.

"You've known me a long time, Feliz," Eastland went on. Wind off the flank of the Coronados stirred his hat brim gently. "You know I wouldn't kill a horse, any horse, unless I really had to. You know that, don't you?"

"No one's going to hurt my mestenos," Feliz said.

"Your mestenos?" Crawford cried. He glared at the rifle in Feliz's hands. "Where the devil do you get that stuff? Mustangs are any man's property who rounds them up. They're no more your mestenos than the man in the moon's."

"Try to look at it our way, Feliz," Eastland said. "It hasn't rained for a long time. The mestenos come down from the Coronados and eat our graze and drink our water. The stallions run off with our mares. Things are going hard for us, Feliz. We don't like it but the mestenos have all got to die."

"The mestenos were here before you came," Feliz said. "If things are going hard for you, why don't you go away? Why blame the mestenos?"

"Feliz," Eastland said, spreading his hands in a pleading gesture. "We're old friends, aren't we? You have always been welcome at my ranch. My wife has fed you. My son has learned all he knows about horses from you. You and I have talked together about the ways of horses many times. Do you doubt me when I say I wish it could be different but there is no other choice?"

"I will not let you or anyone kill the mestenos."

"He's loco," Crawford said. His face was full of angry color. "He's always been loco. Look how he used to hunt mustangs, tracking them on foot, living with them until they took him as one of their own. Now that he's old he's more loco than ever. Are we going to let a crazy man tell us what to do?"

"He might be loco," Ainsworth said, "but he's got a rifle."

"There's five of us," Crawford cried. "Are we going to let a crazy half-breed buffalo us?"

"You want to start it?" Bailey asked. "You want the first slug?"

"Stop that kind of talk," Eastland said. "We're not going to have any trouble. Let's give him a couple of days to think it over."

"You always had a soft spot for the crazy coot," Crawford told Eastland. "You think a couple of days will make him change?"

"It won't hurt to try."

"I'm tired of waiting. Dammit, I'm almost out of graze. If it don't rain pretty soon—"

"A couple more days won't hurt you," Eastland said.

"You trying a stall, Eastland?"

Eastland turned on Crawford. Eastland's mouth was tight, his eyes hard. "I'm in the same fix you are, Crawford. In fact, I've got more to lose than you. I'm not going to sit on my rump and let myself be wiped out. But we are giving Feliz a couple of days."

Eastland's eyes moved back to Feliz. "Listen to me, Feliz. Listen to me as a friend. The old days are over. They are gone for good. The mustangs are through here in the Coronados."

They are not through, Feliz thought, as long as I have breath to breathe and bullets to shoot and a knife to cut.

"But there are other places, Feliz," Eastland went on. "There's a lot of open country to the south. Why don't you take your best mestenos and lead them there?"

"This is my home," Feliz said.

"I know," Eastland said, "and no one is trying to chase you away. But the mestenos have got to go one way or another."

"This is their home, too. We will never leave the Coronados."

"Two days, Feliz," Eastland said. His eyes softened. "Will you try to understand? Will you take your best horses and leave? If you are not gone in two days—" His mouth drew tight and thin. "I swear to it, Feliz. Two days. No more . . ."

Feliz picked up the tracks of the manada heading north and he turned his dun in pursuit. In the distance Carrizo Peak loomed high and ragged and awesome. The wind blew hard down from the Coronados, filling the tracks in fast, but not too fast for Feliz.

Roano, he thought happily, my beautiful Roanito. I would know your hoofmarks on solid stone. You will be mine yet. You are wild and wary but you will be mine.

He topped a rise and there below he saw the mustang band, drinking at the water hole. Some of the mares were rolling on the ground. Several colts frolicked. The roan stallion stood to one side, head high as he spied Feliz in the distance.

Feliz reined in the dun. He dismounted and tied the horse to a juniper. Then he started down the slope on foot. The stallion snorted and pranced, watching Feliz come on.

Oh, you are a great and wise stallion, Feliz thought. From out of nowhere you came and took the manada away from the grullo. You will make a great sire and you will be mine. Some day soon you will be mine.

The wind took his scent and carried it down to the manada. The stallion snorted and shied and pawed at the ground with a front hoof. Several of the mares watched Feliz docilely.

Ho, you know my smell already, he thought. That is good. You would already accept me because you know I mean you no harm. But you, Roano, you big red devil, you do not trust me yet, do you?

He moved on steadily, without hurry. The whole band was watching him now, even the colts. The stallion nickered angrily and tossed his head. The long mane fluttered in the wind.

It is good that you are so careful, Roanito, Feliz thought. You must be more careful than ever now. Those cobardes will kill you if they get the chance and you must not give them the chance. You must be very careful, Roano.

The stallion blew loudly and pranced nervously. One of the mares started toward Feliz and the stallion jumped in front of her and nipped her in the neck. The mare turned back.

You are a good stallion, Roanito, Feliz thought. You still do not trust me even though I am not like the other men-animals who would like to kill you. Leave the Coronados, they said to me. Leave? When the Coronados are our home?

He moved on. The stallion trumpeted a cry of alarm and anger. He wheeled and started nipping the flanks of the mares. They were reluctant to go but he started them. They left in a cloud of dust with the stallion trailing them, biting and kicking to urge more speed out of them. Feliz watched until even their dust was gone. Then he started back up the slope to get his dun.

Your day will come, Roanito, he thought. The day will come, and soon, when you will accept me. Every time you let me come a little closer. But it is good for you to be so careful. Be very careful. If anyone ever harms you or any more of my mestenos—"

Feliz awoke next morning with a strong feeling of apprehension. He came to his feet and for a while he stood stock still, head flung up, sniffing the air. He could discern nothing out of the ordinary but still the uneasiness would not leave him.

Roano, he thought, are you in trouble, Roano? I have not seen you in two days. The other manadas I have seen but not yours. Where have you gone?

He saddled the dun and rode off, chewing on a piece of dried jerky. Once he thought he heard shots and he reined the dun in and rose up in the stirrups and listened with his head cocked to one side. The sounds had been so faint, however, that he could not be sure he had heard anything. Nevertheless, his heart quickened. Dread made him ill.

Roano. Have they hurt you, Roanito?

When he saw the vultures gathering in the sky a hand of ice closed about his heart. He lifted the dun into a hard run. The vultures kept gathering, floating and wheeling high in the sky on wide-spread, motionless wings.

Is that for you, Roanito? If it is, I'll—

His hand closed about the handle of the knife in his belt. A burst of rage made him tremble but it was quickly gone. Only the dread remained now, the sick, cold dread.

He found them, what was left of them, at the foot of a mesa. Several vultures rose and left with a foul flapping of great black wings. Feliz stared at the rim of the mesa over which the manada had plunged and then down at the smashed, bloody carcasses. He began to weep when he saw the stallion.

"I will make them pay, Roanito," he said aloud. "I swear to you, you will not go unavenged. With my gun and knife and even my bare hands I will make them pay. If I could I would bury you, my beautiful Roanito. Little horse, I will never forget you. . . ."

In the cold, gray dawn Feliz waited. He lay in a small depression on a knoll and there below him he could see the ranch buildings and the corrals. His rifle lay on the ground beside him.

Five, he thought, five cabrones. I remember you. The two Ainsworths, and Bailey, and that hijo de puta Crawford, and you, Eastland. I will kill even you but it will be the Ainsworths first, father and son. When they come out . . .

Smoke curled from the chimney of the house. The elder Ainsworth came out and went to the corral and pitched some hay to the horses penned there. Feliz picked up the rifle but he did not shoot.

I will wait until I have them both, he thought. I want them both.

The elder Ainsworth was through now and he went back in the house. Feliz watched the smoke curling out of the chimney. His fingers grew numb from holding the cold rifle and he put it down and shoved his hands underneath his buckskin jacket to warm them.

The boy came out after a while. He went to the corral and saddled two horses. He led them out and stood there, waiting. The elder Ainsworth came out then. He was carrying two rifles and a pack. He walked toward his son and the horses.

Feliz picked up the rifle. He put the stock against his shoulder and looked down the sights.

So, you are ready for another day, are you, cabrones? he thought. Well, you will kill no more mestenos. I will make sure of that. Now, and now, and now, and now.

The first shot dropped the elder Ainsworth suddenly and limply. The boy turned to run for the house. The second shot missed him but the horses were squealing and wheeling in panic. One of them struck the boy and he went sprawling. As he started to rise the third bullet hit him, knocking him flat. He stirred and kicked feebly and the fourth bullet stilled him.

A woman was screaming as Feliz rose to his feet and started for his dun. . . .

Feliz knew they were after him. They had learned about the Ainsworths and so they would be after him. He had not seen anyone yet but he could feel it in the air, ominous and deadly.

Let them come, he thought. Cabrones. Go ahead and come. I am ready for you. Kill my mestenos, will you?

Once he heard a flurry of shots and he came up erect in

the saddle. He began to tremble with rage. With each shot he flinched. It was as though every bullet was tearing into his own body. He started to weep.

You have not stopped, have you, cobardes? Even with the Ainsworths dead you have not stopped the killing. But I will kill, too. Not innocent mestenos but every one of you. I will not stop until the last one of you is dead.

He knew it was folly but he had to see. Which manada was it this time? The bayo coyote's, or the grullo's, or the negro's, or the tostado's? He had to see no matter what the consequences.

He found them scattered over a small plain. He counted fourteen mares and colts and the white-stockinged black. They had all been shot to death. The smell of blood and dying still lingered in the air.

Tears welled in his eyes but they were as much of rage as of sorrow and pain. He rose up in the stirrups and brandished a fist.

"Cabrones," he cried aloud. "Tonight. I will get you tonight. All of you without exception. You will kill no more horses. After tonight you will kill no more."

He was taking one last look at the black when the bullet hit him. It took him in the back and smashed him forward. The saddlehorn dug into his belly and he felt himself begin to slide off on the side and so he made a desperate grab for the horn and caught it. He had already touched the dun with his heels and the horse was off at a gallop. He pulled himself back up in the saddle and then flattened himself along the dun's neck. He heard the roar of several other shots but none of these seemed to hit him.

Faint behind him came shots and a rumble of hoofs and a shot now and then. He did not look back. He urged the dun into a great burst of speed down a slope and then veered him sharply into the mouth of a canyon. He knew of a hidden pocket far up the canyon, a pocket whose mouth was concealed by a growth of junipers and scrub cedars.

Feliz made this pocket. He sat in the saddle with the dun blowing hard under him. At first there had not been much pain from his wound but he began to really feel it now. It sent searing streaks across his eyes and frightening intervals of blackness. He reeled once in the saddle and almost fell but he caught himself in time.

His pursuers passed him and swept up the canyon. He could have shot them as they went by but he was too weak and unsteady. His whole back was a mass of hurt. Some of the blood was running down a trousers leg. He waited until the riders passed from sight around a bend and then he sent the dun out and back the way he had come.

By late afternoon he knew he had eluded them but he kept going until nightfall, even though he could hardly stay in the saddle. He had torn strips from his shirt and fashioned a crude bandage for his wound but it still bled. He realized he could not lose much more blood. Already at times he grew light-headed and drowsy. So when he came to the water hole at nightfall he reined in the dun.

He could not step down from the saddle. All he could do was work his right leg over the cantle and then slide down. Even so his legs refused to support him and he sprawled on the ground.

He lay there, gathering his strength. When he had a little of it back he crawled on his belly to the edge of the water and drank. The dun drank beside him.

After a while he tried to rise to get his blanket off the saddle but the best he could do was get up on his elbows. A few attempts at this and his strength was so far gone that he couldn't even do that. So he rolled on his back and lay on the cold ground and stared up at the stars.

I can't die, he told himself. Not as long as one of those cobardes is alive. I must protect my mestenos. I must live long enough to kill every one of those cabrones. So I will not die. I will not let myself die. I will sleep and rest tonight. In the morning I shall be all right. All I need is a little sleep and rest.

He closed his eyes and lay there awhile, listening to the sounds of the dun stirring about and to the night noises. Gradually they grew fainter and soon he slept. . . .

Something woke Feliz. He had no idea what it was and he opened his eyes and saw that it was dawn. The world looked gray and unreal. Tendrils of mist hung over the land. The sound that had waked him came again.

He was sure it was the dun but when he looked the dun was nowhere to be seen. Instead another horse was standing there. Feliz came up on an elbow, heart quickening.

"Roano," he whispered. "Roanito mio. Is that you, Roano?"

The roan's ears pricked forward. He was standing there at the water's edge with arched neck, all wary and suspicious and alert. He nickered softly when Feliz spoke.

Feliz sat up. He was surprised at the ease with which he moved. It was like in his younger days when each movement was effortless and flowing. He thought he'd try to stand and he gained his feet without trouble. He seemed a little weak but his wound no longer pained. The blood was crusted dry and black on his clothing. He could hardly feel the earth under his feet.

"Roano," he said, taking a step forward. "Then you are not dead, Roano? Every one was so smashed and broken. I was sure it was you but I was wrong. You fooled them, didn't you, wise little horse? I always knew you were too smart for them."

He took another step ahead. The roan snorted softly and shied a little.

"Little horse, I will not hurt you," Feliz said. "I am the only friend you have. I am not like the other men animals who want to kill you. I want to be your friend. Don't you know that?"

The roan nickered again, a plaintive, lonely sound. He watched Feliz take another step ahead.

"You are in trouble and so you've come to me," Feliz said, "because at last you know you can trust me. Roanito, you can always trust me. You and I together. Little horse, don't shy."

He reached out a hand and for a moment it looked as though the roan would flee. He snorted, nervously, and shrank back slightly, then paused there while Feliz moved his hand ahead a little more and touched the stallion's muzzle. The roan shuddered but he did not flee.

"There. You see?" Feliz said. "I have not hurt you. Don't tremble, Roanito mio. We are going to be great friends. We are going to have many wonderful times together. Don't be afraid, little horse."

He moved in close to the roan. He reached up and grabbed a fistful of mane.

"I am going to ride you," Feliz said. "Without a saddle. You want me to ride you, don't you? We have a long way to go and you are going to take me, aren't you?"

The roan nickered gently. Not a muscle flickered in his body.

Feliz did not know if he had the strength to climb on the roan. He felt weak yet somehow buoyant. His hands grabbed the mane and when he threw himself up something seemed to lift him and carry him gently up on the roan's back.

For a moment the roan hesitated. Then he wheeled, gently however, and started off. In Feliz there was hardly any sensation. The smoothness of the ride made him marvel.

The roan's speed increased. Soon he was running at the fastest pace Feliz had ever known. They seemed to float over the ground with the roan's hoofs not even touching the earth.

Like a bird, Feliz thought. We are soaring along like the birds. Oh, I always knew you were a wonderful horse, Roano.

Somehow they seemed to be rising even higher. Ahead of them Carrizo Peak loomed, high and lofty and jagged in the first bright light of the sun.

To the top, to the very top, Roanito, Feliz thought. We must reach the very top.

As if in response the earth seemed to fall away beneath them. Feliz looked down and saw nothing. So he lifted his eyes and looked straight ahead and all he saw was the ultimate crest of Carrizo Peak and in this moment Feliz at last knew where he was going. . . .

The three riders reined in beside the water hole and stared down at Feliz, who lay on his stomach with one hand reaching out, pointing at Carrizo Peak. The dun stood to one side with trailing reins.

"He's dead all right," Eastland said.

"Nothing like making sure," Crawford said. He drew his six-shooter and aimed it at Feliz.

Eastland jumped his bay in front of Crawford and batted Crawford's gun up.

"I said he's dead!" Eastland shouted.

"What you so worked up about?" Crawford shouted back at him, face heavy with anger. "He killed the Ainsworths, didn't he? And he'd have killed every one of us if he'd got the chance. Fill him full of lead and trample him and leave him for the buzzards, I say."

"The buzzards will never touch him," Eastland said. "I'll see to that."

"Well, I'm not going to waste my time burying him." Crawford growled, reining his horse away and riding off.

"I'll help," Bailey said.

"Thanks, John," Eastland said. "But I'd rather do it alone."

When Bailey, also, had gone, Eastland dismounted. He stared down at Feliz. "Old friend," Eastland said, then words failed him. He stood there, looking down at Feliz.

After a while, Eastland went and started gathering stones. . . .

LONG GUNS AND SCALP KNIVES

William R. Cox

PULP Western stories were not restricted in setting to the mountains, ranges, deserts, and towns of the Far West, nor in time to the post–Civil War period. Some of the most interesting and entertaining were set in such locales as Alaska, Louisiana, Illinois (as we've already seen), and the Ohio River country; and some of these, too, chronicled dramatic events that happened as far back as the 1770s, before *the signing of the Declaration of Independence.*

"Long Guns and Scalp Knives" is one such story. The blurb accompanying its publication in a 1942 issue of Dime Western *sums it up nicely: "Wilderness lore has no stranger or more fascinating story to tell than that of the half-pint little greenhorn, Ben Palmer, who stowed away with that grim party of west-bound buckskin pioneers, and who became the deadliest woodsman—with long rifle, scalping knife or bare hands—in all that uncharted and wild Ohio River frontier!"*

The long and distinguished career of William R. Cox (1901–1988) began in the mid-thirties, with boxing and baseball stories in the sports pulps. He soon branched out to other fields—notably, Westerns and detective stories—and, later, to the slick-paper magazines, to adult and young-adult novels, and to movies and TV scripting. In all, he wrote more than eighty books, one hundred films and television shows, and a thousand magazine stories. Many of his novels are Westerns of high caliber, among them the controversial Comanche Moon *(1959),* Moon of Cobre *(1969),* Jack O'Diamonds *(1972), and a recent series of paperbacks featuring gambler and lawman Cemetery Jones:* Cemetery Jones *(1985),* Cemetery Jones and the Maverick Kid *(1986), and* Cemetery Jones and the Dancing Guns *(1987). He was also the author of a definitive biography of frontier gambler Luke Short,* Luke Short and His Era *(1961).*

CHAPTER ONE

Scourge of the Savage Border

Leaving Fort Pitt, the party was a bit astonished to find Ben Palmer among them, but no one suggested that he was not welcome. The little man from Jersey was no bigger than his octagon-barreled rifle, and sometimes it seemed as though a strong wind might catch in his flapping ears and blow him away, but about him there was a quiet air which disarmed the giants of the scouting party.

Casper, the bearded, loquacious leader, told a lot of tall tales that would frighten a greenhorn to death if he believed them, but Ben Palmer just listened and said nothing. Jenkins, the oldster, tough as nails; Hoseby, the young Southerner who had taken a dozen scalps; Paul Patou, polished Frenchman now long settled on the Western Frontier, all took turns in playing small jokes upon the newcomer, but Ben grinned and kept his own counsel, learning as he went.

Casper gave up, finally, and being a naturally talkative person, began instructing Ben in the lore of the western woods. One day he talked of squirrels, or the exceedingly rare albino, of the black squirrel only found in the hushed depths of a trackless forest. He pointed into a high oak and said, "Up yonder's one of the common gray critters—or kin you see that far?"

Ben upped with the long rifle and shot with seeming carelessness. A small body came hurtling down, striking lightly among the branches. Casper picked it up and looked where the head should be. No one spoke for a moment.

Then Ben said apologetically, "I shoulda just blown the top of his skull off. Back home in Freehold we used to try and hit them at the base of the ear."

After that he was one of them. He hunted the turkey, the deer for their provisions. They took delight in filling his agile mind with facts beyond price.

Casper said, "He's just a natural ranger. Never seen a little man take so to the woods." The others concurred.

Ben opened up, when he knew it was safe. He told them about Jersey, and the farms, and his tough old father who had beaten him because Ben would rather hunt than work. But he did not tell them about Susan Gratcorn.

He had been willing to settle down for yellow-haired Susan. At a barn dance, under a harvest moon, he had broken down and told her so. She was a buxom, sweet lass, taller by an inch than Ben, and all the swains were after her.

Jason Huntley, indeed, came looking for her just as Ben stammered his protestation.

Jason, skulking, overheard. Susan laughed. Ben, the little, homespun-clad ne'er-do-well, was trapped between them, speared upon that ridicule. The undersized man never lived who could endure laughter directed at him. Ben swung right and left fists and Jason went down. Then he whirled upon Susan, his love curdling, and said harshly, "There's your big man. Take him. You'll live to hear my name and be proud to say you knew me, and that I wanted you!"

Then Ben Palmer came to the frontier, to seek a name for himself.

One night, far along the journey which was to take them to the Ohio, where a flatboat would pick them up en route to Fort Tarry, they were cooking a rabbit for a stew made with roots Casper had pronounced succulent. The rabbit was scarcely turned brown when a man walked into camp and kicked at the fire, scattering it, upsetting the kettle.

Ben stared up, his knife drawn, but Casper restrained him, saying, "Kelly!"

The stranger was a giant, towering over Casper by four inches. He was dark as any Indian, his hair was black and long, to his shoulders. He had a jutting nose, like a buzzard, and his mouth was a slash in a hunk of mahogany. He carried two knives and a tomahawk in his belt, besides his rifle.

His voice was strangely sweet, like a young boy's. He said, "Delawares, Casper. Right behind you. A dozen."

Casper said, "Have they spotted us?"

Kelly nodded. "But not me. Get going. I'll wait."

Casper said, "We'll double back."

It was very exciting. Kelly disappeared, almost at once. Casper and the others grabbed their packs. Ben hadn't as much to tote as the others, so he stayed in the rear, with Moseby.

They went along the trail, in the black of the night, under trees which above them joined branches to hide the skies. This was a place the sun never saw, in the deepest forest of the Valley. This was a place for ambush.

Casper muttered, "The Delawares been peaceful—I never checked much for Injun sign. I wonder what happened? I bet that Kelly stirred 'em up. I bet that Kelly killed some of 'em. Never happy, that Kelly, unless he's killin' Injuns."

Jenkins said, "There's good and there's bad on the Border, but Kelly's the queerest."

Ben went along, his heart beating like a trip-hammer. He had heard myriad tales about the Indians, but those he had seen around Fort Pitt had been blanketed, sodden with rum.

He had begun to think the Indian tales were all myth, that the nineties had been the end of them. He had scarely believed there was such a man as Kelly. Casper had told him about Kelly, but he had thought it just another tall tale. . . .

a

Kelly (said Casper) was born on the frontier, in West Virginia, sometime in the sixties. His father had been a great, roistering Irishman, but his mother was quality, people said. Padriac Kelly had taken up a section among the Hurons, as the French called the Wyandots, and had prospered.

But in 1774 a canoe-load of Wyandots had been massacred down below Yellow Creek by some fool whites, and that had set them off. Padriac got along with them for years by giving them rum and presents—said Casper—and by keeping his word to them. But one day he had an altercation about some skins, and although the Wyandots went away, they came back.

Young Kelly was then about twenty. He was a gawky, big youth, always in the bush, roaming around, spending half his time with Indians. He was the fastest runner in the West, and his speed had impressed the redskins, so that they pampered him and taught him forest tricks. When his father had that argument with the chief, Matanwa, Kelly was out on a hunt.

In the course of his hunt, young Kelly came across a deer track and went bucketing along at top speed towards a salt lick, hoping for a certain big buck.

When he got to the stream, a stout-bodied big man was lounging about, making some noise, giving orders to a trio of lazy Delawares who seemed dominated by him. Kelly recognized Francois Boulogne, the *coureur de bois,* trader with the Indians, dispenser of rum which demoralized and ruined Kelly's friends.

Especially Kelly was angry because Boulogne had corrupted Winawa, the Swift, Wyandot sub-chief and the only redskin who could come near the Irish lad in a footrace. Being upset about the loss of his shot at the big buck, Kelly proceeded to speak his mind to Boulogne.

He said, "You filthy, low, stinking son of a raccoon, you should be run from the Border. If I ever catch you giving rum to Winawa again, I'll cut your throat and hang you up by the heels."

Boulogne let out a roar and came at Kelly with a knife, and the youth met him halfway and there was quite a struggle. Kelly beat Boulogne almost to death in about a minute, but the Indians had been drinking, and when Francois called for help, they flung themselves upon Kelly and dragged him off.

So he had to fight loose from them, grab up his rifle and run for it. Being a huge, strong fellow, he managed to do this, leaving Boulogne to bathe his wounds and work up his hatred.

Kelly went a long ways on that hunt, looking for game which seemed unusually scarce for that season. But Boulogne went swiftly to the Wyandots and gave out with rum until he got them excited, and then Matanwa groused about Padriac Kelly and the skins, and that was Boulogne's opportunity. He got together a band of them and sent them over to Kelly's farm.

There was just Padriac and Moira, his wife, and little Moira at the farm. The Indians did not wear war paint, and seemed to want to argue—while Boulogne sat back and sneered at Padriac.

It was a scene Padriac had been through many times before. But this time there was a difference, as he soon found out, because a couple of the redskins seized Moira and intimated that if he did not see their side of it, things would happen to Mrs. Kelly.

Padriac, you see, was a giant. He also had a temper and some brains, and he saw what was happening and knew he did not have a chance. He smelled the rum and he saw the hatred in Boulogne's eyes and he did only what he could. He seized a long-handled axe and went to work.

That was a bad thing. Matanwa struck once with his tomahawk and poor Moira was dead. Padriac, himself, killed two of them with the axe in less time than it takes to tell it. The little girl got underfoot and Matanwa cut her almost in two. Padriac killed another brave, and another, trying to get at Boulogne. They closed with him, but he stretched a couple more, and then Boulogne had to draw his pistol and shoot

Padriac in the head, or there would have been no more Indians left.

But that was not the worst of it. Young Kelly had cut the trail of the party and become alarmed. He ran for the farm as fast as he could, and as he burst out of the clearing, they were killing his father, and before he could recover from his stupor, Matanwa had driven an arrow through his shoulder, and he was a prisoner.

They bound him, and he had to watch the farm and all the crops and implements burn to the ground, while the Indians drank rum which Boulogne had thoughtfully brought along. Then they beat him along the trail to their camp and tied him up for the squaws to torture.

A funny thing happened then—Casper said. The squaws threw stones and prodded Kelly with sticks, but after staring at his ugly face and those funny red eyes he gets on him when he's mad, they stopped and went away. They said it was no fun, that Kelly wasn't afraid. But that began the tale they tell of Kelly and the women—that no woman can withstand him, that women are attracted to him by his very ugliness and terrible reputation.

Well—said Casper—Winawa would have probably saved Kelly, for the Wyandot was really his friend, but Boulogne got Winawa drunk, and the torture went on. They made him run the gauntlet that night, and if that ever happens to you, Ben, remember that the strongest men are first in the line. If you can battle past them, you may live. . . .

Kelly near killed a couple of them with his one good arm, and then he came down to the squaws only half dead and they didn't do much. So they took him and painted his face black and put him in a tent and laced it up, and Kelly knew he was going to be burned tomorrow. And there was nothing he could do about it.

The way these Indians have of burning you is not good. They tie your hands and let you walk around on a short rope, and under your feet is hickory charcoal. It takes a long while, usually. . . . No, it is not good.

Kelly spent part of a bad night in that tepee. Some people say Kelly is mad, and they may be right, for that is a thing which would drive a man out of his mind, knowing the dawn would bring such torture to his body, and with his soul racked by memory of his dead parents and little sister and his home gone and nothing left to live for anyway—except revenge. A time like that would do things to any man. . . .

Towards dawn, Kelly says, a guard came in to taunt him, and Kelly kicked the guard, downed him, got his knife and cut himself loose. Then he sneaked into the woods and ran, all battered as he was, to the nearest settlement.

That is what Kelly says—continued Casper—but Winawa's sister, Moon Over Tree, dove headfirst to her death off a cliff soon after. And the Indian guard talked to a man who told me . . . but never mind. Kelly got away and brought back some scouts and they killed and killed for a while, until Winawa got his tribe away.

Winawa never came back to the Ohio Valley and Kelly just kept killing Indians, Casper ended. It's a religion with him. He's even been arrested for it—at first he even murdered them in settlements, wherever he saw them. He's the best bush ranger in the country—picked up a lot of tricks from Wetzel, like reloading his rifle while running, and tracking stunts, and things which only Wetzel and the Indians themselves can do. Kelly is the greatest name on the frontier, but I wouldn't want his killings on my conscience—not all of them!

That was Kelly, who now stalked behind them, ambushing the Delaware war party.

Ben Palmer tingled with expectation. He had no horror of Kelly nor his deeds, only a great curiosity.

Ben, in many ways, was a strange little fellow. . . .

CHAPTER TWO

Hell at Fort Terry!

The others of the party deployed themselves with their backs to the Ohio, but Ben climbed a tree. It was a giant elm, and its foliage was thick enough to hide Ben's small figure, and as he looked westward he could see the morning light reflected over and beyond the forest which had seemed endless. There was a mist, which rose slowly, pink-tinged by the dawn.

They had moved fast all night, and there had been no trace of Kelly, nor had they seen an Indian. Ben might have thought it all another frontier joke, save that Casper and his company were sweating too hard and moving too fast. Now, with the sun rising, they were making a stand. The mist lifted still further and a ray of clear sunshine broke through. Ben gulped and forgot to look for Indians.

The broad Ohio lay beneath him. The majestic stream wended sluggishly through the valley, lined on the one side with cliffs brown and green, on the other by the stately trees of the forests. It poured westward, the way toward adventure, leading into lands known to only a few of the hardiest white men. It was the road to empire, and Ben felt it, roosting in his tree, his rifle cocked over a branch.

There came, then, the call of a turkey gobbler, *"Chug-chug-chuk-kaw-ka,"* repeated at intervals. Casper had told him of this. Ben's eyes snapped front, his gun came up. Nothing seemed to move in the forest save small animals, a bird or two. Then a partridge fluttered up and a bush swayed.

Ben's gaze focused, his sharp eyes narrowed. With infinitesimal care, the fronds of the bush were parted. A face, striped hideously, dark as a Negro's, peered out. One feather tilted from the scalp lock of the closely shaven head. The arm which held the bush aside was sinewy, the chest was broad, the neck solid. For a long moment the savage remained immobile and Ben held hs breath at sight of his first rampaging Indian.

Then the brave stepped into the glade which Ben's tree commanded, and Ben had sense enough not to fire. Casper and the others were within range, he thought. It was not up to him to begin the fracas. This might be merely the advance guard of the war party, and shooting at him might be an error.

Other movement caught Ben's eye. Tree trunks seemed suddenly alive. Red-skinned figures which melted into the landscape began to take form as the morning sun filtered captiously through the thick foliage and dappled the scene. There were at least a dozen Delawares under the chief with the single feather.

Still Ben was breathless, waiting. This was new to him, but he was eager to learn. Somewhere about was Kelly, and even Casper deferred to the big man of the woods. The chief was reading sign now, his noise almost on the ground, as though he was suspicious of something. The Indians seemed to be young men, very brawny, a typical war party.

The chief grunted and they were all grouped for a moment over the footprints. Ben remembered then that Casper had dispersed his forces from the clearing, and that the tracks must lead in various directions. The chief raised his head. He was alarmed, it was in his painted face, his rolling eyes. Already his men were starting for shelter. The canny Delaware had sensed the ambush!

Ben's finger was on the trigger. Surely, Casper would fire now! They would retreat to the woods and harry the whites with a running battle, at which they excelled, were the Indians not now dispatched.

From the east, then, came the wail. It was almost inhuman. It was neither complaint nor boast nor appeal to the gods. It was plain, unadulterated threat, such as the howl of the wolf, the roar of the lion. The sound of it echoed among the trees, and the Delaware were frozen for a split instant.

In that tiny space of time, the guns roared. Ben saw the chief with the feather stagger, but continue to run, and Ben aimed and fired carefully. The Indian leaped into the air, shrieked a strange cry, and fell prostrate. Even while Ben's nimble fingers reloaded his rifle, he watched the victim of his slug beat a tattoo with his heels and die upon the leafy ground of the forest.

At that range, the scouts could not miss. Five Indians were down, seven were rushing away. The farthest was almost out of sight among the trees when Kelly appeared. He just stepped out and swung a tomahawk in one fierce, quick blow. The leading Indian flopped like a fish upon a riverbank, blood spurting from his torn skull.

Kelly's rifle was over his arm, carelessly. Ben rammed home his shot, detached the rod. The second Indian leaped at Kelly, who sidestepped almost effortlessly, then swung the hatchet at the brave's chest. So sharp was the blade that this redskin also died.

The third, using discretion, swerved and sought to flee from the waiting, indolent Kelly. Ben remembered to raise his rifle, then, but saw that Kelly was using his own long gun in a quick snap shot at the departing Delaware.

Kelly got him, too, right between the shoulder blades, but the two remaining flung themselves in desperation upon the big man. They were agile, athletic bucks and they had recognized Kelly now, and were imbued with fear. One seized Kelly's gun, the other plunged in with shining long blade. It was good teamwork.

Ben sighted with exceeding care. There was a chance that as they struggled, Kelly might be switched into the range of Ben's fire. He waited, holding his breath. The Indian with the knife had missed and was gathering himself for another try. Ben fired at him, squeezing gently, holding the gun up as he had been taught, against the recoil.

The Indian spun about, started to run away. He stopped and fell down as though he had been tripped. Ben nodded happily and already he was reloading, tamping down the powder, the little rag between his teeth, reaching for the powder horn.

There was sudden fire from the thicket and then Kelly had the first attacker by the throat, holding him at arm's length. Ben had one look at the dark, despairing face of the brave caught in the grasp of the terrible buckskin man, then the axe descended, inexorably, blotting out forever the hawk-nosed face.

And Kelly stood there, spattered with blood, holding the Indian by the throat until the last breath was gone.

Ben scrambled down from the tree, and when he had reached the forest floor, Kelly had already taken the scalp of his latest victim.

Casper was sweating a little although the morning was cool, and the others, particularly the Frenchman, Paul Patou, looked a little sick. But Kelly was busy gathering scalps, and Ben was strangely fascinated by the quick expert lift of the sharp blade, the dangling bits of hair and skin. This, then, was the West—here were scalped Indians, here the West's greatest hero. He stared at Kelly, and that worthy turned and returned the glance.

Kelly's high, immature voice, said, "You were in the tree, weren't ye, little man?"

"My name's Ben Palmer."

Kelly showed his teeth, but his eyes, gleaming like fiery coals, did not smile. While Ben watched, the fire died and the eyes became normal again, brown and clear and watch-ful.

"That was good shootin' on the buck with the knife," Kelly said.

Casper, recovering his aplomb a bit, said, "Ben's a mighty fine shot—for a greenhorn."

Kelly shrugged. "You can prob'ly all outshoot him in a

match. But when Injuns are howlin' around, it takes nerve to make a shot like he made. Saved me a wound, I reckon."

He stepped forward and held out two scalps to Ben. In the most friendly manner possible, he said, "I generally keep 'em, because others don't care much and I save 'em. I got reason to keep count. But these are fairly yours, I reckon."

Ben accepted the gift, holding gingerly to the coarse, straight hair of the scalp locks. He bowed a little, remembering his manners. Then inspiration came to him.

"I sure appreciate it, Kelly," he said, "but I'll give them back to you, as a gift from me, for your collection." He handed them back, solemnly, and Kelly's eyes flickered again.

The big man stood for a moment, looking up and down the small figure. He said softly, "That's a genteel thing to do, Ben Palmer. I won't forget you." He raised his hand at Casper and the others, gave them a wolfish smile, and turned on his heel. Before Ben could say Jack Robinson he was gone from sight, the scalps swinging from his belt.

Casper said, "And that's Kelly! There's Injuns would give their lives to know where he caches them scalps. He must have a thousand!"

Ben turned and looked at the others. He said, "Well, he's a great fighter. Cool. He's not a man you could really like, though, is he?"

Casper roared with laughter as the tension broke. The others joined in, going to recapture their packs. Casper said, "No, he ain't a man to cotton to, right off. By golly, Ben, you're a card, now, ain't you?"

But Ben was not attempting to be humorous. Kelly interested him. Kelly was a hero, and Ben meant to be a figure of some consequence himself, so that his name might go back to Susan Gratcorn in such a way that she would know he had made good his promise.

He no longer desired Susan—the laughter had finished that. But he did desire fame, and in this great, unfinished land, so different from Jersey, there seemed to be opportunity to gain this renown. At least, he thought, he had made a start!

Then they came to the river, and there they rested, rehashing the fight, bragging a little, but giving credit to Kelly for his flanking operation. That, they said, no other white man could possibly have managed, because none other could have gotten around an Indian party to come up on their rear except Kelly the great runner and tracker. Then they told more tales of his prowess until the river boat came nosing through the mist to take them down the Ohio to the Fort.

Fort Terry was a bulging pile of blackened logs and stockade fence, but around it had grown a settlement of considerable size and great fertility. The Fort had stood so many sieges without crumbling that the frontier was becoming almost tame, Casper said, half jokingly.

River traffic had become increasingly safe and goods were being floated down in exchange for produce from the farms. Farmers were coming to take up land in the fertile valley, and many of the fiercest chieftains of the various tribes were dead, or had moved west.

They went to see Colonel Brandon, in command of the Fort. Ben found him a stout, agreeable man with pink cheeks and none of the gaunt sobriety of the frontiersman.

He shook hands with Ben and said, "Glad to have another woodsman. Since Wetzel wandered away, we have more need of scouts. Casper, I hear bad news. Winawa is back."

Casper shook his head. "I was afraid of it. Boulogne, too?"

"Yes," said Brandon. "Boulogne and his rum, Winawa and his tribe. Five other chieftains are arrayed with them, our informer tells us. They are up near the Mad River, but are heading this way. I must have information about them."

Casper said, "We're ready to go. Let us go down and drink up and rest."

"If you should see Kelly," said Brandon, frowning a bit, "send him in. I don't like Kelly, but we need him. . . ."

Casper laughed and told him about Kelly. Colonel Brandon pursed his lips, shook his head at the tale of the last Indian, the one Kelly had killed with such obvious enjoyment. He nodded at Ben's part, carefully built up by the kindly Casper.

He said, "Let the others go down and drink rum, young man. I'd like to talk with you."

So Casper and his friends left, and Ben remained in the big house, which was located about two miles west of the Fort itself, upon a fine piece of farm property. The Colonel had certainly prospered—Ben had never seen such fine house furnishings in the backwash of Jersey. While he sat there, a door opened and a girl came into the room.

She was a small girl, much shorter even than Ben. She had freckles across her nose, which was upturned, and her hair was red and abundant. She wore a gray linsey dress which fitted her quite closely, and her figure was slight and totally unlike that of Susan Gratcorn. But Ben's eyes would not go away from this tiny girl.

Colonel Brandon said, "My niece, Mary Brandon. Darling, this is a new scout, Ben Palmer."

The girl's eyes were hazel, and very sharp. She said, "I didn't mean to intrude. I thought they were all gone."

However, she did not leave, but busied herself about the room. Colonel Brandon said, "Ben, are you sure you want to join the scouts? I need a farmer to look after my place. It's overlarge, and I'm gouty at times."

Ben said, "Thank you, sir, but I was raised on a farm."

Brandon nodded, as though that was a good answer. "I know . . . I know. . . . But scouting pays nothing except sustenance. The reward often is death, or worse—capture by Indians. This West will be built by farmers, workers. . . ."

"Saving your presence, sir," said Ben calmly, "I did not

come here to build the West, but to protect it from depreda-
tion. I have no ambition for fortune, only for fame!"

He was very tiny, even standing erect, with his shoulders
back, and there were people who would have laughed at his
earnestness. But Colonel Brandon did not laugh, nor did the
small girl at the far end of the room.

The good Colonel sighed, remembering his own youth,
and his service under Lord Dunmore, and the smoke of
battle and sound of musketry. The girl stood quite still and
her glance was steady upon Ben's tight face.

Colonel Brandon said, "Well, no use to talk against youth,
but I do need a farmer. Everyone is so prosperous here he
will not work for another, but takes up his own land! Make
yourself free of the place, Ben. Mary, take him out and show
him the horses. . . ."

Mary came forward without shyness. She said, "We have
fine horses. And milk cows. But I guess you wouldn't want to
look at a milk cow. . . ."

They looked at each other, and then Ben went outdoors
with her and said wonderingly, "How is it that we feel as
though we had known each other before?"

Mary Brandon nodded. She said, "Here, on the frontier, I
am out of place. I cannot ride the wild steers, nor plow in
the fields. I am too small and weak. Unlike the other men,
the big men, you don't stare at me in wonderment. That is
all I know—it's comforting to have another little person
about."

For once Ben did not bristle at reference to his lack of
stature. He understood this girl, and it was in that moment
that Susan Gratcorn became a dim memory which in truth
was somewhat distasteful. . . .

There was a black colt in the enclosure which held the
horse—the corral, Mary called it—and Ben promised to
break it and tame it for Mary to ride. They grew very well
acquainted in those hours, and Ben ate in the kitchen, a vast,
homey room presided over by a giant Negress, and Mary sat

with him. Casper and the others got roaring drunk and beat up a couple of farmers that night, but Ben stayed at the Brandon house and drank only cider purveyed by the red-haired, slant-eyed niece of the Colonel.

He was quite at ease, quaffing his third cup, when there was a scratch on the kitchen door and the Negress went to it and peered through a peephole, then opened it to allow a figure to slip through.

Mary Brandon, across the table from Ben, turned pale as a ghost. She said, "Paddy!"

The tall man seemed to fill the room. He wore fresh buck-skin, fringed and clean, and his moccasins were beaded. His long, black hair was combed to his shoulders and his face was unlined, serene, ugly. His eyes lighted upon Ben, and he smiled, and that was the first time Ben had ever seen Kelly smile. The effect was amazing.

The brown eyes were soft, the slash of a mouth upcurved in gentle lines. Kelly's high, smooth voice said, "I've been looking for you, Ben. They told me you might be held here by the little queen of the settlement." Kelly bowed toward Mary. He was an entirely different man, jolly, tremendously attractive, his ugliness driven from mind by his smile.

Ben said, "You wanted—*me*?"

"Sit down, Paddy," breathed Mary Brandon, and Ben was then aware of the effect of the big man upon the girl. She was flushed, yet in her eyes there was a certain repugnance. She was like a bird charmed by a snake, and the hand that poured cider for the famed scout trembled so that she spilled some on the checkered cloth.

Kelly sat upon a chair and accepted his cup. He said, "Kelly travels alone."

His tone was abrupt—he had a strange habit of plunging into a subject without preamble. "Everyone knows that. Al-most no one can keep up with Kelly." For a moment the arrogance crept through, then he leaned forward and fixed

Ben with his brown eyes. "But comes a time when a man must use canniness. Winawa, Boulogne, have evaded me for years by strategems. They always ran before I came. If I were beating slowly, with a partner who seems puny—begging your pardon, Ben—they would not run.

"And if that partner was not weak, but a great fighter, a cool man in a pinch, I could take Winawa and Boulogne and this impending war would be averted. You understand?" His very speech was different than when he talked to the scouts, back there in the woods. It was clipped, almost erudite, and Ben could see then that Kelly's mother must have indeed been of quality folk.

Ben said quietly, "I am a greenhorn, Kelly."

The big man leaned back, as though satisfied. Over the edge of the cup he laughed a little. "A week, a month with Kelly—which no man has before been able to take—and you'll be the greatest woodsman on the frontier, next to Kelly, in the West!"

Ben sat quietly, not answering. His eyes went to Mary Brandon, and it seemed impossible that they had only met a few hours before. He sat there, asking her what to do. Without words, he conveyed his message and saw that she knew. . . .

Mary moistened her lips with the end of a red tongue. She said, "Paddy—don't take him. He's new here. He's—he's a farmer. The Colonel needs him."

Kelly laughed softly. "Why, Mary, I'm not taking him unless he wants to go. And if he wants—it must be strongly, to go with Kelly!"

She said, "Don't go, Ben. Paddy is too strong. . . ."

But she knew that was the wrong thing to say, and she desisted. She waited a moment, then said, "But you must go, of course. You came here to find fame, you said. With Paddy you'll become famous—or dead. And that's a chance all men take who dare to chance anything."

Kelly stared at her, then, and put down his cup. Kelly's

strange eyes narrowed and he purred in his thin voice, "Mistress Mary, you're a fit queen for a king. I've said it before, and I'll say it again. And I could say still more."

The girl shuddered and rose, still quite pale. She said, "I'll bid you good-bye, for now. I must go to bed. . . ."

She caught Ben's hand, pressed it, averting her eyes from Kelly, striving to cement a bond between herself and the small, still man from Jersey.

She said, "Come back! Get your fame, then come back to the farm. . . ." She was gone.

When Ben turned back. Kelly's face had made one of his startling changes. He was frowning, his mouth was again a stark slit.

He growled, "She's already fond of you. For two years I've—but never mind. Are you ready to come, Ben Palmer?"

Ben said, "After I see Casper, who was kind to me."

"You do not hesitate?" said Kelly curiously.

"I came here to find fame," repeated Ben. "Should I flinch when it is generously offered?"

Kelly extended a huge hand which was sinewy and long, rather than thick and hamlike. Ben's little fist was engulfed in a firm but gentle clasp. In that moment he was amazed that he had ever thought Kelly unlikable—he was drawn to the man as never before had he been close to anyone.

And so they went out together, Kelly's long stride eating up two of Ben's short ones. And from a darkened upstairs window Mary Brandon watched them, a prayer upon her lips, her heart in a strange turmoil.

CHAPTER THREE

Death in the Dark

Far to the northwest of Fort Tarry, Ben lay behind a huge fallen log and listened to Kelly's voice. The scout whispered, although they seemed buried deep in the woods, far from sight or hearing of man.

"Sure, you're weary. No one can keep up with Kelly and not be worn. But you're a tough little man, and you learn quicker than anyone I ever saw or knew. We're comin' close to Winawa's new encampment."

Ben stayed quiet, knowing Kelly needed no response. It had been a bitter time, since leaving Tarry. There had been a million things to learn about the wildlife and how it affected tracking, about the topography of the country, about various and sundry Indian signs, wolf signs, bear signs—a myriad of varied signs which were commonplace to Kelly and brand-new to Ben. It seemed he would never learn them all.

He remembered Casper's warning when he had departed. "Kelly's one idea is to kill Injuns. He don't really care for his own life nor yours! He'll lead you into hell, and let you get out your own way. That's Kelly!"

Jenkins and Moseby and Patou had nodded solemnly. They had not wanted Ben to go. They had been afraid to speak out in front of Kelly, but Ben—and Kelly—had known. Yet Ben had gone ahead, that very night, and now they were in the country Winawa had picked for his new stronghold, and Ben was thinner, his face strained and his belt tight. His stomach rebelled against jerky for breakfast, jerky at noon, jerky at night, and his hide was prickled and bitten by insects and torn by brambles.

Yet he had learned, and so far as he could, he was ready for any circumstance. Kelly said so, and here in the forest Kelly's word was gospel. In the morning they would begin their toilsome reconnaissance, and Kelly would have a scheme.

Kelly always had a scheme, reflected Ben. He was smart. He should have been a great general—a leader of men, instead of a skulking tracker of savages.

Ben fell asleep. Kelly stopped talking and lay upon his

back, staring at the stars. He should have awakened Ben to stand the first watch, but he did not.

He himself watched all through the night, yet in the morning he appeared as fresh as a daisy in a field, and laughed off Ben's protestations with, "I want you sharp as a lynx today. Eat and come along."

Ben could not eat more jerky, but he pretended to do so, and drank heartily at the cool stream upon which they had camped. They started for the hill in the distance, and Kelly had said there would be scout patrols out, so they went quietly through the woods.

It seemed ridiculous, with nothing but wildlife about them, but Kelly insisted that they make progress from tree to tree. Ben saw no sign of Indians.

Kelly whispered, about noon, "We must imagine them before we see them. That's the difference between a scout and a diamond fool. This is the place for them—therefore they got to be here. Stay behind at this tree and wait for my signal."

Ben waited, seeing to his rifle, loosening his tomahawk in his belt. He had practiced with the hatchet, too, on this trip, throwing it at trees under Kelly's direction. He was rather proud of his progress in that science. Ben had a quick eye and marvelous reflexes, so that anything to do with aiming at a mark came easily for him. He drew the Indian small axe which Kelly had given him, and hefted it in his palm.

Kelly was gone up the hill, and there was no sound save the chattering of squirrels, the occasional rustle of a chipmunk rustling for fodder. Yet now the tomahawk froze in Ben's palm. He melted closer to the tree trunk, his senses quickening. It was, Kelly said, like smelling a skunk, only most times there was no actual odor, just the feeling of a foreign, inimical body in the vicinity.

There was no movement. Ben retreated to windward of the tree, crouching, his rifle under one arm, the hatchet in his right hand. If he had to fire a shot, Kelly would be caught in the middle. He stared westward, and after a moment the shadows of the morning sun became clearly defined to his sharp eyes.

He saw a flitting movement. He retreated eastward of his tree. There were some willows nearby, and he longed for their shelter, but he knew better than to attempt them. He remained still.

There was another figure, and another, then more! Ben gasped as the truth began to bear down upon him. For once the great Kelly had miscalculated. Not only had the Wyandots failed to run from him, but they had laid a trap for him.

The ego of Paddy Kelly had not allowed for this. He had been keen enough to realize that they were close to the camp he had never seen, he had come silently and swiftly through the woods with his greenhorn companion, he had allowed for every contingency—save that he had underestimated his enemy.

A tall man in breech clout and war paint, with two feathers, knotted into his hair, was gaining on his companions. He was very swift, so that Ben could scarcely detect his movements, despite the fact that all the Indians were close enough to shoot at now. Ben knew it must be Winawa, once Kelly's friend, now his bitter enemy. There were at least twenty others.

They had completed the arc now, and in their eagerness they had not seen Ben at all. He remained where he was.

The Wyandots would not kill Kelly unless they had to, of course. They would attempt to stun him, capture him, and put him to torture. Kelly had reasserted this point a thousand times in cautioning Ben not to attempt a vain rescue.

Ben could do nothing but stand and wait, unnoticed, inglorious, while Kelly met his doom.

❧

Twice he raised the rifle, drawing a bead upon Winawa. Each time the chieftain moved so swiftly the shot was chancey. Ben dared not miss—only by killing Winawa could he throw the

attack into confusion, he was aware. He reclaimed the tomahawk.

Before he could act, the war cry sounded. He heard Kelly's
shouted defiant answer in the same second, then the unmistakable heavy bang of Kelly's rifle. That would be one dead
Indian, Ben knew. He bethought himself of his old tree
strategy, and slinging his rifle, he went like a monkey up the
trunk.

He had to go high, but he could see the action when he
reached the top of the giant oak. Below him, Kelly and the
big man were running along the hillside, making such leaping strides that the Indians fell behind.

He prayed a little, aiming the rifle. He banged away. An
Indian leaped, rolled down the hill. Kelly's arm flung up in
salute, even as he ran, and then Ben knew he had done right.

Of course, the Indians were also aware of him now. He
came down out of the tree like a squirrel, loaded his gun and
changed position. He found another handy tree and climbed
again. When he could see, the scene had changed.

Winawa was running up a ledge of rock, with Kelly beneath
him. They were out of range, now, and Ben lowered his rifle,
restraining as impulse to shout. Winawa was running on level
ground, fleet as a deer. Kelly was still hampered by uneven
ground. Indians were swarming from all directions. . . .

Winawa's bronzed, splendid body took off in a flying leap.
Before Ben's horrified gaze the chief landed smack atop of
the flying Kelly, even while two big braves appeared on the
angle from the hilltop and were able to plunge in to the aid
of Winawa. Kelly was captured!

Ben stayed in the tree. A party of braves came back and
searched diligently for him. He did not move, high up in the
branches, hunched in a fork between two hefty limbs. They
came beneath the tree several times, talking among themselves in deep gutturals, but they were too excited about
catching Kelly.

Kelly had said that Indians were not so imperturbable as

most people thought; that when they were elated they became frenzied and lost their heads. Otherwise, said Kelly with reason, they would have easily defeated every white force sent against them, both by superior numbers and by their woods guile and undoubted courage in combat.

Kelly was right, and Ben stayed in the tree until nightfall. Then he came down, although he knew there were still patrols out, and that they would be looking for him. He started for the hilltop where Kelly had been captured. And beyond which must be Winawa's encampment.

The way he started was the way Kelly had taught him. He lay upon the dark ground. He reached out before him, sighting on a tree ahead, until he got a firm grip on the moss. Then, careful of twigs and other obstructions which might rustle, he would pull his body forward. That was slow progress, almost torture. Yet he kept on.

But the Indian who leaned against a tree trunk as sentinel of the farthest outpost of the camp did not hear Ben eeling his way forward. The tomahawk in Ben's hand steadied. He gathered his wiry, short legs under him. He sprang forward and upward in one motion, using the blunt edge of the weapon so as to stun and eliminate outcry.

The savage fell without a word. The hardest thing Ben ever had to do came next. He almost closed his eyes as he reversed the hatchet and sank it into the skull of the unconscious Indian.

He crept on, to the top of the hill. In his mouth there was a strange, bitter taste. He could not keep his thoughts from Mary Brandon, her strange demeanor when Kelly had entered the room, her actual horror of the man, even through the fascination his presence held for her, something no one could fathom. . . .

Killing in the dark—that was a strange pastime for a Jersey farm boy who sought fame!

Yet he must go on—Kelly was a prisoner, and what they

would do to Kelly was worse than murder, either in deepest
night or brightest day. . . .

CHAPTER FOUR

Buckskin and Iron

There were fires in the night. The Wyandots were far from
a white settlement; they had patrols all through the land,
they were unafraid of attack.

Ben clung to the other side of the hill, getting his eyes
accustomed to the scene. There seemed to be hundreds of
the lodges and wigwams on the bank of the stream. In the
dim light of the fires there was a milling of many bodies,
shouts came up to Ben's ears.

In the center of the scene was a larger tepee than the
others, and a grouping of wigwams about it made a clearing.
There came a brighter light as fuel was added to the fire in
that space, and the Indians remained a respectful distance
but continued to circle and to cry out.

Kelly was bound to a post. There was blood. Men bore
faggots and piled them.

Kelly's head was high, Ben saw. Winawa, pretending to
ignore him, leaned majestically against another post. Ben
could imagine the taunts which Kelly was loosing at them.

A fat-bodied, gross man in buckskin came out of a tepee,
followed by two squaws and a couple of half-grown brats. He
was, by his walk, a white man. He went up to Kelly and
ponderously swung a fist against Kelly's face, and then Ben
knew that was the Frenchman, Francois Boulogne, who had
joined the Wyandots to escape Kelly's vengeance.

Ben froze there, watching the brave man. Even Winawa
reached out and restrained Boulogne, who would have struck
again. Kelly's mouth moved in the ever-increasing light of
the fire, and Ben could imagine the brown eyes, turned red,

spitting venomous hatred more rapidly than Kelly's quick tongue.

It was a ghastly, fascinating show, and Ben had a grand-stand seat. He could stay, and then backtrack to the Fort and warn the Colonel.

The Colonel could send for precious reinforcements and be ready for the attack upon Fort Tarry. It was Ben's duty to follow this course, and well he knew it.

Still, Ben remained under the clump of willows. Solemnly, he was weighing the situation, weighing himself.

Had he stayed on Colonel Brandon's farm, he would have taken the road to fortune. That was simple, and Ben was essentially a simple person. That would have been another thing, a different thing.

But he had averred that he came West for fame. He had refused the advice of Casper. He had elected to go with Kelly, to seek advancement in the eyes of strong men.

He had been wrong, he knew now. Not because disaster had fallen, not because Kelly was taken and he himself was helpless and forlorn upon his hill, with the road to fame blocked by an avalanche.

But he was wrong because he no longer had reason to garner fame. Susan Gratcorn and her laughing swain were no longer of any consequence. Ben Palmer was out on a limb, with nothing to hope for should he be able to cling to it safely. The only thing he wanted, he found now, was to return to the small, understanding girl with the red hair and hazel eyes.

Of course he could not do that. He had set his feet upon a course and it must be followed. There was in his small frame no compromise with fate. He started edging down toward the stream of water.

It took a thousand years to reach that water. From the village came shouts, from time to time, great loud noises of pleasure, and what they were doing to poor Kelly Ben could only imagine. But he kept edging for that water.

There was another sentinel, this one wide awake and disgruntled because he could not be in on the death of Kelly.

Ben jumped upon his back and holding the scalp lock with one hand, drew his razor-sharp knife across the throat. He picked up the man's rifle.

He found the stream shallow enough to wade and deep enough to immerse himself if necessary to avoid detection from the bank. He dared not remove any of his clothes in fear of what might come, if his reckless and daring plan was successful.

He wondered a little if fame would come to him after he died; if the Indians would tell his story and if it would get back to Fort Tarry. He thought it might, and the idea gave him pleasure, for he knew Mary Brandon would understand.

That was the thing about her, that instant understanding which had flashed between them, almost visible, cementing them in one common bond. He went on, above the camp, to where he heard the nicker of horses.

He was a farm boy; he knew horses, probably better than the average frontiersman of his time.

So he came up to the band of hobbled Indian horses without disturbing them. The stunted ponies nuzzled the little man who walked among them with a plaited rope he had loosed. He found hackamores and placed them on a dozen of the steeds. He ran the rope from one to the other, through the bone rings of the hackamores, until he had them loosely strung together.

The time had come to take action. He waited a moment, holding the end of his rope. He picked out a gray mustang upon which to ride, petted it, soothing it. He took a hitch at his wet pants, removed the tomahawk from his belt, put his knife at hand. He had all the horses loose, now.

An Indian came reluctantly to check upon the mounts. Ben slid under his horse's belly and waited. The brave grunted, sensing something wrong. Ben hit him.

This time he was taut and ready to die, but he had a plan and he was going to execute it as his last act on earth.

He slipped easily onto the back of the gray. He rode in a little circle, managing the others as easily as though he had trained them, chirping between his lips. He got the main body of the herd ahead of him. He arranged his dozen in the rear. He gathered his breath, and let out a howl that could have come from a covey of banshees.

In a moment the stampeding animals were dancing and driving through the street. Braves sprang up waving their arms, attempting to head them off. Squaws scuttled from underfoot. A clear path to the wigwam of Winawa and the clearing where Kelly was bound appeared as if by magic.

Ben rode low, his sharp eyes alert, clinging to the gray with his knees. Then he saw Kelly.

The big man's head was up, his eyes alert. They had his hands still bound, but they had tied him to a short rope which allowed him to walk. They had been on the point of strewing bright hickory charcoal beneath his feet, for his last dance.

The rope went around the post. In the bright light, it was a shining mark. Ben held the knife in one hand, the toma-hawk in his right fist. He came down behind the horses, directing the twelve with the rope in his teeth. He jerked his head once, almost dislodging all his molars. The twelve obediently swerved for the chief's tent, forming a barricade of horse flesh between Ben and the stake where Kelly waited.

There was no time for cutting Kelly loose. There was no chance, as braves realized what went on and dashed for weapons. Ben had to try it, though. He leaned out a little and gauged the speed of his horse, the short distance to the post. His arm went out. He tossed the hatchet, using his wrist for accuracy rather than his arm for speed.

The tomahawk sped through the air. Kelly stood very still, his eyes following its course. It glinted in the firelight, and a squaw shrieked. A pony kicked at Francois Boulogne, upsetting him. Ben rode behind the flight of his axe.

The sharp edge thudded into the pole. Kelly leaped forward. The axe had cut the rope which held him captive!

Ben was leaning farther out. Kelly turned, quick-witted as ever despite the scars upon him, his face, black-painted for the burning. Ben reached and slashed at the thongs which tied Kelly's hands behind him. Kelly whirled with magic speed. A buckskin pony came running. Kelly reached for the mane, made a leap.

Shots sounded, now, but Kelly was on the horse's back. Ben rode hard and low, kicking the ribs of the gray. They went for the end of the village street, straight through milling, yowling braves.

Hands snatched at them, and Ben slashed and cut with the knife, red bodies fell away. Kelly beat at them with fists of iron. Arrows hummed around them, crude leaden slugs cut the wind above their heads.

They reached the end of the avenue of wigwams. Kelly, in the lead, swerved right, up the hill. Ben kicked his pony up and came abreast.

"Not that way!" he panted. "Around, and over the plain below. We can get clean away from them and back to the Fort. We can take the low road and warn the Colonel!"

Kelly sat up straight, riding the horse easily. He said, "By Gad, I came here to kill Indians! I want Winawa and Boulogne, and I'm going to have them!"

"The Fort!" said Ben. "They're started, now. They'll move, now that we got away!"

Kelly said, "I want Winawa and Boulogne!" and his eyes were mad again.

Kelly was slowing down. The pursuit was forming. The big man said calmly, "Ben, that was the greatest stunt was ever pulled on the Border. I'm not forgetting it. You ride for Tarry. I'll round up a gun from these redskins and tree me my men. Go ahead, Ben."

They were halfway up the hill. Ben trembled a little, but he said, "Let me tether the horses. They understand me." He got down, ignoring Kelly's further pleading for him to go. He hobbled the horses with the two hobbles he'd had the foresight to string at his belt.

For once Kelly followed in silence, knowing Ben had something in mind. After a moment, Ben got oriented and found the spot. He pointed, and Kelly exclaimed at the dead sentry with his rifle and horn and bullet pouch intact.

They worked their way half down the hill. Winawa was immediately discernible, shouting orders, rallying the panicked Indians. Boulogne was examining the spot where the pony had belted him.

It was a downhill, a long shot. Ben would never have attempted it. But Kelly sighted, lowered his gun, placed a ball, the horn and a patch close at hand, then raised the long barrel once more.

As calmly as though on a turkey hunt, Kelly pressed the trigger of the strange Indian gun.

It was Boulogne who collapsed. The fat man seemed punctured, like a balloon. He fell face forward, into the fire, and by the way his arms waved, Ben knew he still lived with his flesh scorching in the embers intended for Kelly.

Kelly's rapidity of motion was unbelievable. He was reloading the gun in the time another man would take to empty a smidgin of powder. This time he scarcely aimed, for Winawa was already running, sprinting for dear life away from the light and danger. The gun banged once.

Winawa gave one more leap, straight into the air. As if by magic, the Indian village was stricken by silence. Their chief lit upon his feet, staggered forward, wailed once, and went down like a felled ox.

They mounted and Kelly headed for the plain, but first he paused and said, "That was a strange thing. It was so easy, killing them. My parents will rest easy now, Ben!"

Kelly's voice was boyish and smooth again, almost a treble,

and he was filled with peace, Ben knew. And they rode through the night, scarcely stopping before they came inside the stockade of Fort Tarry.

Mary Brandon sat in the big kitchen, with the pitcher of cool cider before her. Kelly had just finished his tale. There was a great difference in Kelly, now. He was all his seldom-seen gracious self, but it was deeper than that. He lacked something that had been in him before, some underlying tragic force.

He ended, "Ben came down and got me. That's all." He arose and looked down at them. He said softly, "Casper and the others are waiting for me. We're going to scout the thing and see if the war is over before it begins, thanks to Ben. He's won his fame. . . ."

"I'll go, too," said Ben.

Kelly shook his head. "You'll stay. You'll farm. You will marry Mary Brandon, get rich—and die in bed. But you'll never forget Kelly—and you'll be known the whole West over as the man who was big enough to pull Kelly out of a hole he got into by his own brash foolishness!"

He bowed once to Mary and for a second his eyes shone redly, the old way. He snatched her hand, kissed it fervently. Then he was gone out of the door and the two small people sat and looked at each other. It was as if a great gusty wind had passed over them, leaving them in peace.

Mary said, "That was a bold thing he said—about us."

"But Kelly is usually right," said Ben.

It wasn't necessary to grab her, or to humble himself, or to do anything but sit there and let their great understanding take its course. The little people would build the West, if they had the courage and the knowledge and iron and buckskin in their hearts. . . .

DIG MY GRAVE DEEP

Talmage Powell

THE Chinese—as was the case with such other ethnic groups as blacks and Mexicans—were for the most part rather shabbily treated by pulp writers. If a Chinese character appeared in a Western story, he was usually a cook or a laundryman, was made to speak in a singsong dialect, and was more often than not played for cheap laughs. Even in the few stories in which Chinese characters were prominently featured, little attempt was made to individuate them, or to examine their relationships with each other, the whites of the time, and their hardship environment.

"Dig My Grave Deep" is a notable exception. It portrays a Chinese miner, old Ming, as a real human being, and explores the nature of his friendship with his white partner, Coggins, in some depth and with considerable feeling. The story has something more to recommend it, too: a quality of claustrophobic suspense not often achieved in pulp fiction, for much of it involves a deadly game of cat-and-mouse deep inside an old mine.

Talmage Powell has been a full-time writer since his first professional sale in 1943. He has published hundreds of mystery, detective, western, and science fiction stories, as well as a dozen novels. His Western stories appeared in such pulp magazines as Dime Western, Fifteen Western Tales, Western Story, Zane Grey, Western Magazine, *and* New Western; *several have been anthologized. His only Western novel,* The Cage *(1969), an offbeat and surprising tale of a manhunt across a southwestern desert, was filmed in France in the 1970s.*

Coggins could feel the wild sweat soaking him, and against the sweat the cold darkness of the mine shaft sent a shiver along his spine. It didn't do to think too much at a time like this, he told himself. Just keep moving, that was it. Down into the bowels of the earth; into the Stygian darkness and musky, earthy smells of the old mine.

He staggered under the weight of old Ming on his shoulder. The Chinese had always looked small, like a wrinkled, yellow doll; but he was heavy now. Maybe it was because Coggins was trying to move so fast. Maybe it was just because old Ming was dying. Coggins had heard once that dying and dead men always feel heavier than live ones.

He was gasping, like an animal in terror. The terror was there, yes, Coggins thought, like cold worms crawling through his belly, but he could control it. There was a lack of air in the old mine, that was all. If he could only have one, deep lungful of fresh air. . . .

Coggins stumbled deeper into the mine. He felt as if he were miles deep in the cold, dark earth. He could hear water dripping slowly somewhere ahead, and a rat skittering across his path. The world above, the world of sunshine and growing green things seemed years in his past, even though it had been only moments since he'd heard the distant echo of the shots and had gone to the mouth of the shaft.

Ming had almost stumbled into his arms, gasping, "They rob us, rob us of all the gold!"

Now with Ming's dying weight on his shoulders, Coggins felt bitterness bubbling in him. In a way, it wasn't so bad for Ming. Ming had lived out his life, and had known from that last visit to the doctor that his days were numbered. The bullet in old Ming put a definite date on his death, and in that sense made it easier for him. Coggins had seen what the waiting under the shadow of death had done to him. Even Ming's opaque eyes hadn't been able to conceal it entirely.

That was one way of looking at it, Coggins thought. But if you looked at it another way, dying was a terrible thing for

Ming. Ming had an ambition, which he had often confided to Coggins. It was to bring Ling Toy, Ming's grandson, across the wide green sea to this new land of promise. The land had offered Ming grinding work, as a chuckwagon cook, then as a member of a railroad gang as the roads pushed ever westward over the towering mountains; even working the mine here, Ming had had to grub like a gopher.

But America meant something special to Ming; something that a mind different from his stoical, Oriental mind could never fully understand. Coggins never tried to understand completely, but he knew that Ming had this dream for Ling Toy, and for Ling Toy's children and children's children. Generations later it would be Ming who had started it all; by the act he would become an Honorable Ancestor, a status more important to Ming than life itself; through Ling Toy's generations, something of Ming would remain in the land, alive and strong, and those generations would pay him respect in their memories because he had been strong and keen enough to make this breathtaking land of green valleys and mountains possible for them.

Under Ming's weight, Coggins muttered soft, almost hysterical sounds in his throat. There was heartbreak and frustration in him at this shattering of Ming's dream, in the mine no one but the old yellow man and Coggins had been willing to work.

Why didn't the old Chinaman say something? As if in answer to Coggins's thought, Ming made a sound, a cough that showed that the bullet was in the lungs. There wasn't a chance in hell for Ming; Coggins knew it and sensed that Ming knew it too.

Coggins was stooped now, almost having to crawl in the low shaft with the old man. His heart was hammering against the lack of oxygen. Something smashed against his shoulder, almost knocking him off balance. He had to pause an instant, gulp for breath.

"Coggins?" Ming whispered, and the word brought another cough tearing out of him.

"It's all right," Coggins said. "An old timber down, but not a cave-in."

Ming coughed again, and like an echo on the heels of the cough, Coggins's listening ears caught sounds from back toward the mine mouth. It took only a moment for the sounds to have meaning, and standing there in the darkness Coggins felt his flesh go to gooseflesh and his throat go alum-dry. They were following him in. They had searched the cabin for the gold, and now, enraged and still empty-handed, they were coming into the mine. They would get the old Chinese and his partner and burn the location of the dust out of them with the tip of a hot knife blade.

Coggins wondered how much time he had before they overtook him. His heart was numb and cold, but a part of his mind was crystal clear. There were two of them; he had seen that from the mine entrance when Ming had fled in. They were Sorrel Sidel and Ed Clane, and they were drunk. They had got together, swigged the crazing yellow liquor in town, and had decided to go out and get their hands on the dust that rumor credited the old Chinese and his partner with having. Here in the lawless Territory men like Sidel and Clane did things that way; liquor, empty pockets, an itch in their palms, and a prize to be taken. Those were ingredients enough for minds like Sidel's and Clane's.

As he moved, Coggins tried to tell himself that he was exaggerating. Sorrel Sidel and Clane would never venture this far into the mine. But he knew that he was fooling himself. Perhaps the wanton shooting of Ming had been reactive, a liquored-up impulse of the instant to keep the old man from fleeing into the mouth of the mine shaft; but now that they had gone this far, now that the shooting was done, Sidel and Clane would go all the way.

The cough racked Ming again; and this time the spasm was so fierce the yellow fingers dug into Coggins's back.

Coggins listened again. Back in the distance of the shaft, a voice shouted, echoing, rolling down the shaft. They had heard old Ming's cough. They were coming forward faster now, like dogs smelling blood. Sidel and Clane knew the old Chinaman was unarmed, and they would guess that Coggins was too. They had seen Coggins for that brief moment at the shaft's mouth. They would guess he had been working, and they weren't too drunk to figure that Coggins didn't wear a gun when he was working.

Misery beat in Coggins's heart. He had never figured his life to amount to anything much; but now he knew, in these seconds before death came swooping out of the dank darkness behind him, what a man's life was worth. He knew that every cell in his body cried out against dying. For an instant agonized frustration erupted in him at dying like this, empty-handed and helpless, deep in a cold, dark, ready-made tomb.

He staggered to a stop, blowing like a horse that has run a great distance. He forced himself to remain calm. He could faintly hear Sidel and Clane coming down the shaft. He pictured a chart of the mine in his mind, trying to remember. The blind shaft at the last bend was the one with the cave-in—or was it? Was the next minor shaft, the one that angled off from the main shaft just ahead, the clear one? Coggins was sure that it was. For an instant his spirits lifted. He'd turn into the small shaft. He had to have a place to lay Ming down. He would find a weapon of some kind, an old pickhead, anything. . . .

But of what use would a pickhead be against two men with guns?

Ming coughed again. Coggins cursed under his breath and moved on down the shaft.

He searched with his free hand along the shaft wall, fingers touching the ragged strata of rock and claylike dirt. The main vein had played out here years ago, and the big Eastern corporation that owned the mine had closed it up. After Ming and Coggins came, there was clearing out to do, cave-ins to move, timbers to brace. They had gambled that they could still take gold from this earth. Ming had put up the money, and Coggins had furnished half the brains and a strong back. They had labored like ants through all the old diggins, before hitting the new, small vein that had been paying off. And laboring through the shafts, Coggins had learned every twisting and turning of them.

But now his teeth went on edge and he wondered if the chart he'd drawn in his mind was as accurate as he'd thought. He'd missed the small side shaft, and he couldn't keep to the main shaft much longer. Sidel and Clane were getting too close behind.

Then Coggins's searching hand touched empty air. He jerked to a stop. Bending low, he pushed his way into the small shaft that angled off the main one. Squatting, Coggins still couldn't keep Ming from brushing against the roof of the burrow. The movement brought down a small shower of dirt. The Eastern corporation had made several tappings like this off the main shaft when the mine had started playing out.

The burrow formed an ell. Coggins wriggled around it and laid old Ming out in the darkness.

"If they go on down the main shaft, they might bypass us here," Coggins said.

Ming said nothing.

Coggins listened. Distantly, he could hear sounds coming on down the shaft. He couldn't risk a light, but his fingers searched blindly until he had Ming turned a trifle and felt the blood on Ming's back. It was hot against his fingers, and he pulled them away, letting Ming settle back slowly.

"I am very sorry, Coggins," Ming whispered. "Now they follow—and Ming has brought death to you, my trusted friend."

Coggins slouched on his haunches and said nothing. He had never been a man of many words, and there were no words that would reply to the bitter heartbreak in the old man's voice. Ming had brought danger to a friend. Better that he should have gone to his ancestors a thousand times and with great pain each time than to have done that to a friend.

"Ming will die with this thing in his heart!"

"No," said Coggins, "you mustn't feel that way. You didn't figure they'd start shooting when you made the break. You didn't figure them to follow you in. Anyhow, it was your only hope, Ming. Any man would have been a fool not to try to make the mine shaft."

"Your words prove your manhood," Ming said in his husking whisper, trying to fight back a bubbling, tearing cough, "which only makes Ming sadder."

Coggins sensed that Ming was weeping. It was a shocking, strange thing to think of those never-blinking almond eyes filling with tears. Even through the fear that was washing through him like dirty, cold water, Coggins felt a great pity for the man, and he was glad the darkness hid Ming's tortured eyes from his gaze.

"I would touch my queue before I die, Coggins."

Coggins eased Ming up, pulled the long braid of hair from under Ming's shoulder, and draped it down across Ming's chest. He felt Ming's fingers brush his and touch the queue. It was the one mark of old China still upon Ming. He might wear blue jeans and a shirt and boots, but that queue would be rolled under his flat-browed Stetson. He claimed it was the most wonderful queue in the world. Coggins could believe that, for the queue was long and glistening-black and belied Ming's age. To the old Chinese it was a wonder because it was the queue of the Mings.

"I have disgraced this queue, bringing danger to you, Coggins." Ming fought a cough. "And now I die here. I have only one hope left—that you, friend dear as a son, will somehow escape. The gold is still hidden under the cabin. You get out, Coggins, take Ming's gold, send Ling Toy. . . ." Ming fell back gasping, fighting a cough, and when he touched the old man's brow, Coggins felt the quickly rising fever.

"If I get out, Ming, I'll send your gold to Ling Toy."

"Ming is happy."

The light grew. He could hear their voices now, Sidel's muttering, and Clane's short replies.

"Hell," Clane said. "Might take two or three days. They both might even die in here, starving rather than facin' us. And somebody might happen along. Can't afford it. Let's git 'em now! They got to be in the belly of this mountain."

Then suddenly the light was waning.

Coggins tried to swallow; he watched the lantern glow grow dim, and listened to Sidel's and Clane's footsteps fading as they went on deeper down the shaft.

The earth was composed of silence and blackness again. Coggins turned, wriggled back up to Ming.

His hands went forward, searching, jerked to a stop; and then he drew his hands slowly from Ming. He was glad the darkness hid the sight before him. All the while he had known with dread certainty that Ming's racking cough would lead Sidel and Clane to them. But Ming had known it too, and Ming had smothered the cough, given his friend the insurance of silence, and the silence had saved Coggins' life.

Coggins pressed against the wall of the burrow, his fingers still twitching from the feel of Ming's queue, embedded and knotted with the last of Ming's strength in the yellow skin of his own throat.

Ming had lifted the disgrace from his queue, Coggins thought; and he sat shaken by things he would never be able to tell any man.

The man who turned and crawled out of the burrow was different from the man who had crawled in. He reached the main shaft, moving in silence on his toes. Caution slowed him down, but finally, through the inky blackness, he saw a pale light ahead. It brought a hammering to his heart, that light, the light of day. Then he was out in it, feeling the glory of the sun on his flesh, the expansion of fresh air in his lungs. He moved across the rocky side of the mountain.

Coggins jerked the cabin door open. A Winchester hung on pegs against the sagging wall. He took the gun down, jacked a cartridge into the chamber, and moved to the window.

The window faced the mine entrance. Coggins flung it open and rested the Winchester on the sill. His cheek was firm against the stock, and eyes like ice sighted along the barrel of the gun as he waited in the bright light of day for the appearance of two figures in the mine's yawning mouth.

THE BIG HUNT

—

Elmore Leonard

BUFFALO hunters were the scourge of the plains states during the last half of the nineteenth century, slaughtering millions of the shaggy animals for their meat, hides, even their tongues and bones. The most famous of the hunters, William F. Cody, is said to have killed 4,280 bison over a period of eighteen months in the 1860s, earning him the nickname of "Buffalo Bill." The slaughter was so overwhelming that Plains Indians bitterly fought the white hunters; the Sioux succeeded for a time in closing the Bozeman Trail, which crossed their best buffalo range.

There was little glamor in the buffalo-hunting trade. The shooters and skinners were hard men, many of them loners and misfits. Elmore Leonard's portrait of two such hunters, young Will Gordon and his alcoholic partner, Leo Cleary, is steeped in raw realism; you can almost hear the cracking of the big Sharps .50 rifle and the cries of the animals, almost smell the dust and the blood. "The Big Hunt" achieves a kind of grim majesty as a result.

Some of the finest traditional Western fiction written in the past forty years has come from the imagination of Elmore Leonard. His pulp stories, which began appearing in the late forties in such magazines as Dime Western, Western Story, Zane Grey's Western Magazine, Gunsmoke, and Argosy, are of a uniformly high quality; two of the best were made into successful films, "3:10 to Yuma" and "The Captives" (The Tall T). His novel Hombre (1961) has appeared on numerous lists of the best Westerns of all time. Almost as fine are The Bounty Hunters (1953), Escape from Five Shadows

(1956), and Valdez Is Coming *(1970). In recent years Leonard has turned to the writing of hard-edged, contemporary-life-in-the-raw crime thrillers such as* Glitz *(1985) and* Freaky Deaky *(1988), with best-seller results.*

It was a Sharps .50, heavy and cumbrous, but he was lying at full length down-wind of the herd behind the rise with the long barrel resting on the hump of the crest so that the gun would be less tiring to fire.

He counted close to fifty buffalo scattered over the grass patches, and his front sight roamed over the herd as he waited. A bull, its fresh winter hide glossy in the morning sun, strayed leisurely from the others, following thick patches of gamma grass. The Sharps swung slowly after the animal. And when the bull moved directly toward the rise, the heavy rifle dipped over the crest so that the sight was just off the right shoulder. The young man, who was still not much more than a boy, studied the animal with mounting excitement.

"Come on, granddaddy . . . a little closer," Will Gordon whispered. The rifle stock felt comfortable against his cheek, and even the strong smell of oiled metal was good. "Walk up and take it like a man, you ugly monster, you dumb, shaggy, ugly hulk of a monster. Look at that fresh gamma right in front of you. . . ."

The massive head came up sleepily, as if it had heard the hunter, and the bull moved toward the rise. It was less than eighty yards away, nosing the grass tufts, when the Sharps thudded heavily in the crisp morning air.

The herd lifted from grazing, shaggy heads turning lazily toward the bull sagging to its knees, but as it slumped to the ground the heads lowered unconcernedly. Only a few of the buffalo paused to sniff the breeze. A calf bawled, sounding *nooooo* in the open-plain stillness.

Will Gordon had reloaded the Sharps, and he pushed it

out in front of him as another buffalo lumbered over to the
fallen bull, sniffing at the blood, nuzzling the blood-stained
hide; and, when the head came up, nose quivering with
scent, the boy squeezed the trigger. The animal stumbled a
few yards before easing its great weight to the ground.

Don't let them smell blood, he said to himself. They smell
blood and they're gone.

He fired six rounds then, reloading the Sharps each time,
though a loaded Remington rolling-block lay next to him.
He fired with little hesitation, going to his side, ejecting,
taking a cartridge from the loose pile at his elbow, inserting
it in the open breech. He fired without squinting, calmly,
killing a buffalo with each shot. Two of the animals lumbered
on a short distance after being hit, glassy-eyed, stunned by
the shock of the heavy bullet. The others dropped to the
earth where they stood.

Sitting up now, he pulled a square of cloth from his coat
pocket, opened his canteen, and poured water into the cloth,
squeezing it so that it would become saturated. He worked
the wet cloth through the eye of his cleaning rod, then
inserted it slowly into the barrel of the Sharps, hearing a
sizzle as it passed through the hot metal tube. He was new to
the buffalo fields, but he had learned how an overheated
gun barrel could put a man out of business. He had made
sure of many things before leaving Leverette with just a two-
man outfit.

Pulling the rod from the barrel, he watched an old cow
sniffing at one of the fallen bulls. Get that one quick . . . or
you'll lose a herd!

He dropped the Sharps, took the Remington, and fired at
the buffalo from a sitting position. Then he reloaded both
rifles, but fired the Remington a half-dozen more rounds
while the Sharps cooled. Twice he had to hit with another
shot to kill, and he told himself to take more time. Perspira-
tion beaded his face, even in the crisp fall air, and burned
powder was heavy in his nostrils, but he kept firing at the

same methodical pace, because it could not last much longer, and there was not time to cool the barrels properly. He had killed close to twenty when the blood smell became too strong.

The buffalo made rumbling noises in the thickness of their throats, and now three and four at a time would crowd toward those on the ground, sniffing, pawing nervously.

A bull bellowed, and the boy fired again. The herd bunched, bumping each other, bellowing, shaking their clumsy heads at the blood smell. Then the leader broke suddenly, and what was left of the herd was off, from stand to dead run, in one moment of panic, driven mad by the scent of death.

The boy fired into the dust cloud that rose behind them, but they were out of range before he could reload again.

It's better to wave them off carefully with a blanket after killing all you can skin, the boy thought to himself. But this had worked out all right. Sometimes it didn't, though. Sometimes they stampeded right at the hunter.

He rose stiffly, rubbing his shoulder, and moved back down the rise to his picketed horse. His shoulder ached from the buck of the heavy rifles, but he felt good. Lying back there on the plain was close to seventy or eighty dollars he'd split with Leo Cleary . . . soon as they'd been skinned and handed over to the hide buyers. Hell, this was easy. He lifted his hat, and the wind was cold on his sweat-dampened forehead. He breathed in the air, feeling an exhilaration, and the ache in his shoulder didn't matter one bit.

Wait until he rode into Leverette with a wagon full of hides—, he thought. He'd watch close, pretending he didn't care, and he'd see if anybody laughed at him then.

He was mounting when he heard the wagon creaking in the distance, and he smiled when Leo Cleary's voice drifted up the gradual rise, swearing at the team. He waited in the saddle, and swung down as the four horses and the canvas-topped wagon came up to him.

"Leo, I didn't even have to come wake you up." Will Gordon smiled up at the old man on the box, and the smile eased the tight lines of his face. It was a face that seemed used to frowning, watching life turn out all wrong, a sensitive boyish face, but the set of his jaw was a man's . . . or that of a boy who thought like a man. There were few people he showed his smile to other than Leo Cleary.

"That cheap store whisky you brought run out," Leo Cleary said. His face was beard-stubbled, and the skin hung loosely seamed beneath tired eyes.

"I thought you quit," the boy said. His smile faded.

"I have now."

"Leo, we got us a lot of money lying over that rise."

"And a lot of work . . ." He looked back into the wagon, yawning. "We got near a full load we could take in . . . and rest up. You shooters think all the work's in knocking 'em down."

"Don't I help with the skinning?"

Cleary's weathered face wrinkled into a slow smile. "That's just the old man in me coming out," he said. "You set the pace, Will. All I hope is roaming hide buyers don't come along . . . you'll be wanting to stay out till April." He shook his head. "That's a mountain of backbreaking hours just to prove a point."

"You think it's worth it or not?" the boy said angrily.

Cleary just smiled. "Your dad would have liked to seen this," he said. "Come on, let's get those hides."

Skinning buffalo was filthy, back-straining work. Most hunters wouldn't stoop to it. It was for men hired as skinners and cooks, men who stayed by the wagons until the shooting was done.

During their four weeks on the range the boy did his share of the work, and now he and Leo Cleary went about it with little conversation. Will Gordon was not above helping with the butchering with hides going for four dollars each in

Leverette, three dollars if a buyer picked them up on the range.

The more hides skinned, the bigger the profit. That was elementary. Let the professional hunters keep their pride and their hands clean while they sat around in the afternoon filling up on scootawaboo. Let them pay heavy for extra help just because skinning was beneath them. That was their business.

In Leverette, when the professional hunters laughed at them, it didn't bother Leo Cleary. Maybe they'd get hides, maybe they wouldn't. Either way, it didn't matter much. When he thought about it, Leo Cleary believed the boy just wanted to prove a point—that a two-man outfit could make money—attributing it to his Scotch stubbornness. The idea had been Will's dad's—when he was sober. The old man had almost proved it himself.

But whenever anyone laughed, the boy would feel that the laughter was not meant for him but for his father.

Leo Cleary went to work with a frown on his grizzled face, wetting his dry lips disgustedly. He squatted up close to the nearest buffalo and with his skinning knife slit the belly from neck to tail. He slashed the skin down the inside of each leg, then carved a strip from around the massive neck, his long knife biting at the tough hide close to the head. Then he rose, rubbing the back of his knife hand across his forehead.

"Yo! Will . . ." he called out.

The boy came over then, leading his horse and holding a coiled riata in his free hand. One end was secured to the saddle horn. He bunched the buffalo's heavy neck skin, wrapping the free end of line around it, knotting it.

He led the horse out the full length of the riata, then mounted, his heels squeezing flanks as soon as he was in the saddle.

"Yiiiiiii!" he screamed in the horse's ear and swatted the rump with his hat. The mount bolted.

The hide held, stretching, then jerked from the carcass, coming with a quick sucking, sliding gasp.

They kept at it through most of the afternoon, sweating over the carcasses, both of them skinning, and butchering some meat for their own use. It was still too early in the year, too warm, to butcher hind-quarters for the meat buyers. Later, when the snows came and the meat would keep, they would do this.

They took the fresh hides back to their base camp and staked them out, stretching the skins tightly, flesh side up. The flat ground around the wagon and cook-fire was covered with staked-out hides, taken the previous day. In the morning they would gather the hides and bind them in packs and store the packs in the wagon. The boy thought there would be maybe two more days of hunting here before they would have to move the camp.

For the second time that day he stood stretching, rubbing a stiffness in his body, but feeling satisfied. He smiled, and even Leo Cleary wasn't watching him to see it.

At dusk they saw the string of wagons out on the plain, a black line creeping toward them against the sunlight dying on the horizon.

"Hide buyers, most likely," Leo Cleary said. He sounded disappointed, for it could mean they would not return to Leverette for another month.

The boy said, "Maybe a big hunting outfit."

"Not at this time of day," the old man said. "They'd still have their hides drying." He motioned to the creek back of their camp. "Whoever it is, they want water."

Two riders leading the five Conestogas spurred suddenly as they neared the camp and rode in ahead of the six-team wagons. The boy watched them intently. When they were almost to the camp circle, he recognized them and swore under his breath, though he suddenly felt self-conscious.

The Foss brothers, Clyde and Wylie, swung down stiff-legged, not waiting for an invitation, and arched the stiffness from their backs. Without a greeting, Clyde Foss's eyes roamed leisurely over the staked-out hides, estimating the number as he scratched at his beard stubble. He grinned slowly, looking at his brother.

"They must a used rocks . . . ain't more than forty hides here."

Leo Cleary said, "Hello, Clyde . . . Wylie," and watched the surprise come over them with recognition.

Clyde said, "Damn, Leo, I didn't see you were here. Who's that with you?"

"Matt Gordon's boy," Leo Cleary answered. "We're hunting together this season."

"Just the two of you?" Wylie asked with surprise. He was a few years older than Clyde, calmer, but looked to be his twin. They were both of them lanky, thin through face and body, but heavy boned.

Leo Cleary said, "I thought it was common talk in Leverette about us being out."

"We made up over to Caldwell this year," Clyde said. He looked about the camp again, amused. "Who does the shooting?"

"I do." The boy took a step toward Clyde Foss. His voice was cold, distant. He was thinking of another time four years before when his dad had introduced him to the Foss brothers, the day Matt Gordon contracted with them to pick up his hides.

"And I do skinning," the boy added. It was like, What are you going to do about it! the way he said it.

Clyde laughed again. Wylie just grinned.

"So you're Matt Gordon's boy," Wylie Foss said.

"We met once before."

"We did?"

"In Leverette, four years ago." The boy made himself say it naturally. "A month before you met my dad in the field and paid him for his hides with whisky instead of cash . . . the day before he was trampled into the ground. . . ."

The Foss brothers met his stare, and suddenly the amusement was gone from their eyes. Clyde no longer laughed, and Wylie's mouth tightened. Clyde stared at the boy and said, "If you meant anything by that, you better watch your mouth."

Wylie said, "We can't stop buffalo from stampedin'."

Clyde grinned now. "Maybe he's drunk . . . maybe he favors his pa."

"Take it any way you want," the boy said. He stood firmly with his fists clenched. "You knew better than to give him whisky. You took advantage of him."

Wylie looked up at the rumbling sound of the wagon string coming in, the ponderous creaking of wooden frames, iron-rimmed tires grating, and the never-changing off-key leathery rattle of the traces, then the sound of reins flicking horse hide and the indistinguishable growls of the teamsters.

Wylie moved toward the wagons in the dimness and shouted to the first one, "Ed . . . water down!" pointing toward the creek.

"You bedding here?" Leo Cleary asked after him.

"Just water."

"Moving all night?"

"We're meeting a party on the Salt Fork . . . they ain't going to stay there forever." Wylie Foss walked after the wagons leading away their horses.

Clyde paid little attention to the wagons, only glancing in that direction as they swung toward the stream. Stoop-shouldered, his hand curling the brim of his sweat-stained hat, his eyes roamed lazily over the drying hides. He rolled a cigarette, taking his time, failing to offer tobacco to the boy.

"I guess we got room for your hides," he said finally.

"I'm not selling."

"We'll load soon as we water . . . even take the fresh ones."

"I said I'm not selling."

"Maybe I'm not asking."

"There's nothing making me sell if I don't want to!"

The slow smile formed on Clyde's mouth. "You're a mean little fella, aren't you?"

"I'm not bothering you . . . just water your stock and get out."

Clyde Foss dropped the cigarette stub and turned a boot on it. "There's a bottle in my saddle pouch." He nodded to Leo Cleary who was standing off from them.

"Help yourself, Leo."

The old man hesitated.

"I said help yourself."

Leo Cleary moved off toward the stream.

"Now, Mr. Gordon . . . how many hides you say were still dryin'?"

"None for you."

"Forty . . . forty-five?"

"You heard what I said." He was standing close to Clyde Foss, watching his face. He saw the jaw muscles tighten and sensed Clyde's shift of weight. He tried to turn, bringing up his shoulder, but it came with pain-stabbing suddenness. Clyde's fist smashed against his cheek, and he stumbled off balance.

"Forty?"

Clyde's left hand followed around with weight behind it, scraping his temple, staggering him.

"Forty-five?"

He waded after the boy then, clubbing at his face and body, knocking his guard aside to land his fists, until the boy was backed against his wagon. Then Clyde stopped as the boy fell into the wheel spokes, gasping, and slumped to the ground.

Clyde stood over the boy and nudged him with his boot. "Did I hear forty or forty-five?" he said dryly. And when the boy made no answer—"Well, it don't matter."

He heard the wagons coming up from the creek. Wylie was leading the horses. "Boy went to sleep on us, Wylie," he grinned. "He said don't disturb him, just take the skins and leave the payment with Leo." He laughed then. And later, when the wagons pulled out, he was laughing again.

Once he heard voices, a man swearing, a never-ending soft thudding against the ground, noises above him in the wagon. But these passed, and there was nothing.

He woke again, briefly, a piercing ringing in his ears, and his face throbbed violently though the pain seemed to be out from him and not within, as if his face were bloated and would soon burst. He tried to open his mouth, but a weight held his jaws tight. Then wagons moving . . . the sound of traces . . . laughter.

It was still dark when he opened his eyes. The noises had stopped. Something cool was on his face. He felt it with his hand—a damp cloth. He sat up, taking it from his face, working his jaw slowly.

The man was a blur at first . . . something reflecting in his hand. Then it was Leo Cleary, and the something in his hand was a half-empty whisky bottle.

"There wasn't anything I could do, Will."

"How long they been gone?"

"Near an hour. They took all of them, even the ones staked out." He said, "Will, there wasn't anything I could do. . . ."

"I know," the boy said.

"They paid for the hides with whisky."

The boy looked at him surprised. He had not expected them to pay anything. But now he saw how this would appeal to Clyde's sense of humor, using the same way the hide buyer had paid his dad four years before.

"That part of it, Leo?" The boy nodded to the whisky bottle in the old man's hand.

"No, they put three five-gallon barrels in the wagon. Remember . . . Clyde give me this."

The boy was silent. Finally, he said, "Don't touch those barrels, Leo."

He sat up the remainder of the night, listening to his

thoughts. He had been afraid when Clyde Foss was bullying him, and he was still afraid. But now the fear was mixed with anger because his body ached and he could feel the loose teeth on one side of his mouth when he tightened his jaw, and taste the blood dry on his lips, and most of all because Clyde Foss had taken a month's work, four hundred and eighty hides, and left three barrels of whisky.

Sometimes the fear was stronger than the anger. The plain was silent and in its darkness there was nothing to hold to. He did not bother Leo Cleary. He talked to himself and listened to the throb in his temples and left Leo alone with the little whisky he still had. He wanted to cry, but he could not because he had given up the privilege by becoming a man, even though he was still a boy. He was acutely aware of this, and when the urge to cry welled in him he would tighten his nerves and call himself names until the urge passed.

Sometimes the anger was stronger than the fear and he would think of killing Clyde Foss. Towards morning both the fear and the anger lessened, and many of the things he had thought of during the night he did not now remember. He was sure of only one thing: he was going to get his hides back. A way to do it would come to him. He still had his Sharps.

He shook Leo Cleary awake and told him to hitch the wagon.

"Where we going?" The old man was still dazed, from sleep and whisky.

"Hunting, Leo. Down on the Salt Fork."

Hunting was good in the Nations. The herds would come down from Canada and the Dakotas and winter along the Cimarron and the Salt and even down to the Canadian. Here the herds were big, two and three hundred grazing together, and sometimes you could look over the flat plain and see thousands. A big outfit with a good hunter could average over eighty hides a day. But, because there were so many hunters, the herds kept on the move.

In the evening, they saw the first of the buffalo camps. Distant lights in the dimness, then lanterns and cook-fires as they drew closer in a dusk turning to night, and the sounds of men drifted out to them on the silent plain.

The hunters and skinners were crouched around a poker game on a blanket, a lantern above them on a crate. They paid little heed to the old man and the boy, letting them prepare their supper on the low-burning cook-fire and after, when the boy stood over them and asked questions, they answered him shortly. The game was for high stakes, and there was a pot building. No, they hadn't seen the Foss brothers, and if they had, they wouldn't trade with them anyway. They were taking their skins to Caldwell for top dollar.

They moved on, keeping well off from the flickering line of lights. Will Gordon would go in alone as they neared the camps, and, if there were five wagons in the camp, he approached silently until he could make out the men at the fire.

From camp to camp it was the same story. Most of the hunters had not seen the Fosses; a few had, earlier in the day, but they could be anywhere now. Until finally, very late, they talked to a man who had sold to the Foss brothers that morning.

"They even took some fresh hides," he told them.

"Still heading west?" The boy kept his voice even, though he felt the excitement inside of him.

"Part of them," the hunter said. "Wylie went back to Caldwell with three wagons, but Clyde shoved on to meet another party up the Salt. See, Wylie'll come back with empty wagons, and by that time the hunters'll have caught up with Clyde. You ought to find him up a ways. We'll all be up there soon . . . that's where the big herds are heading."

They moved on all night, spelling each other on the wagon

box. Leo grumbled and said they were crazy. The boy said little because he was thinking of the big herds. And he was thinking of Clyde Foss with all those hides he had to dry . . . and the plan was forming in his mind.

Leo Cleary watched from the pines, seeing nothing, thinking of the boy who was out somewhere in the darkness, though most of the time he thought of whisky, barrels of it that they had been hauling for two days and now into the second night.

The boy was a fool. The camp they had seen at sundown was probably just another hunter. They all staked hides at one time or another. Sneaking up in the dark they could take him for a Kiowa and cut him in two with a buffalo gun. And even if it did turn out to be Clyde Foss, then what?

Later, the boy walked in out of the darkness and pushed the pine branches aside and was standing next to the old man.

"It's Clyde, Leo."

The old man said nothing.

"He's got two men with him."

"So . . . what are you going to do now?" the old man said.

"Hunt," the boy said. He went to his saddlebag and drew a cap-and-ball revolver and loaded it before bedding for the night.

In the morning he took his rifles and led his horse along the base of the ridge, through the pines that were dense here, but scattered higher up the slope. He would look out over the flat plain to the south and see the small squares of canvas, very white in the brilliant sunlight. Ahead, to the west, the ridge dropped off into a narrow valley with timbered hills on the other side.

The boy's eyes searched the plain, roaming to the white squares, Clyde's wagons, but he went on without hesitating until he reached the sloping finish of the ridge. Then he moved up the valley until the plain widened again, and then he stopped to wait. He was prepared to wait for days if necessary, until the right time.

From high up on the slope above, Leo Cleary watched him. Through the morning the old man's eyes would drift from the boy and then off to the left, far out on the plain to the two wagons and the ribbon of river behind them. He tried to relate the boy and the wagons in some way, but he could not.

After a while, he saw buffalo. A few straggling off toward the wagons, but even more on the other side of the valley where the plain widened again and the grass was higher, green-brown in the sun.

Towards noon the buffalo increased, and he remembered the hunters saying how the herds were moving west. By that time there were hundreds, perhaps a thousand, scattered over the grass, out a mile or so from the boy who seemed to be concentrating on them.

Maybe he really is going hunting, Leo Cleary thought. Maybe he's starting all over again. But I wish I had me a drink. The boy's down-wind now, he thought, lifting his head to feel the breeze on his face. He could edge up and take a hundred of them if he did it right. What's he waiting for! Hell, if he wants to start all over, it's all right with me. I'll stay out with him. At that moment he was thinking of the three barrels of whisky.

"Go out and get 'em, Will," he urged the boy aloud, though he would not be heard. "The wind won't keep forever!"

Surprised, then, he saw the boy move out from the brush clumps leading his horse, mount, and lope off in a direction out and away from the herd.

"You can't hunt buffalo from a saddle . . . they'll run as soon as they smell horse! What the hell's the matter with him!"

He watched the boy, growing smaller with distance, move out past the herd. Then suddenly the horse wheeled, and it was going at a dead run toward the herd. A yell drifted up to the ridge and then a heavy rifle shot followed by two reports that were weaker. Horse and rider cut into the herd, and the buffalo broke in confusion.

They ran crazily, bellowing, bunching in panic to escape the horse and man smell and the screaming that suddenly hit them with the wind. A herd of buffalo will run for hours if the panic stabs them sharp enough, and they will stay together, bunching their thunder, tons of bulk, massive bellowing heads, horns and thrashing hooves. Nothing will stop them. Some go down, and the herd passes over, beating them into the ground.

They ran directly away from the smell and the noises that were now far behind; down-wind they came, and in less than a minute were thundering through the short valley. Dust rose after them, billowing up to the old man who covered his mouth, coughing, watching the rumbling dark mass erupt from the valley out onto the plain. They moved in an unwavering line toward the Salt Fork, rolling over everything before swerving at the river—even the two canvas squares that had been brilliant white in the morning sun. And soon they were only a deep hum in the distance.

Will Gordon was out on the flats, approaching the place where the wagons had stood, riding slowly now in the settling dust.

But the dust was still in the air, heavy enough to make Leo Cleary sneeze as he brought the wagons out from the pines toward the river.

He saw the hide buyer's wagons smashed to scrap wood and shredded canvas dragged among the strewn buffalo hides. Many of the bales were still intact, spilling from the wagon wrecks; some were buried under the debris.

Three men stood waist-deep in the shallows of the river, and beyond them, upstream, were the horses they had saved. Some had not been cut from the pickets in time, and they lay shapeless in blood at one end of the camp.

Will Gordon stood on the bank with the revolving pistol

cocked, pointed at Clyde Foss. He glanced aside as the old man brought up the team.

"He wants to sell back, Leo. How much you think?"

The old man only looked at him because he could not speak.

"I think two barrels of whisky," Will Gordon said. He stepped suddenly into the water and brought the long pistol barrel sweeping against Clyde's head, cutting the temple.

"Two barrels?"

Clyde Foss staggered and came to his feet slowly.

"Come here, Clyde." The boy leveled the pistol at him and waited as Clyde Foss came hesitantly out of the water, hunching his shoulders. The boy swung the pistol back, and, as Clyde ducked, he brought his left fist up, smashing hard against the man's jaw.

"Or three barrels?"

The hide buyer floundered in the shallow water, then crawled to the bank, and lay on his stomach, gasping for breath.

"We'll give him three, Leo. Since he's been nice about it."

Later, after Clyde and his two men had loaded their wagon with four hundred and eighty hides, the old man and the boy rode off through the valley to the great plain.

Once the old man said, "Where we going now, Will?"

And when the boy said, "We're still going hunting, Leo," the old man shrugged wearily and just nodded his head.

PLAGUE BOAT

Frank Bonham

THE major forms of transportation in the Old West—railroads, steamboats, stagecoaches—provided colorful backgrounds for hundreds of pulp stories. Writers found the history of riverboats and rivermen particularly rich in story material, for stern-wheelers and side-wheelers plied every important river in the western United States—the Mississippi, the Missouri, the Yel-lowstone, the Colorado, the Sacramento, and the Columbia— and were influential in the often turbulant settling of the frontier. And the individuals who operated and worked on these river packets made fine pulp heroes and villains: owners, pilots, captains, deckhands, engineers, gamblers.

In the 1940s, Frank Bonham (1914-1988) wrote a number of first-rate tales about steamboating (and about railroading and stagecoaching as well) for such better magazines as Blue Book, Short Stories, Dime Western, *and* Argosy. *"Plague Boat," which first appeared in the adventure pulp* Short Stories *in 1942, is perhaps the best of these—a tense account of trouble between riverboaters and shantyboaters in the Loui-siana bayous, compounded by a ruinous flood and an outbreak of yellow fever.*

Bonham made his first professional sale in 1935, of a mystery story to Phantom Detective, *after which he spent three years learning the craft of fiction writing as a "ghost" for the legendary pulp hack, Ed Earl Repp. Between 1941 and 1951, he contributed millions of words of Western and histori-cal adventure fiction to a wide range of pulp titles, as well as to such "slick" magazines as* Liberty, McCall's, *and* Esquire. *His first novel,* Lost Stage Valley, *appeared in 1948; his twenty-first and last Western,* Eye of the Hunter, *was published earlier this year. A collection of his best Western short stories will also be published in 1989, by Ohio University Press.*

At dusk Ben Worden came up from the texas and took the wheel from Ord McDan'l. He scowled down at the opaque surface of the river, as thick and red as tomato soup in the sunset. Ezra Church arose from his plush chair at the back of the wheelhouse, and crossed to where Ben was standing. In the dusk, he loomed behind Worden like a fat, soiled ghost, his wrinkled, white duck trousers and flannel shirt gray in the gloom.

He cleared his throat. "As I recall it," he said. "Whiskey Creek empties into the river about a mile above that shack, yonder."

Ben said curtly, "It's less than half a mile, and the mark's a burned stump on the near shore. Maybe you didn't know, but I've been up this river before."

Ezra Church, who owned a dozen steamboats four times the size of Ben's little packet, glowered at the back of the pilot's head. He said nothing, but the promise of an early explosion was in his purpling features and the small, shrewd eyes.

Night, sinister and full of dark portents, moved upon the river. Fear came out of the bayou and walked the wheelhouse, and its hard pressure was in the face of each man. Even Ben Worden, who had been at odds with danger before and had not moved one step out of its path, shared the general uneasiness.

Ben and Ord McDan'l and Ezra Church all knew that the shantyboaters of the Whiskey Creek region were more dangerous than rattlesnakes, because they gave no warning when they struck. In the last month, three pilots had dropped beside their wheels without knowing that they had come into a shantyboat man's sights. They had slumped to the deck and their boats had gone hard aground before the relief man could reach the wheel.

They'd had their differences, the men who piloted the gleaming white palaces that traversed the ol' Mississipp' and the men who slept and fished and drank on their ramshackle houseboats. But it was a bloodless feud which had become a habit with each group. No one could have foreseen a war.

Shantyboaters' dinghies had been swamped by careless pilots for generations. Trotlines were forever being cut by the paddles of a packet working inshore uncommonly close. But these were hazards of the trade, which were cursed roundly and endured, like malaria and the spring shortage of good corn liquor.

But when a shantyboat full of river folk was run down at Whiskey Creek and seven men and women lost their lives, the shantyboaters declared open war. No matter that the raft had been in midriver at midnight and jammed to the bull-rails with river people celebrating a wedding, all of them more or less drunk. *Murder had been done.*

The River Commission stewed over the sniping of steam-boat pilots but did nothing, while cargoes mysteriously caught fire, and snags, moored just under the river's surface, took out the paddles of a dozen boats.

Ben's eyes, brown as the river at flood, squinted in a face that was lean and hard with constant perusing of the river's face—the book that a pilot must learn to read without stumbling. He strove for ease of mind and did not find it, for he knew that old Catfish Clemens himself was likely in this bayou. Old Clemens, who was to the shantyboat clan what Neptune is to the deep-water man—part legend, part god, mostly devil.

To Ord McDan'l, Ben said, "Tell them rousters to chunk that torch in the river and shoot craps in the boiler room. I'm gettin' a reflection on the brightwork."

McDan'l, a stocky man in a blue box coat, grimaced at Ezra Church and went below. On the *Majestic,* flagship of Church's

Red Star fleet, McDan'l was chief pilot, but he was only a humble relief man today on Ben Worden's down-at-heels little tub, the *Annabelle*.

Church's glance sought the wall clock. "Six o'clock," he muttered. "Too bad we couldn't have got here on schedule. We'll be crowded to get out of the bayou before sun-up. Flood'll be on us in less than twelve hours." His pendulous jowls worked like those of a bulldog. He bit the end off a cigar and his teeth locked upon it.

"I knew what we were getting in for," he went on. "The idea of personal safety is my last concern. I'm thinking of the men and women who are dying of yellow jack at Bayou Grand. It's worth any risk if we can save as many as two or three of them. But as for being a hero—" His fat shoulders shrugged. He struck a sulfur match and twisted the cigar in the flame until it smoldered.

Ben Worden's hand shot back over his shoulder. He ripped the cigar from the boatman's mouth, slid open a window, and hurled the cheroot into the night. "If you can't do any better than that," he snapped, "go down to the saloon. Maybe your pilots have to put up with your lightin' flares in the pilothouse. I don't."

Ezra Church came sputtering out of his stunned silence. All the indignities of the last two days were loosed within him. "By God, you won't ever make another pay-haul if I can help it! I'll see that the commission blacklists you from one end of the river to the other."

At the companionway, he glared at the lean form of the pilot, framed against the rusty skyline. "You can put a shantyboater at the wheel of the biggest boat on the Mississip', and he's still a shantyboater," he said bitterly.

"That," said Ben Worden, "ought to be good enough for anybody."

He was glad Catfish Clemens and his long-legged daughter, Jolean, hadn't heard him say that. For in a way Ben was proud of his shantyboat ancestry, though he knew that there

would be no more nights when he sat on the foredeck of
Catfish's boat with Jolean, and talked and stole an occasional
kiss. No more nights spent in spinning windies with other
shantyboat men, while the air of the cabin thickened with
smoke and the whiskey jug sat in the middle of the floor,
and men's hearts warmed to each other.

All those things had ended two years ago, when Ben
Worden had forsaken his father's honored calling to pilot his
own packet boat. All Ben's kinfolk lived on the river. They
said, "Trust a cottonmouth or the muzzle end of a gun, but
never a steamboat man."

Ben's father had died like a good shantyboat man. He was
setting his trotlines after dark when the steamboat hove upon
him. And because he knew he couldn't get out from under,
he stood up and shook his fist and cursed the pilot until he
was run down. But he was full of corn and out in midchannel,
so nothing much had been said about it.

There was plenty of talk, however, when Ben acquired the
Annabelle. Her owner-captain had picked a night of hell and
high water to tie up at Natchez, dismiss the crew, and get
drunk. Ben found her on a sand bar, put in his claim for ten
thousand salvage, and had it honored by the River Commission. Her owner swore she wasn't worth it and refused to pay.
So Ben Worden gave his trotlines to Catfish Clemens and
went on the river.

He knew the smaller tributaries as he knew the palm of his
hand. He was lean and tough, the way the river makes a man
who works hard and leaves whiskey alone. He was tall and
his eyes had small lines at the corners, pinched in deep
through reading the river's fine print.

The *Annabelle* was the smallest boat on the lower Mississippi. Thus she got a lot of jobs the bigger boats couldn't
take, when the river was too shoal or the haul was up some
small backwoods creek. And that's why the *Anabelle* had been
chartered by Ezra Church, heading a committee for the
relief of the yellow fever victims at Bayou Grand, to make

the trip to the flood-marooned village with medical supplies and equipment.

Darkness came, and an ache behind Ben's eyes sharpened . . . feud, and flood, and fever—three grim foemen to try any pilot's heart. Ben knew he was risking his boat, for if the oncoming flood took him out of the channel, he would never find it again. Sniper's bullets, or the horrible death that men called black vomit might do for him or all the members of his skeleton crew, even after they reached the plague victims.

With the *wash-wash* of her buckets behind, the packet poked her curious nose deep into Whiskey Creek. Glutted with spring torrents, the bayou was virtually a foreign passage to Ben. The clock was bonging off eleven strokes when Ben's eyes found a curious redness in the trees some distance ahead. Hearing his grunt of surprise, McDan'l and Ezra Church came forward.

"Grand Bayou," Ben frowned. "Though what—God in heaven! The town's afire!"

They had come around the bend into full view of the town. Great piles of flame poured a redness onto the water. Up this carpet of liquid fire the packet glided with her paddles dragging. The town's outlines were starkly silhouetted by the surging light. Tumbledown shacks crowding the riverbank, wharves leaning slantwise to the water, a mountain of baled cotton on the dock.

"Them's sperrit fire!" McDan'l said. "Colored folks build 'em to keep the sick-devils off."

As they warped in to the dock, the dismal monotone of Negroes' voices came to them from the high ground back of town. The wailing traced a cold finger down Ben's spine. He sent the steamboat's shrill whistle through those mournful sounds.

Roustabouts threw the boat's stout hawsers over the mooring bitts. The flame-soaked streets were crowded with men and women hurrying toward the dock, and there was a medieval, plague-town malignance to the setting that made

Ben's skin pimple with gooseflesh. In the noxious air he could taste horror and disease.

He raised his eyes from the wharf and let his glance wander down to where the flood-choked river had burst its banks and taken the south end of town. And there he saw Catfish Clemens's shantyboat.

He grabbed the speaking tube. His voice echoed harshly back from the engine room. "Keep them drums a-groanin'! We put out in an hour!"

The landing stage was run out and Ben was the first man on the dock. Lumbering behind him came Ezra Church, and at his heels Ord McDan'l, while behind timber and stanchion flashed the perspiring, scared faces of rousters.

Ben saw Church move busily among the piles of cotton, inspecting tags, counting bales, standing in the middle of it while he let his small eyes, quick and mercenary as adding machines, rove over the dock. Moving to the landing stage, Church cupped his hands to his mouth.

"Lay me a gangway! *Stir,* you scared louts! Stow those bales aboard!"

With his words, a slow wonder grew on Ben. But movement suddenly spirited his glance to where three figures were coming onto the dock. He strove for recognition and when it came he stood with his spine gone stiff.

To Church, his voice coming with a quick thrust, he said. "Catfish Clemens. Watch him. When he's drunk he's tricky as a tinhorn gambler's left hand."

Catfish stopped within a few feet of them. He was tall and stooped and had a nose like a buzzard's beak. Malaria had yellowed his skin like an old hide and left his body a gangling rack of stringy muscle and bone.

"Of all the boats to get through," he said, "it had to be your stinking little tub. But it's any old port in a storm—"

There was corn liquor in his rusty-hinge voice and blood-shot eyes, but Ben answered coolly, "If you think I came up here to pull your damned raft to safety, you're drunker than usual. Where's those sick folks?"

"That's what Pop's saying." Jolean stood at Catfish's elbow, slim and straight in a white jersey and brown skirt, a slender, high-breasted girl with auburn hair caught back by a ribbon and eyes that were blue with flakes of gray in them. To Ben, her beauty was always as startling and as moving as the sun breaking through leaden clouds at sunset, after a day of storm. "We've got the sick 'uns in houseboats, but we can move them onto the *Annabelle* in an hour's time."

Ezra Church made a sound like that of a man strangling. "Move the plague onto my boat? Turn the thing into a pest ship? I reckon *not!*"

With Catfish and Jolean was a lean, rawboned young man in dirty white coat and trousers. He could not have been over thirty. He was tall and excessively slender, and his eyes were keen in dark pockets.

"Pest ship?" he echoed, with the trace of a smile. "I'd call it a mercy ship. By tomorrow Bayou Grand will be under three feet of water. We're evacuating the able-bodied to high ground and the sick to boats. But those dying men and women won't have a ghost of a chance when the flood hits."

Church looked at him coldly. "And who are you?"

"The shanty folks call me Young Doc. I reckon that'll do. I've escorted a dozen of those same shanty people out of this world in the last three days, not to mention a score of townsmen. The rest must be taken out quickly. When the black vomit strikes, there's not much I can do without medicine."

"Medicine—" Church's strained features relaxed a little. "Medicine, of course! Will you come aboard, gentlemen? We came for that very purpose."

Rousters were back-and-bellying the hemp-netted bales of cotton onto the boat as they ascended to the texas. Ben had said nothing yet, but his mind was busy, and he thought he had finally accounted for Ezra Church's unprecedented gen-

erosity in chartering a boat out of his own pocket to do
rescue work.

The boatman lugged a box onto the deck and set it by a
water barrel. He was sweating; his silk shirt stuck to his chest
like a mustard plaster.

"You said medicine. There you are! I can't take your sick
folk on board, but our supplies will insure that they get the
best care possible."

Young Doc's knuckly fingers opened the box and removed
a bottle. He read the label and nodded. "I'm grateful, Captain. But it will take more than medicine to save these people,
I need clean beds, fresh food—pure water!"

Church's jaw set harder. He sopped his handkerchief in
the water barrel and placed it folded across the top of his
bald head. "I couldn't bring a whole hospital with me."

Ord McDan'l shifted on his stocky legs. "Reckon there'll be
plenty of room, Captain, even with your cotton aboard. I
don't see why—"

"Then I'll tell you why! No town on the river would let us
land, with the damn' tub crawling with yellow jack! We'd be
afloat for weeks, until the last man was back on his feet—or
dead. What's more, my cotton would go begging after we did
dock. Ten thousand dollars worth!"

"You can stop right there," said Ben Worden. "Your own
words damn you to hell. Cotton! I thought that halo was a
size too big for you, Church. An angel of mercy grindin' a
private axe under his robes. Don't you savvy, Young Doc? He
bought this cotton on futures and knew he'd lose every bale
of it if he couldn't take it out before the flood hit."

Church stood motionless, his eyes aflame with fury and
desperation. "The cotton was a secondary consideration," he
protested, almost shouting the words.

"You can prove that," Young Doc suggested, "by letting us
bring the patients aboard."

Ezra Church's jowls worked. "I am under no obligation to

defend my motives. I'm putting out in an hour. I have a feeling you'll make out quite nicely without any further help."

He dipped a tin cup full of water and was raising it to his lips when Young Doc rapped. "Captain Church!"

"Well?"

"Take my advice and don't drink that stuff. Call me crazy, if you like—plenty have. But I have a theory that yellow fever grows in contaminated water."

"Bah!" Church noisily drank off the brimming cup. Then he wiped his mouth and let it fall to dangle by the string. "I've drunk river water all my life and never caught a bug yet."

"I hope you can say as much a few hours from now—if you've been drinking that stuff all the way up."

His expression was somber.

There was a frowning interval of silence. Then Ben Worden said grimly, "I'm going down with you, Doc, and we'll load 'em on."

Ord McDan'l stared hard at Church, quite obviously undergoing an inward struggle to break from the manacles of convention. "I'm with you!" he said, finally.

Church pointed a swift finger at Ben. "Then it will be the last cargo either of you ever moves. I've got my rights. Until we hit New Orleans, I'm in command. If you men persist in mutiny, I'll see you both stripped of your licenses, and you, Worden, of your boat!"

Ben was conscious that Catfish Clemens was watching him, his amber eyes full of poison, his lips twisting in silent sarcasm. He knew Jolean was waiting to hear how an ex-shantyboater would answer Church's ultimatum.

It was McDan'l who first grunted response. "Bluff! With these witnesses you'd never touch us."

Ben's eyes were unsteady, touching in succession the faces of Jolean, Catfish, and Young Doc, and finally wandering to McDan'l.

"That's all right for you. You could apply for reinstatement if he did pull your teeth. But what about my boat? If I carry a plague cargo they'll tie her up at a bonded dock till she rots or wharf charges eat her up."

Catfish began to curse in a bitter monotone. "You yaller mud-sucker! You misbegotten offspring of a rouster pappy and a she-wolf mammy—"

"Pop!" Jolean made it a command, and while Catfish got his breath she confronted Ben. "You haven't got this far away from the river, have you, Ben? To let folks die rather than risk losing your boat? Wash Gray's down with the plague, and Jube Milton's family. Remember them?"

Ben said, "I remember Wash Gray hammering a bullet under my nose last month, a mile above his shanty. Would Wash or any other cussed shantyman risk so much as a mess o' channel cat to help me out of a fix?"

"You know they would. We've taken aplenty from you high'n mighty steamboaters, but we can forget a grudge when there's a need."

"When you're a-needin' help, leastways," said Ben.

Jolean's face was tired and her shoulders were slumped under the thin sweater. She passed Ben without a word, and the heart of him turned sharply, so that he had to clench his fists to keep from reaching for her.

Catfish followed, pausing at the rail for a last thrust. "I've held 'em down as best I could," he muttered. "But I'm cuttin' the hawsers now. What happens from tonight on ain't on my conscience."

Young Doc went with them, carrying the box of drugs under his arm. In his very silence Ben felt scorn that was like a lash.

Church went forward. Ord McDan'l would have gone off the guard for a smoke, but Ben drew him into the shadows.

"A shantyman's pride is a sorry thing," he said. "It kept me from saying before those two what I'm going to say to you."

McDan'l filled his pipe without looking up. "I've called many a pilot many a bitter name, but never coward."

"Don't break the record for me," Ben said, beginning to smile. "Go catch Young Doc and tell him what I say—"

The older man listened; then smiled and struck Ben between the shoulder blades. "You've a fool's pride but a riverman's heart!" he said.

❧

It was just after one o'clock when Ben Worden reached for the go-ahead bell and the *Annabelle* warped out into midstream. Ord McDan'l slumped in a chair in a dark corner of the wheelhouse, but Ezra Church was right there at Ben's elbow, seeing the job done right.

Sluggish under a wallowing weight of cotton, the steamboat swung a circle and headed out. Not until Bayou Grand was well behind did Church stir from his position. He rubbed his sweaty forehead with a moist palm.

"I'll grab a few winks," he said. "This cursed swamp air's given me a gadawful headache."

At dawn the *Annabelle* shouldered heavily against the tawny flood-heads of the Mississippi. Familiar landmarks along the shores were all erased, and where those guiding snags and cut-banks had been, the pilot's tired eyes found only the suck-and-boil of a brown blanket of water that lapped deep into the fields on each side.

Ben had hardly straightened up for the downstream haul when Ezra Church came charging into the wheelhouse like a mad water buffalo. "Worden!" he cried. "That damned shantyboat is towing behind us!"

Ben tied the wheel and looked aft. A hundred feet astern, Catfish Clemens's shantyboat was throwing off huge bow waves like a harrow coming through a wheat field. She was loaded to the gunwales. Beds occupied every inch of deck space. Jolean was on her knees beside one of the victims, administering Young Doc's medicine.

It was right then that Young Doc himself came up from

the saloon into the pilothouse, picking his teeth after a hasty breakfast. Ben gave him a quick glance.

"You know, I thought she handled mighty sluggish," he said. "I reckon Young Doc, here, must have tied on as we were leaving."

"You do, eh? It couldn't be that you thought you'd beat a mutiny charge by telling the commission they stowed away without your knowledge?"

Ben made his eyes round. "Captain Church! You don't trust me!"

The captain started for the door. "Have your little joke. But give an extra belly laugh when I cut that pest-raft loose."

Young Doc remarked quietly. "It would just about ruin a big man like you to have such a tale of cold-blooded murder bandied up and down the river."

Church halted, slowly turned around. He knew the doctor held aces. But he was not easily stumped. "Then I'll sure as heaven unload them at the first town we hit!" he muttered. "And if the townsmen cut them loose, it won't be my fault. Stand from the wheel, pilot. I'm taking over."

He thrust Ben out of the way. His face was flushed; his skin looked hot and dry, and he had ceased to perspire.

Seeing that, Young Doc stroked his chin. "Well, Church, you can't say I didn't warn you."

"About what?"

"About that river water. Why don't you admit you're sick? Your head's splitting with fever. Your throat aches. Your belly's tied in knots. Yellow jack!"

"Rubbish!" snorted Captain Ezra Church. "If you intend to stick with your outfit, mister, get back on the shanty. I'm cutting you off at Tobacco Point. McDan'l—send me up a bottle of brandy."

The little town of Tobacco Point had kept the plague out, thus far, and by the looks of the committee on the dock, she meant to remain healthy. Townsmen and shantyboaters stood close-packed, hats tugged down on their faces, jaws jutting. Rifle and shotgun barrels ran red, dipped in sunrise light, as the *Annabelle* warped in.

Standing between the chimneys with McDan'l, Ben Worden winced as he saw gun bores level off at them, and suddenly he and the other man both were sprawling on their bellies, as gunflame ran redly the width of the dock. Heavy duckload spattered the packet's windows. A rifle ball whanged off an iron chimney.

Up in the wheelhouse, Ezra Church shouted curses at the townsmen, and steered back into the river. Lead continued for some time to chew into plank and stanchion, and the yells of the Tobacco Pointers was their only farewell.

Ben got on his feet. "Maybe now he'll have sense enough to know he ain't going to land them that way."

"Don't you think it," said McDan'l. "He won't give up that easy and risk havin' his cotton burned at the dock."

Ben thought of that, knowing that a plague-fearful mob would not bother to take cotton off the boat before burning it. He had thrown his boat, his livelihood, his last penny, into the fight to save a boatload of people who wouldn't give a damn what happened to him so long as they got off safely.

At Brewster, four miles south, a group of armed townspeople met them on the jetty that ran out into the river from the little red-brick and clapboard town. Their shouts rang across the water.

"Keep a-rollin', pilot! You ain't unloadin' your pest-cargo here!"

Ezra Church thrust his head out the window. Through a leather megaphone he shouted, "We've a load of flood victims, neighbors! No yellow jack aboard, you understand? Just let us drop this shanty—"

Someone bawled, *"Keep a-rollin'!"* and a bullet shivered the window beside his head.

Later, Ben looked back from the hurricane deck and saw something that chilled him to the marrow of his bones. Young Doc and Catfish Clemens raised a plank to the rail of the raft and let a body, wrapped in a sheet, slide into the water. It went straight down, and a trail of bubbles rose and was lost in the wake. But the remembrance of those bubbles remained as an image of horror in Ben Worden's mind.

Behind the locked door of the pilothouse, Church steered a wild and perilous course. Two more towns drove the *Annabell* off. They could see Church up there behind the wheel, sick, drunk, possessed of the blind fixation that he must unload his pest cargo at any cost.

The *Annabelle* ran full upon a dozen sawyers. Church barely missed them by climbing the wheel, and each time the shantyboat rolled wildly, shipping waves that soaked the sick, lying on pallets on the deck.

Fear came into the packet, like a plague itself. Fearful roustabouts bunched on the foredeck, praying, wailing, terrified by the grim raft that followed like the shadow of death. The knowledge grew that Ezra Church was fever-racked, and half out of his mind. Young Doc told Ben that there was no doubt as to what ailed him. The full force of the yellow jack would hit him before nightfall.

The day wore on. A succession of river towns approached and were found hostile. There came a time when Church passed a town without making any effort to land. The significance of that put a cold weight in Ben's breast. But Ord McDan'l now seemed relieved.

"He's given up. Maybe he'll let us take over."

Ben went up with him, but he shook his head. "He ain't givin' up. He's too sick, too crazy to know when he's licked. I got a fear for what comes next, McDan'l."

Church grunted some response to their knock and they heard the door unlocked. The boatsman had tied the wheel. He stumbled to a chair. Dropping into it, he let his head fall against the back.

"Take the wheel, Worden," he muttered. "McDan'l, fetch me a pitcher of water."

Ben took the smooth spokes into his grasp. He heard the

other man leave and then, oddly, the grate of the lock. But the towering chimney of a Red Star boat took his attention right then as it moved past a near bend and into midriver, plowing north. Only a few hundred yards behind it came a second boat, pushing a string of towboats before it.

Until Church spoke, Ben did not realize he had come close. "Steer closer to her, pilot. Starboard to starboard."

"We'll risk the current sucking us together!"

A gun barrel touched Ben's spine and Church croaked, "Spoke off!"

McDan'l was at the door with the ice water, pounding. The captain breathed noisily through his mouth and the pressure of the gun remained above the small of Ben's back.

"What are you trying to do?" Ben demanded.

Through the panels came Ord McDan'l's command to open the door. For a split second the gun left Ben's back and the roar of an exploding shell pounded against his eardrums. Again there was the nudge of cold steel at his spine.

"Right close, now, pilot!" warned Ezra Church.

It was the *Henry W. Bean,* and they passed so close that their bull tails traded coats of paint. During the passage, Church lowered his gun and turned his back on the *Bean.* Ben saw the officers of the boat at the pilothouse windows. He could hear the captain cursing him, and a man shouting, "It's that shantyboater—Ben Worden! Full o' corn, I'll wager!"

In an instant the passage was completed. Ben reached for the tie-down, and with his hand still groping staggered against the wall and fell. Church's gun barrel had struck him glancingly on the back of the head.

He was brought harshly back to consciousness by the sound of yells rising from below. Strongest of them was McDan'l's hoarse shout at the door. "Ben, for God's sake, stop him! He's fixing to wipe the shanty off on the towboat!"

Ben sat up, feeling blood move dully through his head. He

saw a red chimney come into the square of a window. With the shock of that, he was on his feet and starting forward.

The *Annabelle* was cutting directly across the path of the big stern-wheeler with its string of tow-boats. The steamboat was so close that he could see the decks crowded with excited passengers, yelling and waving their arms. The forms of officers moved jerkily in the wheelhouse. The sound of the boat's whistle was a frantic, hoarse snore.

Ben staggered towards Church. Get away from that wheel!" he ordered, his voice choked with rage.

Church twisted to fire. The muzzle blast of the gun was deafening. But though it burned Ben's cheek the bullet passed harmlessly. Ben stepped in, reaching for the gun. He gripped the warm barrel and another shot ripped past him.

Ben tore the weapon free, and with a backhand blow smashed the butt of it against Ezra Church's forehead. With his foot, he shoved the ponderous body away and swung the wheel. He hung on the steam cord. He was acting purely by boatman's instinct, knowing that to try to swing upriver would send the shantyboat crashing broadside into a raft; to try to cross in front of the string would mean the shanty'd get cut in two.

Ben headed down-river, hoping the shantyboat would follow true. He came in beside the stern-wheeler so close that their loading booms crashed together. A fancy scrollwork railing was ripped from the bigger boat. He had a glimpse of the captain in the pilothouse shaking his fist at him.

Then Ben knew why Church had made him pilot the boat past the Red Star craft. There would be witnesses to swear that Ben Worden had been piloting the *Annabelle* three minutes before the shantyboat was wiped off on a towboat—

At the last instant, he looked back. The shanty was wallowing into the river giant's path. He climbed on the wheel.

Ord McDan'l was yelling. "Hard a-starboard! Hard a-starboard!"

The *Annabelle* heeled far over, as if she would capsize.

Bales of cotton toppled like sugar lumps into the brown river. And now the first of the towboats slid in beside the shanty.

Bow waves piled upon the shallow deck. Young Doc planted a boat hook against the sheer strake of the steamboat. The force of that contact hurled him against the wall of the cabin, and he slipped down and lay stunned, while Catfish ran past him to retrieve the boat hook.

Then one of the heavy waves got under the raft and shoved her away gently, so that the protruding fantail of the steamboat grazed by her within a foot, and a landing stage crashed against the crooked sheet-metal chimney and toppled it into the water.

With clear water ahead, the *Annabelle* pulled her burden to safety and steamed on. Ben Worden tied the wheel and unlocked the door. His face was the color of a bloated channel cat.

"She's yours," he said to Ord McDan'l. "Like the feller says, I feel the need of a stimulant."

Sometime after midnight the *Annabelle* nosed into a berth at the foot of Canal Street in New Orleans. Ezra Church was not aboard. During the night yellow jack took him, and Ben and Catfish quietly gave him a river man's burial.

The sharp-eyed ferret of a man from the health department, who arrived in the morning, showed considerable curiosity regarding Church's death. He poked about the texas and finally came back to the wheelhouse where Ben, McDan'l, Catfish, and Jolean waited on tenterhooks.

"Whichun's the room Mr. Church died in?" he demanded, and Ben thought, *Here it comes! They'll burn her before sundown.*

But Catfish answered, corking his jug of corn and setting it at his feet. "Matter of fact, Church died on my boat."

"On the shantyboat! Why in heaven's name did he set foot on that thing?"

"Well, you know Mr. Church. It was everybody else first,

and him last. He was up all night, carin' for the sick. And when he knew he'd caught yeller jack himself and had to go, he said, 'Don't waste no medicine on me, Catfish. Save it for them other poor souls that has a chance.' "

Catfish choked a sob by taking another pull at the jug. The health officer gazed reflectively through a rear window at the empty shantyboat, from which all the sick had been removed.

"A pity," he murmured. "Mr. Church was a fine man. But it doesn't alter any the report I have to make."

He made a notation in a little leather book. "Mr. Worden," he said to Ben, "as your boat now floats, she's a menace to the health of the entire community. That menace must be removed. I shall send down a box of sulfur candles this afternoon, which you are to use to fumigate your boat from bull rails to whistle. After that, you may obtain your free-bill."

Ben sat woodenly, not trusting his ears. The ferret-eyed man froze Catfish's grin by remarking from the door, "I'll send a tug down today to tow that raft out to sea and burn it. Good day."

Worden watched Catfish's lean features twist and saw his eyes squint shut. "I'll make up for your loss, Catfish," Ben said quickly. "That was a right fine thing you did for me."

"For you!" sniffed Jolean. "If they'd burned the *Annabelle*, we wouldn't have had any way to get a tow back up the river. And now we haven't even got a shanty to go back in."

"You can have better than that, if you'll take it," Ben said. "I need a good freight clerk. I'll give you good pay, good grub, and rooms with real mosquito-bar screens. We couldn't finish this feud any better than by joining forces."

Catfish swore. "If you live long enough, you may see a steamboat sailing on dry land, but you'll never see Catfish Clemens working on a steamboat."

"You figure you've got to keep on feuding for the sake of your honor?"

Catfish scratched his head. "Didn't say so. After your

bringing folks like Wash Gray and Jube Milton down the river, there ain't much we can do but admit a steamboater has his points. I'll make you a proposition. You keep an eye out for trotline jugs and dinghies and I'll see that the boys save their bullets for 'possum."

They shook hands on it. With Ord McDan'l, Catfish went out on the hurricane deck to smoke a sad pipe over the fate of his floating home. Jolean's back was straight and uncompromising as she stood at the window. Ben came quietly behind her. He slipped his arm about her shoulders and felt the tension go out of her body.

"Let's end this feud all the way," he said. "With a shanty girl on my packet, wouldn't be a man on Whiskey Creek could say a word against the *Annabelle*. If she was good enough for the daughter of Catfish Clemens, she'd be good enough for anybody."

Jolean turned, and put her hands on his shoulders, her eyes sober. "She's good enough for me, Ben. Do you reckon a shanty girl and a steamboat pilot would ever make a go of it?"

Ben kissed her. "I've still got corn bread and catfish in my blood, and I reckon I'll never get so civilized but what folks will know I was brought up with the river for a backyard. And you'll find yourself lovin' the sound of the paddles and the songs the rousters sing down in the boilers on a cold night. We'll make out, honey. A few years from now Catfish will be showin' our kids how to set a weir and bait a fish-trap."

"And telling them how their daddy took a packet up a bayou during a flood and saved a whole parcel of shantyboaters. He's a stubborn old critter, Ben. But a loveable one when you get to know him."

"It's a failing of the whole family," Ben said.

THE LAST PELT

―――――

Bryce Walton

BOUNTY hunters were widely despised on the Western frontier. They were considered vultures, little better than the men they tracked down—gun artists who would just as soon bring a fugitive in dead as alive. Many in the pulp-writing fraternity chose to ignore these historical facts, however, and portrayed the bounty hunter as an heroic loner whose sense of justice far outweighed his greed. So did the producers of the popular sixties TV show, Wanted: Dead or Alive, *starring Steve McQueen.*

Bryce Walton's picture of Barston, the protagonist of "The Last Pelt," is much closer to the truth. Grim and unrelenting, with an equally grim and unrelenting desert setting, the story derives both its realism and its tragedy from the fact that there was very little fundamental difference between the bounty hunter and his quarry—in life and in death.

Before he turned his hand to writing, Bryce Walton (1918– 1988) traveled extensively and held down such diverse jobs as placer miner, migrant fruit picker, sheepherder, sign painter, combat correspondent for the Navy during World War II, and staff correspondent for Leatherneck Magazine *after being transferred to the Marines. He sold his first pulp stories in 1945, and was soon a frequent contributor to the better magazines in the Western, mystery/detective, and science fiction categories. He remained a full-time writer until the last year of his life, selling stories to the digest-sized genre fiction magazines, men's magazines, literary magazines, and such "slicks" as* The Saturday Evening Post; *nonfiction pieces to various publications; one adult mystery novel and six young-adult adventure and science-fiction novels; radio scripts to* CBS Radio Theater *and other programs; and TV scripts to such shows as* Alfred Hitchcock Presents *and* Captain Video.

Barston was no longer tired as he raised the big Buntline special. He was no longer so tired of the long hunt that he almost wanted to be dead. He softened the sound of the hammer with the flesh of his hand, and the outlaw's gut was hooked on the fang of Barston's sight.

He savored the moment. It had been so long coming it would be a shame to end it fast. His levis and hickory shirt were stiff with sweat-caked alkali. His face was wind-burned to an Indian black. Lying there Barston was as inconspicuous as a lizard, blending into the desert like some gaunt-bellied Gila waiting for its fly.

For a year he had run, rode, swum muddy rivers, climbed dizzying heights, left dead horses under the buzzard's circle, crawled and preyed and clung to the wily spoor of the hunted.

The blood beat in him and the breath was quick in his throat. At this range he couldn't miss and Red Fowler seemed too tired to care. Barston had the line of the sights, all he had to do was pull the trigger.

Fowler sat down there in the feeble shade of a granite rock, shrunken by the sink's glittering immensity around him, spent and too tired for alertness, looking like an old, dusty, shabby bear, his shaggy red head down between his knees and resting on his hands. His pinto stood over him wobbly on wide-spread legs.

Barston sucked the last bit of gratification from the moment, then shot the outlaw through the stomach.

Fowler didn't die any easier than he'd lived, and that was the idea. Barston could have put the bullet into the brain and ended it abruptly. But he didn't. He wasn't that type of man.

Barston stayed down and watched Fowler cough as he stretched himself upward through pain, slapping instinctively at his holster. Then he fell to his knees and yelled up at the naked hot skin of the sky and pressed at the hole in his belly.

Then, knowing it was safe, Barston slid down the hot shale on his bootheels to watch Fowler die. He hated Fowler more than he had ever hated any man. He hated Fowler because he'd depended on him so long, and because Fowler had stretched out that dependency almost too long to bear.

"Going back home was your mistake," Barston said. "Hear me, Red?"

Barston grinned and rasped his nails through his graying beard stubble. His sun-whitened hair clung as he raked off his hat to reveal a fishbelly band of white.

Fowler stiffened out slowly on his back and dug his boots into the blistering hot shale. His hands fell away from the hole in his belly, and he put them over his eyes. His breath shuddered.

"Hear me, Red?" Barston touched the red hair with his blunt fingers. "Five thousand dollars. Nobody would start ridin' back across hell without a good reason and I figured you was headin' back home, back to White Rock."

"Home," Fowler said. And died. . . .

With Fowler tied across the pinto—which seemed to appreciate Fowler's mastery even in death—Barston led five thousand dollars' worth of human bounty across the sink's glittering face.

As a bounty hunter, Barston had collected his last human hide. He thought about that as he made camp and ate jerked beef and then slept. He dreamed about a big spread on the Powder River where the grass was hock-high and rich. Once he woke and thought that, too, a dream as Red Fowler seemed to move uneasily in the moonlight. Then Barston managed to laugh at his own fears.

After so long, after starving and shriveling in desert heat

and shrinking in winter cold, why now should he somehow feel a fearsome thing like loneliness because Fowler was dead?

And he was dead. Even Red Fowler couldn't be any deader. He was nothing but a pelt worth five thousand dollars. He was a lot more valuable than anything a trapper ever found in his waiting steel.

But Barston had a hard time getting back into the numbness of sleep. He licked his sun-broken lips and cursed his own fears. Maybe he shouldn't have seen to it that Fowler died so hard. Maybe that was it. Someone had said that a man who dies too hard doesn't sleep easily in his grave.

Fowler had no grave.

Barston was up before dawn to take Fowler where he could be buried. First there had to be witnesses. Before he could collect the five thousand, someone had to know and be able to testify to the fact.

❧

White Rock was a mining town that wouldn't admit it was dead. It had four buildings left standing comparatively intact. On the right of the dusty road curving up the valley and into town from the east was a graveyard surrounded by a sagging peeled-pole railing. Two concrete foundations shone whitely like skeletons never given form by flesh. There were two saloons, one still serving its original functions. The other was a church on Sunday. It was vacant the rest of the week.

White Rock's inhabitants were old-timers, old men impaled on the hope-softened barbs of the new strike, the great bonanza that would never come again. They did some prospecting in the mountains and thought about how it had been when the town throbbed with the hope only gold can bring.

Barston rode in past the graveyard three hours after sun-up, leading Fowler's horse with Fowler doubled over it, his stiffened fingers dragging as if in longing for the ground denied him.

Already the heat was intense, a hazy, blinding whiteness reflecting from the mountains as from furnace slabs. Dust filtered into his eyes. Barston's throat was swollen. He needed whiskey. Heat waves rose and dust devils danced in the silent street.

He clumped up steps and through creaking batwings. He made his way through a welcome if musty coolness to the end of the bar nearest the broken windows. Through the fly-specked fragments of pane he saw Fowler, his head hanging obscured in a cloud of hungry blow flies.

The old-timers were spotted around the big room, some at a table over cards, three others by the windows looking out. Old bearded men in faded levis and patched corduroy. Nobody spoke. Nobody looked at Barston.

There was a piano, the keys cobwebbed to silence. When Barston hit the top of the bar, dust filtered out of the cracks.

"How about a slab of beef, some beans and a bottle of Sam Thompson?" Barston yelled at the barwiper who came toward him past rows of bottles, their labels covered with dust.

The barwiper was beanpole thin, chinless and bald. He looked as though he were about to cry. A dirty expanse of muslin nuzzled his thighs. He didn't seem to hear Barston.

"What the hell is this?" Barston said. "I ain't ate nothin' for three days but jerked beef. My throat's dryer than a dead buzzard's bones."

The bottle of Sam Thompson made a solidly comforting sound and the heavy-bottomed shot glass had a real thud against the worn mahogany. Barston washed three shots down his throat and waited, but still nobody spoke.

The barwiper went into the back, then reappeared, and Barston smelled sizzling steer meat. When the platter came out loaded with steak and Mexican beans Barston forgot for a while the feeling of hostility.

Then he glanced up slowly. The old-timers at the card tables were looking at him. The three at the window were doing the same thing. The barkeep halfway down the bar was watching him, but out of the side of watering eyes.

The unease in Barston was no longer vague. He turned slowly and hooked one elbow on the bar.

"I'm sure glad to have pulled into White Rock," he said. Nobody said anything. Barston brushed the heel of his hand across his upper lip. "I sure am," he said. The words seemed loud in the oppressing stillness.

The men at the window moved slightly to either side. One man was big with a black beard and a red shirt. One was short, with his belly hanging over his levis. The third was very old, his skin like that of a lizard.

The black-bearded one said. "You be a marshal? Or maybe that poor gut-shot fellow there be a friend of yours?"

Barston said. "No marshal. A bounty hunter. And I just brung in the fox." He grinned stiffly. Inside, his heart seemed to swell.

Maybe it was some kind of grim humor. But this was Red Fowler's home town. He'd pulled his first job here, shot down two and rode fast from his kin. They sure knew him! *They surely did!*

Barston hesitated, wondering. "That's five thousand dollars' worth of henyard outlaw, gents," he finally said. "And I brung him home to roost."

Without saying anything, the other old-timers rose from the card tables, walked over and looked out the window. Barston tossed off another shot and walked up behind them. He might have been pouring the rot gut on the sawdust. Nothing seemed to displace the painful emptiness in his stomach.

"Reckon you fellas ain't forgot what Red Fowler looks like," he said.

The black-bearded prospector looked back at Barston. There was a definite expression on his face, but Barston couldn't quite figure what it was.

"I don't guess Red Fowler'd ever come riding back to his

old home town that way," the prospector drawled. "Would he now, Long Tom?"

The short pint shook his head in agreement. "No siree. Red Fowler'd come into town yellin' like a Comanche and shootin' the sky full a' light with his .44s."

"That's right," the barkeep whined and wiped at his watering eyes wth the bar rag. "Red Fowler'd come into town of an evening yellin' and shootin'. And he'd have a poke of money and he'd be droppin' it where it was needed."

"You gents tellin' me that ain't Fowler?" demanded Barston.

"Not the one we knew," the barkeep said. "A dead man gatherin' flies in the street that way—guess that just couldn't be the Fowler we used to drink with."

Barston felt the quiet then, heavy and oppressive. He felt the dust of the years grinding in his eyes, caking his scalp. He felt the sweat pour down his ribs. He felt the awful weariness of the long hunt flooding down his length, settling in his knees, in the exhausted hamstrings of his thighs. But somehow he fought down the panic that pawed at him.

If he couldn't get the body out there identified, an affidavit signed that it *was* Red Fowler—then it might as well be anybody, or nobody, or Barston himself.

These men knew. All of them knew, all right. But if they didn't admit it, then all the hellish miles and the starving and fighting the dust and sun and winter cold and the muddy swirls of rivers, all would be for nothing—or worse than nothing. The triumph would be only failure, the bounty money would have no meaning. He'd never have the rich spread on the Powder.

But what was that other thing—this thing that had started to haunt him and that was even more haunting and fearsome because only its shadow was there? A kind of feeling that aside from the five thousand, the rich spread on the Powder, Red Fowler was important to him.

He had to get paid for bringing in Fowler. Somehow, the world had to know.

"Listen! Now you all listen," he yelled. "That's Red Fowler. I oughta know! I been trailin' him for years! I been everywhere trailin' him. Nobody else coulda done it! Nobody else would have cared even five thousand dollars' worth to have done it! That's Red Fowler, and you gents know it!"

"He'd never come ridin' back to us that way," the black-bearded man said.

"If he'd come back in sittin' his saddle straight," said Long Tom, "then nobody'd have no doubts who it was."

"That's him!" Barston yelled. "By Gawd that's Red Fowler!" He turned, poured more Sam Thompson down his throat. He didn't feel anything. A whole bottle of the rotgut wouldn't make any damn difference.

"You got a sheriff here?"

"He's right next door," Long Tom said. "In what used to be the barber shop. Only Mike there's got any hair left to trim. The regular barber just got tired of no business and up and died."

"Hell. I don't want no haircut!" Barston yelled. "I want to see the sheriff."

"Right next door," said Mike the black-bearded prospector.

Barston went outside. The near noon sun hit him full in the face, a naked and merciless blow. He went along the cracking boardwalk, then stopped and stared at Red Fowler hanging there waiting to have the right label put on him. He's laughing at me, Barston thought. Now he's dead and he don't care whether he was once called Red Fowler or not. No pride any more.

Barston saw his own hand reaching out and he jerked it back from Fowler's head. The flies were swarming thicker. This kind of heat urged quick burial.

Barston stumbled back down the walk, half fell through the door of what had once been a barber shop. Shaving mugs of dead and departed men were buried in dust, strung together as beads on skeins of cobweb. The barber chair was falling apart.

It was quiet in there. The kind of stillness that man-made things seldom claim, the stillness found a long way from anywhere.

"Sheriff!" Barston said. "Hey, Sheriff!" He waited. He kept on waiting for a long time.

He thought about White Rock when it had kicked and laughed and roared and screamed with life, oblivious of its impermanence, its saloons dragging in gold and spilling light and music and death out into the dusty streets. He saw Red Fowler alive and laughing and saying, "Another round, Beanpole, another round on me!"

They're all his friends, that's it. All of them. Everywhere else he was a killer worth good hard cash, hunted from sun-up to sundown across the land. But here, Fowler was a friend and he'd been heading back home where he'd know he'd be safe.

"Sheriff!" A door squeaked and Barston spun, sweaty fingers moving nervously for the walnut butt of his Buntline.

The beanpole barkeep stood wiping his face with a greasy towel.

"Where in hell's the sheriff?" Barston yelled.

Barston started for him, dragging at the Buntline. Mike and Long Tom moved in behind the barkeep and Barston saw the glint of heavy .44s.

"No need for a legal lawdog round here no more," Mike said. "Not since all the fun's gone away."

Barston leaned against the barber chair. "Listen," he said. "I got Red Fowler. Five thousand dollars worth of killer. You gents admit you're friends of a mad dog killer like that?"

They didn't say anything.

"It took me over a year to bring him in," Barston said. His voice got higher. "You know it's Red Fowler! Now all you got to do is sign an affidavit, put your names to a statement!

Swear it's Fowler I got. If you don't, what good will it have done me to track a man the way nobody else could?"

"But we reckon you made a mistake," the barkeep said softly. It sounded almost kindly, with a suggestion even of pity. "Like we already said, Red Fowler wouldn't come ridin' back to his town that way."

There was something blurred about them as they drifted away from him, looking sorry for the way things were.

The Buntline's roar was a product of Barston's pain, hate and fear. The bartender slammed back into the wall. He clawed at it, rolled around the door jamb and stumbled into the bright sunlight.

Barston went to the window and the shelter of the wall. A .44 slug tore into the dried wood and little lines of blood trickled from Barston's peppered face. He fired through the window. But all at once the street was empty; Long Tom had disappeared around the saloon corner supporting the wounded barkeep, and the black-bearded prospector had dodged around another corner.

He'd get them. Somebody was going to sign an affidavit. He stumbled out into the glare of sunlight. The dry hot wind hit him, burned into his eyes and into his lungs.

The emptiness was the more terribly quiet for the thunder that had gone before as Barston ran up and down the boardwalks, ran in and out of buildings and listened to the hollow echoes of his desperate shouting.

Even the saloon was empty. But they'd have to come back to the saloon—it was cool here. There was the friendly glitter of glass, and the cards on the tables, and the smell of sawdust.

He dragged out two bottles of Old Sam Thompson, dragged a table to the wall between the end of the bar and the batwings and sat down. Here he could watch both entrances. They'd have to come back to the saloon. They'd have to sign the affidavit, too. He'd see to that, he thought, as he poured the rotgut down his dried throat.

He finished one bottle and started on the second. The

emptiness left his belly and he felt the blood beating in his temples. He stood up and waved the second bottle and started to laugh.

They'd come back. They'd sign. He'd gut-shoot 'em one by one until somebody signed. Red Fowler had to be named.

He stumbled to the end of the bar and turned, dragging deep at Old Sam Thompson. He roared at the haze of bravery that moved over him . . . and the old piano began playing. Bright women in red skirts swirled ghostlike across the sawdust. White thighs flashed and there was the smell of rich perfumes and sounds of poker chips and the clinking of golden eagles.

He saw the strong-limbed pinto of his dreams, the silver-studded saddle, the big green spread on the banks of the rushing Powder. He saw the big ranch buildings, the corrals full and kicking, and he saw himself riding the line through grass, hock-high and rich.

He raised the Buntline and blazed away at the fly-specked panes, at the bottles behind the bar. He stumbled down the length of the bar and stood with knees bent facing the batwings.

Dimly out there, he saw Red Fowler hanging over the horse.

Swaying and slipping drunkenly, Barston slammed into the batwings and fell on his hands and knees in the street's dust. He dragged himself up, threw back his head, and roared with laughter until his voice filled the dying town.

"I don't need you old fools!" he yelled. "Hear me! I don't need nary one of you!" Beyond the town he heard the sweet water of the Powder roaring down from the mountains. He heard the bunch grass rustling and the longhorns bawling. He saw the rich spread looming and calling outside the town.

"We can make it, Red and me," he shouted and his laughter roared out again. "We'll make it to another town!" Any other town they'd be glad Fowler was dead. Any other town they'd celebrate Barston, honor him, the man who'd got Red Fowler.

Swaying in the saddle, an almost empty whiskey bottle in one hand, Barston rode fast back out of the town in the direction from which he'd come. He scarcely saw the broken panes of abandoned false fronts, the bleached concrete foundations of buildings never finished, the sagging doorways and the Boothill plot around which the peeled-pole railing was rotting.

He looked back once, just long enough to see the blurred figures of the citizens of White Rock standing there watching him go. He looked back just long enough to laugh. Then he turned and kept on riding toward where the sweet water waited, and the rich grasslands—toward the dreams a man must have to keep on going.

He moved out, suddenly small, a speck that got smaller as it disappeared into the sink's glittering, lifeless immensity. Over the stove-hot sand he rode, feeling the numbed horse under him weakening with every dragging movement of his tortured limbs. Behind him, Red Fowler's body danced in senseless rhythm, its hands reaching toward the earth.

After a while there were only Barston, the sun, and a Red Fowler who couldn't be left behind. For somehow, undefinably, Barston knew that if he left Fowler he would lose himself. That became a great fear, so great that finally it was his only fear. It was no fear of the sink after that. How far he had come across it was incomprehensible, and the distance he had yet to go was more incomprehensible still. There was only the sun that shone blindingly from the sink's cracked surface, and the fading whisper of dying hoofs scraping and slipping over the immeasurable miles.

At first there was agony in his back and shoulders, but then after a while he wasn't conscious of those things either. He was only aware of the fear of losing Red Fowler.

* * *

He remembered dimly the moment when whatever spirit was left of the flesh that had carried him burned out. The horse went down and Barston fell kicking on sand hot as flame.

He got up and moved his feet over the sand, the reins of the other horse around his waist as he leaned into the weight, Red Fowler swaying behind him. The baked earth and rock, which had reflected the enormous heat into his face, now flamed up through the muscles of his legs.

He looked down at his feet, at each of them in turn, alternately, and watched each of them rise and fall.

Once he turned and saw the horse that carried Fowler, and felt the brackish, gusty breath of death from its foam-encrusted mouth. He caught some faint sense of warmth and sympathy in the animal's strange begging eyes.

He crooned and coaxed and begged for a long time before he realized the horse was dead.

After a while, Barston whispered, "We're gonna make it, Red."

He moved his knees through the sand, not feeling the flame anymore, feeling nothing but searing hunger that seemed to feed only on that insatiable fear of losing Red Fowler. "We got to make it, Red, you and me." He felt the puffy flesh, his nostrils deadened. Below, the sands blazed; above, the sun was a mass of flame.

He got his arms under the corpse and after a while managed to stand up with it, Fowler's weight plowing his ankles under the sand. His knees shivered as he stood there holding Fowler in his arms, trying to see where to go. He stood there for a long time—or seemed to.

There was only a reddened hazy glare around him then, and he knew vaguely that the sun had burned his eyes too deep for seeing. "Red!" he shouted, as his seared eyes looked directly into the sun. "Red! You got to show us the way! You got to show us the way, cause I can't see it no more."

The old-timers found Barston and Fowler at the end of the street, the end of a circle Barston had made out around the edge of the sink. The barkeep, his arm in a sling, dropped down on his knees and looked at Fowler.

"Guess Red Fowler's come back to us," he said finally. "Guess he's come back at last."

Everybody nodded.

"We ought to bury him now," Long Tom said.

They finished the job at sundown. They put Barston under the ground beside Red Fowler; there was never any doubt that he belonged there.

COMANCHE PASSPORT

Will Henry

*THERE are two situations so often repeated in Western litera-
ture and films that they have achieved classic status. One is the
"walkdown," in which two armed men draw against each other
to determine which is the fastest gun; the second is a pitched
battle between the U.S. Cavalry and a warring band of Indians.*

*Cavalry-versus-Indian stories reached the height of their
popularity in the forties, thanks in large part to the pen of
James Warner Bellah and the filmaking prowess of John Ford.
Ford's cavalry trilogy starring John Wayne—*Fort Apache
(1948), She Wore a Yellow Ribbon *(1949), and* Rio
Grande *(1950)—are each based on a Bellah short story. A
fourth film,* Sergeant Rutledge *(1960), also based on a
Bellah story, has a similar theme.*

*The Western pulps carried their fair share of cavalry stories,
many of which were told from the Indian point of view. An
entire magazine, in fact, briefly published by Fiction House in
1950, carried the title* Indian Stories *and was in large part
devoted to frontier skirmishes between red men and white.
"Comanche Passport" is one of the best of the cavalry stories as
seen through the eyes of the horse soldiers. This tale of how
scout Bass Cooper, a quarter of a troop of green cavalry, and
ten rawhide-tough Santa Fe Trail skinners go about outguessing
a hundred hostile Comanches is not pleasant, but it is realis-
tic—much more so than Ford's cinematic treatments. One has
the feeling that, like it or not, this is the way it really was.*

*The Western fiction of Henry W. Allen, whether it appears
under the pseudonym of Will Henry or that of Clay Fisher, has*

been widely praised for its provocative exploration of both the myth and reality of the Old West. He has won more Spur Awards from the Western Writers of America than any other writer, two for Best Historical Novel—From Where the Sun Now Stands *(1960) and* The Gates of the Mountains *(1963)—and a pair for Best Short Story: "Isley's Stranger" (1962) and "The Tallest Indian in Toltepec" (1965). Much of his fiction is quite sympathetic to Native Americans; "Comanche Passport" may in fact be considered an atypical, if no less powerful, Will Henry story.*

The officer's eyes, watery and red-hawed from ten hours of High Plains sun, squinted through the smoke of the night fire at the silent man across from him, his words coming slow and careful the way a wise man's will when he's talking to a hard case like Bass Cooper.

"You and I aren't exactly new to one another, Cooper, and I feel I can speak frankly to you."

His companion's answer was a flat stare, unvarnished by any other acknowledgment, and the cavalryman, flushing to its direct challenge, finished lamely.

"I may as well tell you, right out, that the men didn't buy your story about that captive Comanche you brought in from Pawnee Fork this afternoon."

The silent one, a medium-tall man, looking taller from the slack way his greasy buckskins gaunt-draped his frame, returned the officer's gaze, level-eyed.

"And me, Captain Hughes, I don't give a hoot what your troopers are buying. As long as I'm scouting for this supply train, they'll buy what I bring in to sell."

Captain Henry Hilton Hughes, Troop B, Fourth United States Cavalry, wasn't just the man you put the spurs into like that, without you got some back-hunching out of it. His words stiffened with the jut-out of his broad jaw.

"Let me remind you, Cooper, that your record in this

man's army smells like a sick dog. And as far as the men in
this immediate command are concerned, perhaps you'd better remember that that *other* supply train was a Fourth
Cavalry outfit. Maybe that'll let you see how this whole thing
looks to these men."

Bass Cooper could see the way it looked without any
trouble whatever. All the while the captain had been getting
his worries into hard words, the lean scout's mind had been
running the two-year-old back trail to the Comanche ambush
that had kept him off the service payroll until this present
outfit's regular scout had come out second in a knife seminar
in Kansas City and young Captain Henry Hughes had reluctantly accepted Bass's plea for the chance to get back to army
scouting.

That ambush, two years ago, had been no more Bass's
fault than it had God's, but the fact he had lived with the
Comanches, spoke their tongue better than he did his own,
and knew half their head chiefs by their *tipi* names, had
made up the army's mind against him. The clincher had
been the particular chief who had done the job—old
Oudlt'ou-eidl, the notorious Big Head.

Bass had known Big Head as well as he knew himself, had
received him as a friend in that army camp the night before
the Pawnee Fork Massacre. The post commanders at both
ends of the Santa Fe had looked at one another and nodded.
And suddenly had no more service for the best civilian scout
in the business.

For two long years, now, Bass Cooper had haunted the
Trail, lonehand, hoping to get at Big Head some way. But
Oudlt'ou-eidl's outsize cranium was stuffed with good red
brains. He had pulled his lodges after the ambush, headed
south for Old Mexico and an easy career at horse-raiding the
big Spanish ranches in Sonora, and been seen no more along
the South Trace.

Bass, looking at Captain Hughes across the fire now, knew
he couldn't blame the youthful officer. Nor was there any-

thing he could say to him. The look-alike of the two cases was too cozy. That other train had been a post-supply outfit, too, even toting along the same kind of Comanche bait as this one, a creamy horse herd of high-class cavalry-replacement mounts. His answer, when it finally came, echoed the resigned bitterness of the condemned guiltless.

"There ain't nothing I kin say, Captain. Either you trust me and follow my scouting, or you don't. I ain't going over my side of that Pawnee Fork Massacre again, for any man. You know my claims about it."

"I know them," replied the other man awkwardly, "and as far as I, personally, am concerned, Cooper, I believe them. Had I not, I would never have signed you on for this hitch. But, good Lord, man, two of the tallest men in Texas couldn't see to spit over that story you brought in tonight. Let alone that shoulder-shot Comanche buck you brought along with it."

"Nevertheless, you'd best believe it, Captain. You and your men, both. I *did* catch this buck trailing me up by Pawnee Fork and I *did* wing him just like I told you. And"—the swart scout paused, meaningfully—"you *have* got a clean hundred war-trailing Comanche braves squatting acrost your path somewheres past Pawnee Fork. And you *are* toting along a horse herd that would suck in any Comanche wolf pack ever whelped."

"I'm sorry, Cooper. What you've told me so far doesn't add up. Comanches along the trail are hardly news to a regular cavalry outfit."

"Well, maybe here's something that is," nodded the scout. "I *know* that buck I brought in this afternoon."

"You what?"

"I know him," repeated the scout, easily. "Name's *Peidei-t'ou-dei*. You can shorten that to Stiff Leg. He's subchief and general handyman to an old Comanche friend of mine. A big one. And mortal bad. Name of *Oudlt'ou-eidl*."

"And how does that come out in English?" Captain

Hughes's short question came edged with the irritation that was growing under the scout's laconic disclosures.

Bass Cooper looked off across the fire, staring south into the prairie-black gut of the spring night. His answer was that soft the officer barely caught it. But what he caught of it jumped the short hairs along the back of his neck straight on end.

"Big Head," said Bass Cooper, and that was all he said.

The following morning, Captain Hughes called his troopers and supply-wagon skinners up in the gray cold of predawn and gave them Bass's amended story without benefit of his own opinions, the men saying nothing, but taking it with many a hard-eyed glance at the somber scout. After that, they set out, the officer riding the head of the wagon line with Bass, the ten members of Troop B clanking along in the dust of the heavily loaded supply vehicles. Ahead lay the fifteen-mile, rising pull to Pawnee Fork, soldiers and skinners, cavalry mounts, and wagon mules settling to it with a grimness that could be felt.

Hour after hour the wagons rolled, jaw-set skinners keeping the ten-mule hitches as far up in their collars as the bite of a blacksnake bullwhip could drive them. Nerves were popping loud enough to outdo the whips, yet the livelong day they saw nothing—not a pony track nor a pile of horse dung fresher than that of the last freight outfit in front of theirs.

Riding the head of the sullen line, Bass Cooper could read the hard questions swept repeatedly at him by Captain Hughes's accusing glance—*Where are your Comanches, Cooper? Where is even any sign of your Comanches, Mister?*—knew, even as he rode, that his last chance of convincing the army man lay in the cold ashes of that big ring of hostile cookfires he had spotted the day before at Pawnee Fork. If the Comanches had played it cute, had scattered and blanked-out those ashes, he was as done as a pit-roasted rack of hump ribs.

Big Head's band had played it just about as opposite of cute as a pack of High Plains hostiles ever did. Captain Hughes, his dust-caked troop of cavalry, and his hardbitten crew of Missouri and Texas muleskinners, took one long, quiet look at that stark ring of ash spots and backed off to do a batch of reconsidering about civilian scouts in general, and dark-faced Bass Cooper in particular.

By the time coffee had been boiled and night had shut, tight-down, around the little prairie camp, there wasn't a man in the outfit but who was hunkered close to the fire, waiting, nerve-set and awkward, for Bass Cooper to expound his professional views on how a quarter of a troop of green cavalry and ten rawhide-tough Santa Fe Trail skinners went about outguessing upward of a hundred hostile Comanches, under the roughest cob in the whole cornfield of South Texas trail raiders.

"All right," Captain Hughes's brittle admission went to the tactiturn scout, "you can count on all of us, now, Cooper. What do you propose doing?"

Bass Cooper wasted no time telling them.

"First off, we can reckon Big Head will go on through with whatever plan's he's made for attacking us. Providing he has any plans. Me, personal, I think he has."

"Yeah," this from Cloyce Travis, a wolf-jawed Texan who was Hughes's boss skinner, "but the hell of it is we ain't got no way of knowing what them plans might be. And no way of finding out."

"That's where you're wrong." The scout's mouth twisted to a fleeting grin. "We got a plumb quick way of finding out, firsthand."

"What you-all getting at, Cooper?"

"When you want Injun plans, get them from an Injun, that's all."

"Meaning that wing-shot buck we got tied up in the lead wagon?"

"You ain't just whistling, I mean him. That's why I brung

him back yesterday instead of blowing his bowels apart. He'll know about any plans them red sons may have hatched."

"Hell," Travis shrugged, "that buck ain't going to tell us nothing. You-all know that. He ain't said a word since we trussed him up and threw him in the wagon."

"He'll talk," said Bass. "You boys just go fetch him. Meanwhile, I'll get me my talking stick."

"What's that?" demanded Captain Hughes uneasily.

"Little Comanche invention for freezing up froze tongues."

"Hold on," countered the young cavalryman. "I don't believe we can allow any Indian torturing, Cooper. We're all Christian people, here. I grant you the red man may know something, but—"

"But nothing—" Cloyce Travis's soft Texas drawl undercut the officer's objection. "I ain't got nothing against Christians but that heathen red scut wouldn't know Jesus from Jed Smith. Let's leave the Lord out'n it. Bass Cooper's running this outfit until we hit Arkansas Crossing and get shut of these here Comanches. Mebbeso you-all want your hair with you in Santy Fee, you'll bear that in mind."

Shortly, the cavalry officer nodded, turned to the waiting scout. "Go ahead, Cooper. Get your stick. I'll have the Indian brought up for you."

When Hughes's troopers returned with the glowering Comanche, Bass straightened up, fetched a foot-long piece of whittled hardwood to view.

"This here's a talking stick. The Comanches call it *dei-n t'ou-e*, the Tonguestick. You give it a twist and talk comes out."

"How's she work?" Cloyce Travis eyed the small stick skeptically.

"On a very artistic principle," replied Bass soberly. "Now pay attention because I ain't going over this twice."

Having warned the white audience, he turned to the scowl-

ing Comanche, addressing him in a short-barked string of
his mother tongue.

"Ho, you, Stiff Leg. You are familiar with this stick? It
comes from the southern tribes, down in Sonora. Now, you
listen. And while you are listening, look, too. Look at me.
Hard. You remember *K'ou sein-p'a-ga?* You remember Black
Beard?"

"You K'ou! You Black Beard. Him you!" The startled
recognition burst from the sullen brave, his quick-following
plea coming with a guileless, widemouthed grin. "Listen,
Black Beard, I've been south. I know the stick. We were
friends, you and I, *kou-m,* real friends. You remember Stiff
Leg? You won't use the Tonguestick on your old friend.
Kou-m, kou-m, there is no need for the stick. Big Head means
your wagons no harm. He doesn't want the horses of these
Pony Soldiers. Hear me. I swear it."

Bass, stepping back into the full firelight, held the little
stick up so the watching white men could see it clearly.

"You'll all observe there's a slot cut in the middle of this
stick. All we do is take a good-honed skinning knife and
open us up a little flap of skin on Stiff Leg's belly. Just under
the button. Then we flay this little strip of skin away from the
meat and fat, and stick it through this slot in the stick, pulling
her on through, tight.

The scout paused, watching the brave for any sign of
folding, saw none, continued.

"Now, we start rotating the stick, half a turn at a twist.
What starts peeling off and wrapping itself around the stick
is the three-inch strip of Stiff Leg's bellyhide."

Bass hesitated again, looking Stiff Leg up and down.
"Depending on how hard this buck don't want to talk, we
keep turning the stick. Looking at him, there, I'd judge him
to be about a three-turn man. Mebbeso, he's tougher than I
think. Depending on that, we'll peel him clean down to the
end of his pizzle."

"*Hiii-eee!*" the Comanche's snarl came with his wild lunge

at Bass. The scout sidestepped as Cloyce Travis and the muleskinners snowed the crazed Indian under.

"Spread-eagle him on that wagon wheel!" snapped Bass. "And stuff his yap with something. We don't want him wailing loud enough for Big Head to hear him."

With Stiff Leg bound and gagged on the wagon wheel, Bass stepped in, close. His skinning knife whipped up, slashing the front of the comanche's war shirt. The captive twisted, driving his teeth furiously into the leather gag. The watching men bit just as hard, gag or no gag.

Bass made three thin cuts, his knife moving like a light streak. When he had made them, he brushed the blood off Stiff Leg's belly with the greasy foresleeve of his buckskin shirt, stepped back, grunted a short Comanche phrase at the hostile. The brave's answer, in Comanche or any other tongue, came out a snarl and Bass shrugged, moving in with the knife again.

Stiff Leg stood up to the flap-flaying, the pulling of the flayed flap through the stick-slot, and a turn and a half of the stick itself. Then he caved in.

At that, he took it better than three or four of Captain Hughes's young troopers, each of whom felt compelled to stumble off in the dark to bark up his sowbelly and beans back of the handiest wagon wheel.

Bass sloshed a dipper of creek water across Stiff Leg's belly, cut him down, laid him out on his back by the fire, daubed his wound with tallow, pasted the flap back in place, and bound it there with a strip of trade muslin. Then he propped him against the wagon wheel and threw another dipper of branch water in his face.

Stiff Leg came out of it shaking his head and whining like a cornered bear. When his head was clear, he talked, and from the sound of it, talked reasonably straight.

His story came out in a mixture of Comanche, broken English, and dramatic hand-sign language that made the confession clear enough for the greenest trooper to follow with eye-popping understanding.

"Big Head, him want the horses. Need ponies. Very long trip up from Sonora. Hard on the horses. Him see you. Him see your ponies. Him remember other time, make big laugh. Him—"

"*Hau, hau,*" waved Bass. "We savvy horses. How about the attack, now? Where will Big Head attack?"

The Comanche hesitated, watching the scout. Bass smiled, encouragingly, twirling the Tonguestick the least bit.

"Sandstone Slot!" Stiff Leg had gotten the point, his answer bursting out hurriedly.

The name sent Bass's mind loping up the Trail to the spot, setting it at two miles past Big Coon Creek, in the very gut of the desolate country ahead. It was a narrow, quarter-mile-long defile, hand-carved by Man Above for the ambush used of his savage red sons.

"Go on," he grunted, flashing the Tonguestick, "keep talking."

"Wagons go in Sandstone Slot. Horses not in yet. When wagons all in, Indians ride in, fast. Get between horses and Slot. You trapped inside. Can't get out to fight. Indians run off horses. *Sat-kan,* it's as easy as that."

After that, there was a little silence, then Bass talked. And the way he talked made a man know he was thinking the thing out.

"I hate to horn in on a man's pondered plans, 'specially when he's made them with such loving consideration of his white brother. What Stiff Leg ain't told us, and which any of you mossyback skinners ought to know, is just this. Once them Comanches get us in that bottleneck wash, with our horse herd run off and all, they'll put a bunch of braves on either end of the Slot and thirst us out. They ain't got nothing better to do, I promise you. Seeing's how I don't hanker to set in that slot till my gizzard shrivels, we'll just go

ahead and do as I say. And that's to run it out Big Head's pet
way—up to a point, leastways."

The night Bass peeled Stiff Leg's belly, the train was thirty-
three miles from Big Coon Creek, the last camp before
Sandstone Slot. That made it a two-day drive facing the
caravan, during which, according to Stiff Leg, they could
expect no bother from the hostiles.

Bass was satisfied he had gotten the gospel out of the
wounded Comanche but he and Captain Hughes outrode
the lead wagon wide and wakeful, all the same. They pulled
the Coon Creek Crossing without a sign that Indians had
ever come near the Santa Fe Trail. So far, so good. Up to
Coon Creek, leastways, it looked like the Comanche Tonguestick was big medicine.

After supper in the Coon Creek camp, Bass called the
men up for the final powwow. "I ain't going to give you my
plot before you sleep. It might keep you awake," he grinned.
"But I allow you'll agree it's a good one when you hear it. I'll
give it to you when I bust you out'n your blankets along after
moondark. Meantime, I got to know for final and sure—am
I giving the orders, or ain't I?"

After a moment's uncomfortable silence, Cloyce Travis
spoke for the skinners. "You-all are giving them, Cooper,"
he grunted. "Leastways, so far as my boys are concerned."

"You've been right so far, Cooper. Go ahead." Captain
Hughes's agreement, for all its grudging dignity, was just as
definite as Travis's.

Bass nodded, facing around to take in the full group. "All
right. Everybody turn in. Get all the sleep you can. When I
roll you out, I want you should roll out quiet. No lights and
no noise. Every one of you clear on that?"

Apparently everyone was, for his only answer was a wave
of sober nods washing around the listening circle. Bass
chucked his head, satisfied.

"Good enough. Truss that buck up again and throw him

back in the wagon. Go on, spread out. I want this here camp dark in ten minutes."

In some minutes less than that, the camp was as out-black as a snuffed candle.

Bass, hunched between the lead wagon's front wheels, smoked his short stone pipe, turned his ears to the night-bird and small-animal talking going on in the low hills to the west.

"Keep your nighthawks whistling, Big Head," he muttered grimly. "And hold them fox barks, steady. Happen things go just so, tomorrow, I'll hand you back something you hung on me two years ago."

At three o'clock, the moon went down and Bass sent Captain Hughes and Cloyce Travis to roll-out the troopers and wagon skinners. With all hands assembled, the scout nodded shortly.

"All right, boys," the low voice carried maybe a wagon length, no more. "what I got in mind works tricky. All the same, it's the best I been able to figure."

He gave them the layout, then, and going along he could sense their agreeing nods, hear their low grunts of approval. When he had finished, nobody had a word to ask. He waited a few seconds, concluded abruptly.

"We'll roll a mite early, while it's still near dark. All the light we need is to see the Slot when we get there. Trail's clean and smooth from here to the opening."

"And she's smooth clean on through," added Cloyce Travis thoughtfully.

"That's right." Bass's voice dropped even lower. "Now spread out and catch-up your mules. And for God's sake rustle them long-ears in here, quiet-like."

Out-trail, west of the night-moving wagon camp, two kit foxes began yapping back and forth. A third and fourth joined the conversation, aided by the faster, more excited tonguing of a dog coyote.

"Listen to them damn 'skins talking it up," Bass whispered

to Captain Hughes, where the cavalryman squatted by his side in the morning dark. "Ever hear a better kit or coyote?"

"Nonsense!" rejoined the young officer uneasily. "Those are the real thing. I've been down this trail enough times to tell a Comanche talking when I hear one, Cooper!"

Bass said nothing. Let the youngster bolster himself. No point in unsettling him more than he and his green boys were already unsettled. No use for a man to josh himself, though. Happen the cocksure captain had been down the Trail more times than a buffalo herd had tick birds, those were still red tongues clacking out there toward Sandstone Slot.

Cloyce Travis drifted noiselessly up through the black. "All set, Bass. We got them all spanned-in and the wagons gang-hitched Injun file, like you-all said."

"Good. Now," the scout's voice picked up speed and urgency, "have four of them troopers to haze the horse herd along, easy and normal, back of the last wagon. When the last wagons are going in the Slot them boys are to leave the horses and hit into the Slot, too. Get that into their heads. They got to get clean away from that herd before Big Head comes down on them. Hump your tail, man!"

"She's humped!" the skinner's answer drifted back, his hurrying figure fading with it. Minutes later, he was back, reporting the horse herd bunched and ready to move to Bass's order.

"It's nigh four—" Bass was thinking out loud. "We can go ahead and slop the hogwash to them."

Cloyce Travis drifted out again, Bass giving him a minute before singing out "Catch up! Catch up!" at the top of his well-trained lungs. Seconds later, the darkness was rent with the hairiest-chested imitation of a wagon-train catch-up that had ever been staged on the Santa Fe. The skinners had forty-five minutes of unnatural silence to make up for in their addresses to their hammerhead hitches, and they didn't miss a four-letter word. They read the skinner's bible backward and forward and threw in a few psalms even Bass had never heard.

"Stretch out! Stretch out!" The scout's final order boomed up the darkened Santa Fe loud enough for every red fox in the next sixteen sections to hear. The five spans on the lead wagon hit into their collars as Cloyce Travis poured the blacksnake to them. Down the invisible wagon line, other snakes were snapping and other hitches digging in. The big Murphy freighters squealed and groaned into motion, the obedient, trail-broke horse herd tagging along behind the last wagon.

Following the momentary letup in blasphemy that always set in after the wagons got under way, a renewed chorus of fox barks and nighthawk cries sprang up around the gully-washed country flanking Sandstone Slot. Turning to Captain Hughes, Bass laughed.

"You still reckon them are the real Johnny Foxes and Willy Nighthawks out there, Captain?"

The nervous officer didn't hesitate with his fervant reply, this time. "If they are, by God, they're a damn sight more interested in army supply trains than they should be!"

Forty minutes down the Trail and the skybelly back of them was lighting to a fish-bloat gray. The pale light bounced off the scrub-beetled brows of Sandstone Slot, staining the face of the escarpment, sick-blotchy. The gaping mouth of the Slot itself loomed blurred and empty as a burned hole in a dirty blanket. Redbird, Bass's bright chestnut gelding, padding along, cougar-quiet, fifty feet in front of the lead wagon, kept crouching and side-skittering with nerves.

The morning wind, blowing straight at them out of the Slot, was a pure blessing. Being dead-on, it caught up the pony stink from the twin gullies flanking the narrow defile, carrying it parallel to the train and scattering it away on the desert behind the trailing cavalry horses. Not a horse or a mule in Bass's outfit caught one whiff of the hostile horse sweat, held into the Slot steady and smooth-stepping.

Bass swung wide of the entrance, checking the hip-shifting Redbird, letting the wagons go in, past him, counting them with breath-held vehemence as they went.

The first of the tied-together groups of army vehicles went in and on down the Slot, smooth as Shanghai silk, the second group following in perfect order. But a sharp eye, given a little closer look than that afforded from the distant gullies, with maybe just a shade better light, would have seen something off-color about that entrance.

As the wagon groups had rumbled past the thin scout at the Slot's mouth, the number two, three, four, and five wagon of each group had discharged a strange, silent cargo. Sort of a long-striding, soft-cursing, two-legged cargo. A cargo that went scuttling up the insides of the brush-choked lips of the Slot, clawing for handholds in the steep going, slipping, scrambling, and dragging the long Sharps rifles by their barrels.

Bass hadn't more than time to count the skinners off their army freighters before he had other worries. Damn, where the tarnal hell were those troopers—oh, yonder they came. Bulking up through the quick-growing light. Riders bent low, horses cat-jumping toward the Slot under the anxious heels digging their ribs. The last four men, the troopers assigned to pilot the horse herd. Moving three and one, with stolid Captain Henry Hughes riding off the flank of the last one.

A moment later, all four had disappeared into the Slot, waving silently at Bass as they passed him.

The scout had a handful of seconds, then, to bat a glance up at the lips of the gully above. He didn't mind what he saw, either. Eight of the ten skinners on one side, the ten cavalry troopers on the other, perfect-hid by the rank sage and mesquite. Bellyflopping and squinting along the three-foot swing of their rifle barrels, his eighteen marksmen waited for Big Head and his Comanches.

Three seconds more for an eye-flick down the silent line of halted freighters in the Slot behind him, showing him the other two skinners straining to hold the long lines of roped-together wagon mules quiet. Two added seconds for another eye-flick out beyond the Slot, checking the empty throats of the twin gullies, and the even, plodding approach of the unguarded cavalry horse herd.

One second, then, and hell gave itself a double rupture, breaking loose.

The startled horse herd went dashing toward the Slot, neighing and snorting their sudden terror—and Big Head was howling the howl of the Texas Comanche and both gullies were puking a vomit of feathers, lance tassels, war bows, and greasepaint. And Bass Cooper and Captain Henry Hughes were banging their faces into the dirt under the rear wheels of the last wagon, where it stood parked in the Slot opening.

Watching the Comanches come, Bass allowed that when Big Head jumped, he jumped with both splayed moccasins. The hostiles came down on that cavalry horse herd like buffalo wolves on a thrown-out batch of hot calf guts.

Sweet? Man, oh man, it was pure sugar. The running horse herd was scarce a hundred yards from the Slot. The Comanches, cutting in between it and the Slot, to block the crazed animals off, weren't fifty yards from the hidden white rifle-men. And hell, a bareface boy couldn't miss at twice that range with a smoothbore!

Bass let the converging Indian charges, one sweeping from the north gully, one from the south, get good and clotted-up in front of the milling horse herd before bellowing "Fire!" The eighteen-gun volley crashed into the packed mass of men and animals with a thud audible above the compounded warwhoops and pony neighs. Indians, Indian ponies, cavalry

horses, gun, hoof, battle scream and wild neigh, went sprawling in a shattered tangle.

Ramming his patch and galena pill home, Bass prayed the
reserves the Comanche chief had undoubtedly left in each
of the twin gullies would hold up their relief charge until he
and the boys could get reloaded, feeling, from what he knew
of the red sons, that they would.

He knew them, all right, and they did.

Indians just didn't fight like white men. Swat them hard
on the first rush and nine times out of ten a man had them
whipped. Big Head's reserves milled in their gullies, awaiting
the return of their chief with his repulsed first waves. The
second of these waves, bearing the raging Big Head in its tail-
tucked van, dumped the chief, black-faced and raving, in the
safety of the north gully.

Immediately, the Comanche leader began yelping his
barking war cry and haranguing his braves to move in on the
still unguarded and wandering cavalry horses. By the time
he had sold them the idea, Bass had his skinners and Captain
Hughes, his troopers, primed and waiting.

"Pick your targets, boys!" the scout's call ran cheerily up
the Slot banks, "but leave the old he-coon to me. Anybody
puts a galena pill in that outsize skull and I'll drill him for
his trouble. Big Head's my meat and I'm namin' him so!"

"Mind what Cooper says!" Captain Hughes barked the
sudden confirmation of Bass's request at his own white-faced
troopers. "Leave the chief for him!"

Before Bass could answer the quick smile Hughes flung at
him with the unexpected order, business was picking up
again out beyond the Slot.

The hidden white riflemen began squeezing-off the return
gallop of the redmen the minute they bombarded back out
of their gullies. Results—the charge never got rolling, and
Bass failed to get his sights near Big Head.

But the Comanche chief had had his share. Back in the
north gully for the second time in three minutes, he waved

Black Dog and four other gun-owning braves, forward. "Fire the five shots!" he growled hoarsely. "Go on, fire them!" The braves nodded, skying their rifles and firing in even rotation. After a moment, the shots were answered by five more from the south gully.

Hearing the signal shots, Bass crawled out from under the army wagon, his grin nearly unhinging his long jaw.

"Get your head out'n the ground, Captain!" he called to the crouching officer. "Them dog eaters is hauling their freight."

"How in hell do you figure, Cooper?" The cavalryman's dirt-smeared face poked out querulously.

"Five's their Bad Medicine Number," Bass replied soberly. "Five's poison to a Comanche or any other Plains Injun. They're through for today. Their hearts ain't good no more." Bass turned, boosting his voice to the watching men above.

"Hold your fire, boys. Them five shots was their medicine signal. We won't be hearing no more red-fox barks betwixt here and Santa Fe."

"By damn, you-all are right, Bass!" Cloyce Travis, highest man on the Slot ridge, called down. "I can see them filing out'n the far ends of both gullies. That bunch easing out'n the near gully is fair close enough to count their coup-feathers!"

"Which one's the near gully?" The easy tones dropped out of Bass's voice, his question snapping with sudden interest. "North or south?"

"North—"

"How near?"

"Three, four hundred yards. They got to hump up over a little cross ridge to get out'n it. We can see them, plain. Why you-all ask?"

"I aim to holler me a 'good-bye' to one of them 'Comanche pals' of mine!" Bass was already halfway up the Slot ridge, his answer scarcely beating him to the Texan's side. "Happen the wind and the light and the luck are just right, he'll hear me, too."

With the scout's words, all eyes swung to the bobbing exits of the Comanches departing the northern jaw of their ill-fated ambush trap. The nervous seconds sped, each one boosting another hard-spurred pony up and across the momentary bareness of the cross ridge.

Captain Hughes, having inched part way up the Slot ridge to join his men in watching the hostile exodus, was counting the Comanches out, his lips moving unconsciously with those of his tight-mouthed troopers, his nerves stretching as the number grew from thrity to forty to near fifty. Still Bass held his fire.

There was a nasty moment, then, when no more Indians came out of the north gully. Damn! What was in that scout's mind, letting the red sons out that way? Sure it was long shooting and not much chance of a clean hit, but why hold down Cloyce Travis and those other center shots among the skinners? It would almost seem as though the moody trail guide was covering to let the red devils make it clean away!

The officer's darkening thoughts scattered and broke for sudden cover—over there at the gully end a last Comanche was kicking his pony up the near side of the crossridge! And up above, on the Slot ridge, Bass Cooper was standing hard against the climbing red of the morning sun, his gutteral voice booming a Comanche greeting across the morning stillness.

"Ho, Oudlt'ou-eidl! It is I, K'ou Sein-p'a-ga! You remember? Your old friend, Black Beard?"

The startled Comanche, caught off guard by the fierce yell, wheeled his painted pony, stood, for one long breath, silhouetted atop the open ground of the cross ridge.

"Wagh!" the warrior's return snarl burst as a single-worded shout of recognition, his rifle swinging up to follow it.

"TH-gyh hou'bH!" shouted Bass Cooper, his Sharps slapping to his hunching shoulder with the words. The gun seemed to explode on contact with the lean cheek, its half-ounce galena pill blending its departing whine with the dull-boomed report of the black powder. Across the silence, a man found it hard to think he didn't hear the soapy swat of that ball going home.

The stricken Indian horseman straightened, hung poised for a second in the saddle of his hunching pony. Even at the distance, what with the clean morning light and the way he sat, so sudden-straight and still, there was no missing the bright flash of that five-foot eagle-crest bonnet, nor of the grotesquely large head its fanning feathers vignetted. The fading roll of Bass's shot was still echoing in the north gully as Big Head's pony leaped sideways and away from the nerveless thing on its back.

The charcoal-and-vermillion-smeared body hit the graveled slope of the cross ridge, rolled, bouncing and flopping, to the bottom of the north gully. There it lay, sky-staring and silent. *Oudlt'ou-eidl,* War Chief of the Cimarron River Comanches, was dead, even before the rattling gravel that was his only funeral procession had ceased following him into his last resting place.

Back on the Slot ridge, Bass lowered his battered Sharps, eyes still on Big Head's distant, sprawled figure.

"Hey, Bass!" Cloyce Travis's friendly call brought the scout's gaze back to the skinners and troopers crowding around him on the brushy slope. "What was that last Comanche yell you-all flung at the chief? The one you-all squeezed-off with?"

"*TH-gyh hou'bH,*" said Bass slowly. "Happy Traveling. Pleasant Journey. It's a thing they say when someone is about to die. About to start up the Shadow Trail. About to put in for his Comanche Passport—"

"Man alive," there was growing admiration in Cloyce Travis's drawl, "I allow you-all are some pumpkins with that Holy Iron of yourn, but that buck was some over three hundred yards! You-all don't aim to say you actually expected to drill him center?"

"You can't very well miss a shot," replied Bass evenly, "that you've been practicing in your head for the long part of two years."

"Well, what do you-all say now that you've made it?" smiled the Texas skinner.

"Yes, Bass"—it was the first time Captain Hughes had called him by that name and Bass didn't miss the frank respect in the young officer's use of it—"what *do* you say, now? I'm waiting for my scout's report—"

The scout looked at the straight-faced captain, and beyond him to the waiting circle of muleskinners and cavalry troopers, his narrow black eyes relaxing as the ring of friendly grins spread around to hem him in.

"Boys,"—his low words, coming haltingly from the crooked, half-shy smile of his twisted mouth, left them all with their hearts full and their mouths empty—"I say let's get them army wagons rolling west. I want to know how it feels to be riding the head of a U.S. Cavalry supply line again. With the wagons and the Pony Soldiers glad to have you out there where you belong—and the sun hitting you from *behind* for a change, as well as in front."

THE NAKED GUN

John Jakes

THE steely-eyed, usually fearless, often amoral gunfighter, as epitomized by Billy the Kid, is a quintessential part of Western myth, and thus is perfect grist for the mills of Western fiction writers. He can be either a hero or a villain; in the hands of the more talented fictioneer, he can even be both. Frontier novels and films have made good (and too often bad) use of the gunslinger, the gunhawk, the shootist; so have pulp Western stories, in which hundreds upon hundreds have fought and died.

"The Naked Gun" stands well above most of the pulp gunfighter tales, flavored as it is with raw realism and a healthy measure of irony. George Bodie is pure myth, yet he might also have stepped from the pages of history. Gunhawks like Bodie did exist; and it is not unreasonable to suppose that one might have met a similarly mordant fate. . . .

John Jakes made his first professional sale (of a science fiction story) in 1950, at the age of eighteen, and followed it with scores of others in a variety of fields. His Western stories appeared in such magazines as Ranch Romances, Max Brand's Western, .44 Western, Big-Book Western, *and* Short Stories. *His only traditional Western novel,* Wear a Fast Gun, *appeared in 1956; but as he himself has noted, the West has been a strong and recurring locale in many of his acclaimed historical novels, and will continue to be in future books. His most recent in a long line of best-sellers is* Heaven and Hell *(1987), the final volume in his North-South trilogy.*

George Bodie sat smoking a cigar in the parlor of Chinese Annie's house on Nebraska Street when the message came.

Bodie had his dusty boots propped on a stool and his heavy woolen coat open to reveal the single holster with the Navy Colt on his hip. He might have been thirty or forty.

His cheeks in the lamplight were shadowy with pox scars. He was ugly, but hard and capable looking. His smile had a crooked, sarcastic quality as the cigar smoke drifted past his face.

Maebelle Tait, owner of the establishment—Chinese Annie had died; her name was kept for reasons of good will—hitched up the bodice of her faded ball gown and poured a drink.

"Lu ought to be down before too long," she said. From somewhere above came a man's laugh.

"Good. I've only been in this town an hour, but I've seen everything there is worth seeing, except Lu. Things don't change much."

Maebelle sat with her drink and lit a black cheroot. "Where you been, George?"

Bodie shrugged. "Hays City, mostly." His smile widened and his hand touched his holster.

"How many is it now?" Maebelle asked with a kind of disgusted curiosity.

"Eleven." Bodie walked over and poured a hooker for himself. "One more and I got me a dozen." He glanced irritably at the ceiling. "What's she doin'? Customer?"

Maebelle shook her head. "Straightening up the second-floor parlor. We got a group of railroad men stopping over around two in the morning." Maebelle's tone lingered half-way between cynicism and satisfaction.

The front door opened and a blast of chill air from the early winter night swept across the floor. Bodie craned his neck as Tad, Maebelle's seven-year-old boy, came in, wiping his nose with his muffler. Maebelle's other child, three, sat quietly in a chair in the corner, fingering a page in an

Eastern ladies' magazine, her eyes round and silently curious.

"Where you been, Tad?" Maebelle demanded.

He glanced at Bodie. "Over at Simms' livery stable. I . . . I saw Mr. Wyman there."

Bodie caught the frowning glance Maebelle directed at him. "New law in town?" he asked.

Maebelle nodded. "Lasted six months, so far. Quiet gent. He carries a shotgun."

Bodie touched the oiled Colt's hammer. "This can beat it, anytime."

Maebelle's frown deepened. "George, I don't want you to go hunting for your dozenth while you're on my property. I'm glad for you to come, but I don't want any shooting in this house. I got a reputation to protect.

Bodie poured another drink. The boy Tad drew a square of paper from his pocket and looked at his mother.

"Mr. Wyman gave me this."

He held it out to Bodie, with hesitation.

"He said for me to give it to you right away."

Bodie's brows knotted together. He unfolded the paper, and with effort read the carefully blocked letters. The words formed a delicate bond between two men who nearly did not know how to read. Bodie's mouth thinned as he digested the message:

WE DO NOT WANT A MAN LIKE YOU IN THIS TOWN. YOU HAVE TIL MIDNIGHT TO RIDE OUT. (SIGNED) DALE WYMAN, TOWN MARSHAL.

Bodie laughed and crumpled the note and threw it into the crackling fire in the grate.

"I guess the word travels," he said with a trace of pride. "Maybe I will collect my dozenth." He raised one hand. "But not on your property, Maebelle. I'll do it in the street, when

this marshal comes to run me out. So's everybody can see."
His hand went toward the liquor bottle.

Maebelle pushed Tad in the direction of the hall. "Go to
the kitchen and get something to eat. And take your sister
Emma with you."

Grumbling, the boy took the tiny girl's hand and dragged
her toward the darkened, musty-smelling hallway.

The girl disengaged her hand, and stopped. Curious, she
lifted Bodie's hat from where it rested on a chair.

Maebelle slapped her hand smartly. "Go along, Tad. You
follow him, Emma. Honest to heaven, that child is the pick-
ing-up-est thing I ever knew. Born bank robber, I guess, if
she was a boy."

"Where the hell's Lu?" Bodie wanted to know.

"Don't get your dander up, George," Maebelle said
quickly. "I'll go see."

She went to the bottom of the staircase and bawled the
girl's name several times. A girlish "Coming!" echoed from
somewhere above. A knock sounded at the door and Maebelle opened it. She talked with the man for a moment, and
then his heavy boots clomped up the stairway. As she returned to the parlor Bodie looked at the clock.

"Quarter to eleven, Maebelle. An hour and fifteen minutes
before I get me number twelve." He chuckled.

Maebelle busied herself straightening a doily on the sofa,
not looking at him.

Bodie helped himself to still another drink, and swallowed
it hastily. "Don't worry about the whiskey," he said over his
shoulder. "I'm even faster when I got an edge on."

Light footsteps sounded on the stair. Bodie turned as the
girl Lu came into the room. She ran to Bodie and kissed him,
throwing her arms around his neck. She was young beneath
the shiny hardness of her face. Her lips were heavily painted,
and her white breast above the gown smelled of dusting
powder.

"Oh, George, I'm glad you got here."

"I came just to see you, honey. Two hundred miles." His arm crept around her waist, his hand touched her breast. He kissed her lightly.

"Well, I'm not running this for charity, you know," Maebelle said.

"I'll settle up," Bodie replied. "Don't worry. Right now though . . . "

He and Lu began to walk toward the stairway.

Another knock came at the door. Maebelle went to open, and Bodie heard a voice say out of the frosty dark, "Evening, Miz Tait. Lu here?"

Bodie dropped his arm.

Maebelle started to protest, but the man came on into the lighted parlor. The cowboy was thin. His cheeks were red from wind and liquor, and he blinked at Bodie, with suspicion. Lu gaped at the floor, flustered.

"Hello, Lu. Did you forget I was comin' tonight?"

"Maybe she did forget," Bodie said. "She's busy."

"Come on, Fred," Maebelle said urgently. She pulled the cowboy's arm. "I know Bertha'd be glad to see you."

"Bertha, hell," the cowboy complained. "I rode in sixty miles, like I do every month, just to see Lu. It's all set up." He stepped forward and grabbed Lu's wrist. Bodie's fingers touched leather, like a caress.

"You're out of luck, friend," Bodie said. "I told you Lu's busy tonight."

"Like hell," the cowboy insisted, pulling Lu. "Come on, sweetie. I come sixty miles, and it's mighty cold. . . . "

"Get your hands off her," Bodie said.

Lu jerked away, retreated and stared, round-eyed, like a worn doll, pretty but empty.

"Don't you prod me," the cowboy said, weaving a little. His blue eyes snapped in the lamplight. "Who are you, anyway, acting so big? The governor or somebody?"

"I'm George Bodie. Didn't you hear about me tonight?"

"George Bo . . . "

The cowboy's eyes whipped frantically to the side. He licked his lips and his hand crawled down toward the hem of his jacket.

"Not in here, George, for God's sakes," Maebelle protested.

"Keep out of it," Bodie said softly. His eyes had a hard, predatory shine. "Now, mister cowboy, you got anything more to say about not bein' satisfied with Bertha?"

The cowboy looked at Lu. Bodie and Maebelle could read his face easily: fear clawed, and fought with the idea of what would happen if he backed down before Lu.

His sharp, scrawny-red Adam's apple bobbed.

His hand dropped.

Bodie's eyes glistened as the Navy cleared and roared.

The cowboy's gun slipped out of his fingers unfired. He dropped to his knees, cursed, shut his eyes, bleeding from the chest. Then he pitched forward and lay coughing. In a few seconds the coughing had stopped.

Bodie smiled easily and put the Navy away.

"One dozen," he said, like a man uttering a benediction.

"You damned fool," Maebelle raged. "Abraham! Abraham!" she shouted. "Get yourself in here."

In a moment an old arthritic colored man hobbled into the room from the back of the house.

"Get that body out of here. Take the rig and dump him on the edge of town. Jump to it."

Abraham began laboriously dragging the corpse out of the parlor by the rear door. Boots, then feminine titters, sounded on the stairs.

Maebelle held down her rage, whirled and stalked into the hall.

"It's all right, folks," she said, vainly trying to block the view. People craned forward on the steps. Abraham didn't move fast enough. "Nothing's happened," Maebelle insisted. "The man's just hurt a little. Just a friendly argument."

"He's dead," a male reedy voice said. "Any fool kin see that.

Bodie stood in the doorway, his arm around Lu once more, complacently smirking at the confusion of male and female bodies at the bottom of the stairs. He heard his name whispered.

The thin voice piped up, "I'm getting out of here, Maebelle. This is too much for my blood." A spindly shape darted toward the door.

"Now wait a minute, Hiram," Maebelle protested.

The door slammed on the breath of chill air from the street.

Maebelle walked back toward Bodie, her eyes angry. "Now you've done it for fair. That yellow pipsqueak will spread it all over town that George Bodie just killed a man in my house."

"Let him," Bodie said. He glanced back at the clock. "In an hour I got an engagement with the marshal anyway. But that's in an hour."

Lu snuggled against him as he started up the stairs. The crowd parted respectfully. Maebelle scratched her head desperately, then spoke up in a voice that had a false boom to it:

"Come on into the parlor, folks. I'll pour a drink for those with bad nerves."

Abraham had removed the body, but she still noticed a greasy black stain on the carpet. Her eyes flew to the clock, which ticked steadily.

Bodie awoke suddenly, chilly in the dark room. His hand shot out for the Navy, but drew back when he recognized the boy Tad in the thin line of lamplight falling through the open door. He yawned and rolled over. Lu had gone, and he had dozed.

"What is it, boy?" he asked.

"Mr. Wyman's in the street, asking for you."

Bodie swung his legs off the bed, laughed, and lit the lamp. The holster hung on the bedpost, with the Colt in it.

"What time is it?" Bodie wanted to know.

"Quarter of twelve. Mr. Wyman hasn't got his shotgun. Said he wanted to talk to you about something."

Bodie frowned. "'What sort of an hombre is this Mr. Wyman? Would he be hiding a gun on him?"

The boy shook his head. "He belongs to the Methodist Church. Everybody says he's real honest," the boy answered, pronouncing the last word with faint suspicion.

Bodie's eyes slitted down in the lamplight.

Then he stood, scratched his belly and laughed. "I imagine it wouldn't do no harm to talk to the marshal. And let him know what's going to happen to him."

Bodie drew on his shirt, pants, and boots. He pointed to the holster on the bedpost. "I'll come back for that, if this marshal still wants to hold me to the midnight deadline. Thanks for telling me, boy."

He went out of the room and down the stairs, a smile of anticipation on his face.

The house was strangely quiet. No one was in the parlor. But Bodie had a good idea that Maebelle, and others, would be watching from half a dozen darkened windows. Bodie put his hand on the doorknob, pulled, and stepped out into the biting air.

Wyman stood three feet from the hitchrack.

He had both hands raised to his face, one holding a flaring match, the other shielding it from the wind as he lit his pipe. Bodie recognized the gesture for what it was: a means of showing that the town marshal kept his word. Wyman flicked the match away and the bowl of the pipe glowed.

Bodie walked forward and leaned on the hitchrack, grinning. The cold air stung his cheeks. Across the way, at Aunt Gert's, a girl in a spangled green dress drank from a whiskey bottle behind a window.

"You Wyman?"

"That's right."

"Well, I'm Bodie. Speak your piece."

Bodie saw a slender man, thirty, with a high-crowned hat, fur-collared coat, and drooping mustache. His face was pale in the starlight.

"I started out to see if I could talk you into leaving town," Wyman said slowly. "I figure I don't want to kill anybody in my job if I don't have to."

"I'll say you got a nerve, Marshal," Bodie said, laughter in his words. "Ain't you scared? I got me my dozenth man tonight."

"I know."

"You still want to talk me into riding without a fight?"

Wyman shook his head. "I said that's why I came, why I started out. On the way I heard about the killing. Hiram Riggs ran through the streets yelling his head off about it. I can't let you go now. But I can ask you to come along without a fight. You might wind up dead, Bodie."

"I doubt it, Marshal. I just purely doubt that."

Bodie scratched the growth of whiskers along the line of his jaw. He lounged easily, but he saw Wyman shift his feet as the rasp-rasp of the scratching sounded loudly in the night street.

"You know, you didn't answer my question about being scared."

"Of course I am, if that makes you feel better," Wyman said, without much malice.

"Nobody ever told me that before, Marshal. Of course most didn't have time."

"Why should I lie? I'm not a professional."

"They why are you in the job, marshal? I'm sort of curious."

"I don't know. People figured I'd try, I imagine." Sharply he raised his heel and knocked glimmering sparks from his pipe. "Hell, I'm not here to explain to you why I don't want to fight. I'm telling you I will, if you won't come with me."

Bodie hesitated, tasting the moment like good liquor. "Now, Marshal, did you honestly think when you walked over here that you'd get me to give up?"

Starlight shone in Wyman's bleak eyes for a moment.

"No."

"Then why don't you go on home to bed? You haven't got a chance."

In a way Bodie admired the marshal's cheek, fool though he was.

Wyman turned his head slightly, indicating the opposite side of the street. For the first time Bodie noticed a shadowy rider on one of the horses at Aunt Gert's rack.

"When I come, Bodie, I'll have my deputy. He carries a shotgun too."

Bodie scowled into the night, then stepped down off the sidewalk, trembling with anger.

"That's not a very square shake, Marshal."

"Don't talk to me about square shakes. I knew that cowboy you shot. He couldn't have matched you with a gun. And there've been others. If you're trying to tell me two against one isn't fair, all I've got to say is, if I had a big cat killing my beef, I wouldn't worry whether I had two or twenty men after him." Hardness edged Wyman's words now. "I don't worry about how I kill an animal, Bodie. If you'd given that cowboy a chance, maybe I'd feel different. But I've got to take you, one way or another. You wrecked the square shake, not me."

Bodie's fingers crawled along the hip of his jeans.

"Can't do it by yourself?" he said contemptuously.

"I won't do it by myself."

"Why not? You can't trust your own gun?"

"Maybe that's where you made your mistake, Bodie. I'd rather trust another man than a gun."

"I don't need nobody or nothing but my gun. I never have," Bodie said softly. "Where's your shotgun, Marshal?"

Wyman nodded toward the silent deputy on the horse.

"He's got it."

"I'll put my gun up against you two," Bodie said with seething savagery. "You just wait."

Bodie started back for the entrance, and from the shadows before Aunt Gert's came a sharp voice calling:

"He might run out the back, Dale."

And Wyman's answer, "No, he won't . . . " was cut off by Bodie's vicious slam of the door.

Maebelle stuck her head out of the parlor as he bounded up the stairs, his teeth tight together and a thick angry knot in his belly. He had murder on his face.

He stomped into the bedroom, was halfway across, when the sight of the bedpost in the lamplight registered on his mind.

His holster —and the Navy—were gone.

Bodie crashed back against the wall, a strangled cry choking up out of his throat, his eyes frantically searching the room.

He lunged forward and ripped away the bedclothes. He pulled the scarred chest from the wall, threw the empty drawers on the floor, then overturned the chest with a curse and a crash. He raised the window, and the glass whined faintly.

He stood staring out for a moment at the collection of star-washed shanties stretching down the hill behind the house. Then he sat down on the edge of the bed, laced his fingers together. His shoulders began to tremble.

He let out a string of obscenities like whimpers, his eyes

wide. He jumped to his feet and began to tear at the mattress cover. Then he stopped again, shaking.

He felt Wyman laughing at him, and he heard Wyman's words once more. Black unreason boiled up through him, making him tremble all the harder. With an animal growl he ran out of the room, stopped in the hall, and looked frantically up and down.

He kicked in the door across the room. The girl shrieked softly, her hand darting for the coverlet.

"What the hell, amigo . . . " began the man, half-timidly.

Like an animal in a trap, Bodie scanned the room, turned and went racing down the staircase. He breathed hard. His chest hurt. He felt a sick cold in his stomach like he'd never known before. Hearing his heavy tread, Maebelle came out of the parlor. Before she could speak, he threw her against the wall and held her. Words caught in her throat when she saw his face.

"Where is it?" he yelled. "Where's my Navy?" His voice went keening up on a shrill note. "Tell me where it is, Maebelle, or I'll kill you!"

"George, George . . . Lord, I don't know," she protested, frightened, writhing under his hands.

He hit her, slamming her head against the wall, turning her face toward the top of the stairs. She choked. The fingers of one hand twitched feebly against the wall, the nails pecking a signal on the wallpaper.

"Emma. . . ," she said.

She sagged as he released her. He cleared the stairs in threes to where the round-eyed, curious little girl stood at the landing in her nightdress, shuffling slowly forward as if to find the commotion, and holding the Navy in one hand, upside-down, by the grip, while her other finger ran along the barrel, feeling the metal. Bodie tore it away from her and struck her across the face with the barrel.

Then he turned, lunging down the stairs again, muttering

and cursing and smiling, past Maebelle. She watched him with a look of madness creeping across her face.

At the top of the staircase, the girl Emma, as if accustomed to such treatment, picked herself up and started down, dragging the leather holster she had picked up near the baseboard. She came down a step at a time, the welt on her cheek angry red but her eyes still childish and round. . . .

Bodie peered through the curtains.

He could see Wyman and his deputy in the center of the street, waiting, their shotguns shiny in the starlight. He had never wanted to kill any men so badly before.

He snatched the door open, slipped through, and flattened his back against the wall, the Navy rising with its old, smooth feel, and a hot red laugh on his lips as he squeezed.

Wyman stepped forward, feet planted wide, and the shotgun flowered red in the night.

Then the deputy fired. Bodie felt a murderous weight against his chest.

The Navy clattered on the plank sidewalk, unfired.

Bodie fell across the hitchrack, his stomach warm and bleeding, the shape of Wyman coming toward him but growing dimmer each second. Bodie felt for the Navy as he slipped to a prone position, and one short shriek of betrayal came tearing off his lips.

Wyman pushed back his hat and cradled the shotgun in the crook of his arm.

Across the street window blinds flew up, and then the windows themselves, clattering.

Maebelle stuck her head out the front door.

Lu came down the stairs, crying and hugging a shabby dressing gown to her breasts, bumping the girl Emma.

With round, curious eyes, Emma righted herself, drawn by the sound of the shots.

She started down more rapidly, one step at a time, toward the voices there on the wintry porch, and as she hurried, first the holster slipped from her fingers and then the bright shells from the other tiny, white, curious hand. They fell, and Emma worked her way purposefully down to the next step, leaving the playthings forgotten on the garish, somewhat faded carpet.

BONANZA!

Dan Cushman

ONE of the most popular pulp magazines from the midtwenties until its demise in 1952 was Northwest Stories *(later North-west* Romances*), which featured "Big Outdoor Stories of the West and North" in its early years and "Stories of the [Northern] Wilderness Frontier" in its later ones. Alaska, the Yukon, the Arctic Circle, the Canadian Barrens, Hudson's Bay, the North Woods . . . these and other Far North locales were the settings. Numerous writers specialized in this type of story, some with considerable success outside the pulps; they include James B. Hendryx, Robert Ormond Case, William Byron Mowery, Frank Richardson Pierce, Samuel Alexander White, Ridgwell Cullum, and Dan Cushman.*

Cushman's "Northerns" were frequently cover-featured in Northwest Romances *in the late forties and early fifties and were highly regarded by readers. None is better than "Bo-nanza!," from the winter 1950–51 issue—a rousing tale of a hunt for lost gold in the Alaskan wilderness. The blurb accompanying the novelette describes it in much more colorful terms: "The Stormwind Cache! A quarter-ton of hidden yellow gold; jackpot bait for hungry adventurers. Jim Ryan swapped his forty-dollar Seattle suitcase for a packsack and moosehide mucks . . . and found himself riding a skin boat into the mouth of hell."*

Dan Cushman's pulp career lasted only a few years. In 1951 he turned to the writing of novels—Westerns such as The Ripper from Rawhide *(1952) and paperback adventure tales such as* Jewel of the Java Sea *(1951),* Timberjack *(1953), and* The Fabulous Finn *(1954). But it was his 1953 novel,* Stay Away, Joe, *a hilarious and yet moving story of a group of American Indians, that brought him his greatest success; it was a major book-club selection and a best-seller, and was later adapted into a play,* Whoop-Up. *Cushman still writes excellent Western fiction—his most recent novel,* Rusty Irons, *appeared in 1984—and historical nonfiction about his home state of Montana.*

Jim Ryan had reached Moyukuk City the hard way.

He'd taken a train up the narrow gauge from Telaqua Bay. At Apex he'd swapped his forty-dollar Seattle suitcase for a packsack and a pair of moosehide mucks, and had traveled afoot northward through the Squawman Hills. It was midnight, and he'd been thirty-six hours without food when he finally waded across windrows of thawing placer gravel to Moyukuk's one long street. He'd saved ten days by not waiting for the river steamboat, but he'd paid for every hour of it.

Seattle had left him soft. His legs ached, his back was stiff. He spat, and laughed from one side of his mouth, and cursed.

Ryan, he said to himself, *here you are back again after all the brags you made. You're back, and worse than being back, you're broke. Ryan, you're a great lad in adversity, but prosperity is more than you can stand. Ryan, what you need is someone to stand beside you. What you really need is someone to stand behind you and kick your seat higher than your shoulders.*

He was about thirty. He was six feet tall, though a breadth of frame developed in the timber camps of Washington made him seem short. His face was slightly battered, and it had a pleasing ugliness. A couple of his teeth had been kicked out and replaced with gold. He had formed the habit of carrying a twig, match, or toothpick in one corner of his mouth, giving the perpetual impression of just having left the dinner table.

It was a twig he was carrying now. He spat it away, hitched

up his sourdough pants, and waded the Alaska muck to the front door of Sky-noo Sammy's Bar and Raffle.

Midnight had brought with it a half-darkness, so lamps were lighted, shining ruddily through the smoked-up windows.

He kicked the door open and stood with his packsack balanced on one shoulder, looking around.

Sky-noo's was a battered, plank-and-tincup saloon with a sour smell of beer and stale tobacco, but it was home to Ryan's nostrils and he breathed deeply of it, just as he'd breathed the odor of the coastal forest when he got off the boat at Telaqua Bay.

A rawboned, muck-smeared miner saw him and bellowed, "My gawd, it's Ryan! There he is, the old Billy-be-damned Guggenheim himself, back for another ton of Chilliwook gold, or did them slickers in the States roll you for a cheechako and skid you out the back door?"

The miner had guessed it. They'd rolled him, all right, and they'd given him the skids.

With a grandiose gesture, Ryan pitched his warbag to the corner and shouted, "To the bar, all of you! Sammy, throw away that leopard milk and set out the best you have in the house. Bonded Kentucky, that's what Ryan buys for his friends." He then turned his attention to the rawboned miner. "Travis, those Seattle necktie-punks never saw the hour they could roll a son of the Ryans and skid him from the back door with his pockets plucked."

He was thinking that he'd got out of Seattle in good shape. However, there'd been a girl named Irene in San Francisco, a horse named Best Regards at Tijuana, and a pair of dice that refused to come up Little Joe over in Carson City. And in all of those places there'd been champagne. Ryan still felt a little throb in his head at the thought of champagne.

He took paper money from his mackinaw pocket and slammed it on the bar in the manner of one who draws on a bottomless supply. Actually, it was almost the end of a twelve-thousand-dollar stake he'd left the country with.

After taking on a couple of bourbons, Ryan said, "It's old Dave Carson I'm looking for. The friend of my heart I grubstaked up on Porcupine Creek. A sick man he is, and I'm taking him back to the States."

The poker game had got under way again, but at mention of Dave Carson a squat, black-whiskered prospector tossed in his cards and walked over, slightly splay-footed in his mukluks.

"You mean there's something wrong with Dave? I saw him ten-twelve days ago at Tonka Landing. He didn't look sick to me."

Come to think of it, Ryan didn't know what was wrong with Dave, either. It was just that a telegram had been waiting for him in Telaqua—

Ryan they're after me. If you want to see me alive be in Moyukuk by the fifteenth. Dave.

Until that moment, Ryan thought it had been the black cough, or whiskey, or some other hazard of the country. Now the message hit him with new significance. He wondered—then he shrugged it off. Nobody'd be after Dave. He didn't have an enemy in the world.

Ryan said, "What day's this? Eighteenth? He should be here in town."

Nobody had seen him. The steamboat had come down but Dave hadn't been on it.

Sammy Grussman, the proprietor, a red-headed Irish Jew, was looking at him grimly from behind the bar. "I don't want to worry you, Ryan, but I heard something. You remember that Russian breed they call Johnny Louse? Well, he came down from that Porcupine country on the tail end of the big Chinook and said Dave had gone crazy."

"Crazy!"

"That's what he said. Of course, I didn't put too much weight in it because the Louse isn't too bright himself, but he said Dave had it in his head somebody was trying to kill him. Wait now. Wait until you hear the rest and decide for yourself whether Dave's crazy. He thought somebody was after him, trying to kill him for something he had. Want to know what it was?"

"Of course I want to know."

"Now, Ryan, steady yourself. They were after a girdle."

"You mean one of those things like a corset that women—"

"Don't ask me about girdles. I'm not the one that's just been to the States. I'm telling you what Louse said. A girdle. And do you know who Carson thought was killing him to get it back? A girl. A white girl with black hair and blue eyes. And from the way Dave talked about her she didn't need any damned girdle."

Everyone was hee-hawing about it. Heat and tobacco smoke and liquor combined to make Ryan feel unsteady. He got outside by himself and let his head clear.

Dave hadn't gone crazy. He wasn't that kind. He was in trouble. He was in a whole hell of a lot of trouble or he'd never have sent the telegram.

Ryan spent a third of his remaining cash for an outfit, and before noon the next day he set out, paddling a canoe upriver toward Tonka Landing.

The Kuskokwim flowed between great barren hills. Snow still lay in the gullies, and a ceaseless wind, cold and damp, blew down on him, making his teeth chatter despite his mackinaw, despite the springtime sun swinging around the horizon.

He slept at a Siwash fishing camp, lulled by the wind and the steady creak of the fishwheels, through the short hours of twilight and night. He went on, fighting the high current of midstream, hunting the quiet waters near shore, picking his way through vast accumulations of driftwood from the high waters of other years. Fatigue lay like paralysis and pain in his body, but he went on, and fatigue left him as his body toughened and the fatty poisons of civilization were sweated off.

The country to the north and east became more rugged. Broad valleys were choked with cottonwoods just coming to bud. He passed the hundred mouths of the Neversink, and on the third evening he brought his canoe up to some steamboat docks with the log and shanty town of Tonka Landing on the hillside beyond.

The warehouse and telegraph office of the Yukon Transportation Company had a new coat of red barn paint, but nothing else seemed to have changed. The same loafers were on the bench at Gilligan's, the same gaunt malamutes barked and showed their fangs from the pens by Cultus Charley's.

He went inside the ramshackle, two-story hotel and found the owner, Blind Tom Addison, behind the desk.

Blind Tom, a scarecrow tall man with a grayish complexion, recognized his voice and cackled, "So you come back like Dave said. Well, they all do sooner or later once they have this Yukon muck in their bloodstreams."

He shook Tom's hand and said, "Dave's here then?"

"He was here." The cheerfulness left him. "That was better'n a week ago. He wasn't drunk and happy like he used to be, though."

"Sick?"

"No-o. Got a room and stayed there. Used to send the Injun out for likker. Sit there and drink it by himself but it didn't get him drunk. When a man drinks and doesn't get drunk there's something bothering him. Then one morning—" He snapped his fingers. "Gone. Just gone. Left owing me twenty-two dollars. Of course, he'd be welcome to stay here a year if he was broke, but just walking out isn't like him. Well, maybe he went to Moyukuk."

"I just came up from Moyukuk." He found a twenty and two silvers, pressed it in the blind man's hand.

"Oh, hell, I'm not worried—"

"Take it. I grubstake him, you know."

Ryan signed for a room and paused a quarter way up the rickety stairs with his packsack on his shoulder.

"Did Dave say anything about a black-haired girl chasing him to get her girdle back?"

Blind Tom doubled over from laughter. "Oh hell, Ryan, you ought to know better'n that. Dave's too old for that kind of stuff."

"They're never too old to talk about it."

Ryan climbed the stairs and walked down the hall. Even in summer it was draughty and cold. One winter he'd stayed in the hotel when the thermometer in this upper hall stood at twenty-two below.

He sat around in the room, smoked, and thought about Dave. He chewed a match and looked out the window. It was cheerless and gray, with a fine, cold rain falling. He lighted a lamp and looked at himself in the piece of rusty mirror. He had a three-day growth of whiskers. He was hungry but he didn't feel like eating. Dave was the best friend he'd ever had, and slowly the certainty had been rising in him that he was dead.

He cursed, and without realizing what he was going to do, turned and swung his fist to one of the door panels. He hadn't done that since he was a show-off kid. The panel was split and two of his knuckles bled. He laughed at himself, but he felt better.

He went to the American Bar and drank whiskies. The swamper had a barber chair in a back room, so he spent a dollar on a shave. Half the men in Tonka were at the American by then, but nobody was able to tell him about Dave.

It was past midnight when he groped back to his room through the dark hotel.

There was no lock on the door. Nobody ever locked a door in Alaska. He went inside, closed the door with his heel, and took the chewed-up match from his teeth to light the lamp. Suddenly he realized there was someone in the room.

He started back, hand by habit going to the place at his waist where he'd carried the .38 Smith & Wesson on his way upriver, but the gun wasn't there. He'd left it in his warsack.

The click of gun hammer stopped him. Then a voice followed it from the blackness. "Stand where you are."

"Sure. I got no gun."

"Well, I have. Don't make me use it."

Ryan remembered the voice from somewhere. It had been a long time before, down in the timber camps, in B.C., or Washington, or off Port Orford. It was too dark to get even a shadow impression of him, but he was a heavy man; Ryan could tell that by the creak of the floor as he moved.

A match flared up in his fingers; he lit the lamp, put the chimney on. Ryan still barely noticed his face. All he could see was the big, round muzzle of the gun aimed at him. It was a bulldog forty-five, the world's most inaccurate firearm, but at that range it would cut him in half.

"Well, Ryan!" the man said with a nasty smile. "So it is you."

Ryan still had trouble placing him. He was in his middle thirties, a rugged, rangy man with broad shoulders, and he might have been handsome if his face hadn't been spoiled by a chin that was long and a mouth too small. The mouth and jaw reminded him of a picture he'd once seen of Napoleon.

"Well, Ryan, what the hell? Don't you remember your old friends? Battles? Bill Battles, Texada Inlet, the Andraes-McConochie timber war? I remember you. I remember that night you lost those front teeth fighting with Big Ole Christopherson."

His eyes kept moving between the gun and Battles's face. "You don't need that thing pointed at me. I hold no grudge for the things that happened at Texada. I never put faith in the story that you got Koval from behind. Anyhow, it's all water over the falls."

"Oh, that." Apparently Battles had forgotten all about Koval. He gestured with the vicious little barrel. "Open your jacket. All right, now turn the pockets out." He saw that Ryan was unarmed, put the gun on the bed, and sat down beside it.

Ryan asked, "Well, what the hell do you want of me?"

He didn't get an answer. After thinking, and running his tongue around his small mouth, Battles said, "I hear you struck it rich."

"I hit a little pay streak. Enough for a vacation outside."

"You mean you left with twenty thousand and went broke in one winter?"

Ryan didn't like to be reminded. He thought of champagne and made a wry face. "I don't know as it's any of your affair. If you're here after what I got left, well, take it and be damned." He took out what he had, tossed it on the table—crumpled bills, small change, matches, and brass beer checks all mixed together.

Battles didn't more than glance at it. He sat forward, elbows on his thighs, a smile on his face that twisted his long, loose jaw to one side.

"Tell me why you came back."

He cried, "I came back because I was broke."

Battles picked up the gun. He cocked it and took aim at Ryan's forehead. "I never liked you, Ryan. I wouldn't mind killing you. Ever see anybody shot right between the eyes? It leaves a big, black hole like the burnt end of a cigar, and the back of your head—"

"Put the gun down!" It made Ryan sick, the gun, its deadly black muzzle, and Battles leering behind it.

"I'll put it down when you tell me what I want to know. You didn't come back because you were broke. You came back because old Dave Carson ran onto a cache just twice as big, and you thought maybe you'd get your hooks into it."

"So you're the one that's been after old Dave!"

Battles didn't answer. He sat with his lips twisted down, the gun aimed. "I'm going to count ten. You start talking. You tell me all about it. We'll see how much talking you can get done before I reach ten. If I think it's enough, you'll walk out of here alive. Otherwise—" He jiggled the gun hammer. "And don't forget to tell what it was Dave sent you down in Telaqua Bay."

"He sent me a telegram saying he didn't expect to live long, and now it's easy enough to see why."

Battles, counting slowly, reached four. "You better get to talking. *Five!*"

"I tell you—"

"What was that package he sent you? *Six!*"

"He sent me no package. If he did, I didn't receive it. I had him grubstaked on the Porcupine, and—"

"*Seven!*"

"Put the gun down, you damn fool! If you killed me, what then? What good would I be to you dead?"

"What good would you be alive unless you tell? If you were dead you wouldn't be running to the U.S. Marshal saying I was here. *Eight!* I'm waiting, Ryan. *Nine!*"

His finger had cocked on the trigger. The tension of his arm, telegraphing itself along the gun barrel, made a tiny tremble.

Ryan had turned hot and cold, sick and sweaty. But at *ten* the fear left him. He took a deep breath.

Beyond the gun Battles's eyes had been the eyes of a killer, but he didn't fire. He jerked back his head with a laugh and said, "You win, Ryan! You got guts, haven't you? You got more guts than I gave you credit for."

Ryan felt dizzy. His ears buzzed. Now that the danger was temporarily removed, he was hot and sweaty again. It was so hot he had a hard time getting air to breathe.

A sound at the door behind him made him gather his faculties.

Battles heard it too, and spoke, "Shorty?"

An unfamiliar, husky voice answered, "Yeah."

"Well, come in."

The door opened, admitting a small, graying man with perfect, fragile features. He seemed slightly jittery. He brought with him the whiskey smell of one who had practically lived on the stuff for weeks, months, even years.

"Well?" Shorty asked. "Find anything out?"

"No, but we will. Draw your gun, Shorty, and get behind him."

Shorty carried a Colt in a half-breed holster beneath his left armpit, hidden by his mackinaw. The holster had a spring mechanism designed to snap the gun upward when the catch was released, and Shorty almost lost it on the floor. He got it with a stab of his hand, and wheeled with it, aiming at Ryan's back. His finger was so hard on the trigger it rocked the double-acting hammer halfway back.

Ryan said, "Be careful."

Battles laughed. He said, "Stand up! Raise your hands!"

The ceiling was low, and Ryan's fingers almost brushed it.

"What was it that Carson sent you in Telaqua?"

"How many times do I have to say—"

Battles moved suddenly. He'd lowered the gun. Now he brought it around in a raking, backhand swing.

Ryan saw it too late and tried to weave aside. The gun hit him. The forward sight ripped him from the base of his jaw, across his cheek, the bridge of his nose.

It sent him staggering. For a second he forgot about Shorty, about the Colt aimed at his back. He caught himself after two half steps, and, arms lowered, started toward Battles. Battles was ready for him. He brought the gun back down, and clubbed him to the floor.

Ryan had no recollection of falling. He was just there, on hands and knees. The room spun around him.

"Get up!" he heard Battles say.

He got as far as his knees. Effort made him black out. Pain was a whirlpool inside his skull, behind his eyes. He could hear Battles's voice. It beat on his eardrums, but the words didn't get through to his brain.

Battles stood in front of him, his logger boots set wide. He lifted one of the boots. Ryan saw it coming. He was like a man in a nightmare whose muscles refuse to answer to his will. He couldn't move. The boot smashed him in the temple, driving him back against the wall.

"Where did he locate it?" Battles was asking for the third or fourth time.

"Locate—what?" Ryan shouted the words, "Locate what?"

Battles hissed, "Quiet or I'll kill you. Where did he locate the Stormwind gold?"

There was a thud of feet running along the hall. He tried to get to his feet. Shorty had his back turned, propping a chair under the doorknob. Ignoring the guns, Ryan lunged forward, but Battles met him and slugged him to the wall. He tried to cover up as Battles repeatedly drove his hobs to the side of his head.

II

Ryan was a long time coming awake. Finally he sat up. Somebody had placed a cold cloth over his face.

He said, with his tongue feeling thick, "Where am I?"

"Alaska," said Blind Tom at his elbow.

He managed to laugh. The sun was shining, just edging the horizon, coming through the smoky windowpane. It hurt his eyes. His neck hurt when he turned. All his teeth ached. They didn't mesh. He'd taken beatings before and it had been like that. His lower teeth weren't built in the same contour as his uppers, and they pained him at each uncomformity.

He got out of bed, finding a handhold on the bedpost until a wave of blackness left his brain. He looked at himself in the mirror. His face was lopsided, there were several deep welts oozing blood from his left earlobe to the bridge of his nose. Both cheeks and his right temple were pocked from hobs and turning purplish.

"Now there's a case of timberjack measles for you," he said. "That's the worst I've had since Big Louie Lamotte worked me over with an ox yoke down in Aberdeen."

"Who are they?" Tom asked.

"Bill Battles and some old fellow he called Shorty." He turned from the mirror and asked, "Is Tonka without the law these days?"

"There's Krause, the U.S. Commissioner."

"You didn't call him?"

"I didn't want to until you came around. It might be some private quarrel and—"

"Sure, Tom. That's just as well. I'm developing a certain fondness for the thought of taking care of this by myself."

His room had been ransacked, warsack emptied, things trod on, kicked to corners of the room. His money was still on the table, his Smith & Wesson was on the floor. They hadn't found what they were looking for, because, whatever it was, old Dave hadn't sent it. There'd only been the telegram.

A memory of something returned. Battles had asked a question about Stormwind. He repeated the word, "Stormwind."

Blind Tom, hearing him, said, "Now *you're* out looking for the Stormwind Cache are you, Ryan?"

That was it! He snapped his fingers at the memory. *The Stormwind Cache!*

Story of the cache dated back to the days of the first gold miners, before the Klondike rush. It was a legend, something that everyone talked about, and only half believed.

Four prospectors were supposed to have come down the Yukon from Circle City with a quarter-ton of gold. At that time, living in Unakitleet, was an outlaw colony of salmon and fur pirates. A group of twenty of these scoundrels had camped on the Yukon, and seeing the prospectors' bateau, they attacked. After an all-day, floating battle the prospectors escaped on shore near the Flattail Muskegs, and under cover of the short, summer night, tried to get out of sight in the scrub timber covering the Kuskokwim divide.

The pirates, however, picked up their trail and fell on them again near the headwaters of Stormwind Creek. This time, the prospectors were killed, but they had cached their gold, which was never found.

That was one of the stories. There were twenty others. For instance, he'd heard that one of the men had escaped and returned later to spend his life hunting fruitlessly for the cache; that one had crawled off to die in an Indian village; that he'd escaped and died behind the bars of the B.C. provincial asylum. Ryan could even recall some gaudy headlines a few years back when a convict at Walla Walla, claiming to be a Stormwind survivor, convinced a group of Seattle businessmen, who used their influence to gain his parole and subsequently took them for eight thousand dollars in a variation of the old Spanish Trunk racket.

He said, "Tom, do you think there's anything to that Stormwind story?"

The blind man laughed. "Well, maybe. But I'd rather go up to Circle and sluice my own quarter-ton of gold. It'd be easier that way."

Ryan saw no more of Battles. He stayed in town, recuperating from his beating, hoping that Dave Carson would learn he was there and show himself. When two days passed and no word of him, he went upriver to the mouth of the Comeluck, and thence up that swift silt-milky stream to Porcupine Flats. There an Aleut half-breed caught up with him, bringing the news Dave Carson's drowned body had been washed up on the rocks below Three Pillar Rapids.

He'd already been buried in the mission yard of St. Paul's five miles downstream when Ryan got there.

"I want the body exhumed," Ryan said.

His request angered the Jesuit. He stood, a big, thick-necked man, with his back to the wind and his cassock blowing around him, and said, "Nonsense, Ryan. I hate to turn a good Irishman down, but what good could it possibly do? The man was drowned. I'm not untrained at medicine, and—"

"I don't doubt your word he was drowned, but they did it. Look at my face. Look at the beating they handed me. Do you think they'd come around and work me over if they could still get to Dave? Whether they killed him or not, they at least knew he was dead when they came for me."

After some consideration, the Jesuit said, "Very well," and called to a couple of Siwash boys who were repairing the shake roof. In an hour their shovels revealed Dave in his rough board coffin.

He was dressed in the same sourdoughs, shirt and mackinaw he'd worn when he'd been washed up on the crags. Women at the mission had washed and pressed them, and put them back on him. His boots were still damp. They were heavy, ten-inch high-cuts.

Ryan pointed to them. "You see? He cracked up in no canoe. I've seen him go barefoot rather than injure a canoe with heavy heels."

Ryan searched him, felt the seams of his clothes, slitted his boot soles, taking them off a layer of leather at a time.

The Jesuit, watching him, said, "What were you looking for?"

"Just looking."

"A key?"

"Dave didn't own a lock, what would he do with a key?"

"I forgot to tell you, but there was a small, brass key inside the lining of his mackinaw. I thought it had slipped through his pocket."

Ryan sat beneath the mission's pole awning all afternoon, smoking, feeling the key in his pocket, trying to get from his mind the picture of Dave's drowned face.

Suddenly he cried, "Fort Baker! The Cudahay Company had some lockboxes there when they ran their express line. What ever happened to them?"

"Why, they're still there, if anybody wants to use them. In the store."

It was twilight, and Ryan had traveled all day. With muscles heavy from fatigue, he turned his canoe ashore and camped on a dry hummock among cottonwoods.

He built a fire, siwashed a salmon he'd bought earlier at an Indian fishwheel, and with midnight sun still hanging on the horizon, rolled up in his rabbitskin blanket to sleep.

He awoke suddenly and sat up. He didn't know what had awakened him.

The sun had slipped behind the mountain horizon for the nearest approach one had to night at that season. A luminous twilight reflected from the sky, the river.

He listened, ears straining. The river made a perpetual roar. There was a slight wind in the cottonwood branches. A coal popped in a dying fire, a whisky jack fluttered and chattered.

His hand, groping beneath the blanket, found the cold steel of the revolver. He felt better then. Holding the gun, he kicked the blanket aside, stood, and spent another three or four minutes listening.

He dressed, and circled, following the river shore for almost half a mile, looking for the impressions of feet in the mud. There was little chance anyone would approach his camp from the river, and apparently, no one had.

He laughed at himself and tried to escape the impression that someone was behind him in the timber watching each move he made. He'd traveled too hard of late. He hadn't been eating enough. He hadn't had the whisky an Irishman needed to keep him going in this country. And the sight of Dave Carson's drowned face had affected him more deeply than he thought.

Stretched in his blanket, thinking these things, he finally fell asleep. When he awoke, the first thing he noticed was a bright strand of hair, tangled in willow, blowing in the gentle breeze.

A spiderweb, he thought, knowing quite well that it wasn't. He pulled it free. It was a hair, almost black, about two feet long.

And while he stood, running the hair through his fingers, Sky-Noo's words came back—A white girl, with black hair and blue eyes.

He looked at his duffle. Nothing had been disturbed. His canoe was as it had been, bottom up on the shore. No sign of moccasin tracks. He tried to forget it, but felt someone watching, watching. . . .

There was no town at Baker, just the ruined army barracks overlooking the river from a high shoulder of ground, the long, log trading post, and half a dozen driftwood shanties occupied by a branch of the Dogrib tribe from the hill country to the north.

It had been three years since Ryan had come down from his claim on Porcupine, so he had to spend some time renewing acquaintances with the proprietor, a huge, filthy man known as Swede Nels.

He dropped the key on the counter and said, "I think Dave left something here."

Nels said, "Yah, sure," and without hesitation started stacking aside sack after sack of dog meal to get at some old-fashioned express lockboxes. "By golly, Ay almost forgot. Dave did come in har and put something away."

"When was he here?"

"Couple month ago. Maybe only sax weeks. There bane plenty snow for sled runner, Ay know that much."

"Mushed down?"

"Yah."

Nels kept trying the key in one lock after another until he

found one that it fit. The lockbox contained something in an old brown paper sack. Nels tossed it over to him.

"He left that old Nanuck dog of his. Sore foot. You can pick her up if you like. Charge you two dollar for feed." Nels didn't seem to attach much importance to the package. He said, "So old Dave bane dead and gone. By yimminy, that's hell."

Ryan looked at the sack. His fingers trembled a little. It wasn't like him to lose nerve. He wanted to rip the package open and see what was inside, but there was an Indian, a stranger, in the big trade room, so he checked himself.

To make an excuse he said, "I'll take a look at that malamute," and went outside.

He walked to the dog pens, opened the sack, and pulled out its contents. There was a single article—a piece of squaw beadwork. He unfolded it, a strip of soft-rubbed buckskin, looked at one side and then the other. He'd expected a message. He could see none. He turned the sack inside out. Nothing there either.

He felt disappointed and let down. He stood by the dog pens, folding and unfolding the beaded strip, wondering if Sky-noo hadn't been right about Dave after all. This thing was a masterpiece of the beadworker's art, worth maybe twenty dollars at the curio stores down at Cook Inlet, but it was nothing a sane man would carry down from Porcupine and lock in an express box.

It seemed to be very old. The buckskin had almost lost its Injun-smoke odor, it was browned and turned rather crystalline from age. Apparently it had never been worn. It was a belt, or a collar-piece, about as long as his arm, four inches wide in the center and tapering to half that width at the ends, which were fitted with tie strings of pliant caribou tendon. The front was a solid mass of beads, a pale blue background worked with figures symbolical of men, animals, canoes, trees, and igloos in red, purple and orange.

Finally he rolled it up and thrust it in his pocket. That last winter of loneliness had done it. Dave had gone crazy trying to find the long end of a square quilt, as the saying went.

Ryan sat at Swede Nels's big, rough-board table, eating lutefisk and drinking home brew. The Swede was half drunk, as he'd been off and on for two days. In the background, moving quietly, keeping more home brew ready, was Nels's wife, a full-blood Aleut from Kulakak Bay.

For what must have been an hour, with no pause except to pour more home brew down his throat, Nels had recounted his adventures in the harvest fields of "Noord Dakota." Then, while taking apart Fargo board for board, he forgot his story and got to bellowing the interminable verses of a song, each alternate stanza of which ended in the words,

> *"Yah, Yah! Vat skal ve ha?*
> *Olga on a buggyride, Yah, yah, yah!"*

Ryan finally got up and went outside. It still frosted each night, and the cold felt good to him. He didn't want to stay there any longer, but he didn't know which way to turn.

The piece of beadwork made a lump in his hip pocket. For the twentieth time that day he took it out to examine it. The sun had set, but enough light remained in the sky for him to make out the intricate bead tracings.

He kept walking, paying little attention to his destination until he was stopped by a heap of fence rails near the malamute pens. One old gray and tan, with his forepaws on the wire, high as a man's head, was barking with his fangs peeled back.

It surprised Ryan, for the malamute had seen him enough to grow used to him.

Suddenly he realized that there was someone else, moving, in the shadow behind him.

He turned with his hand dropping instinctively to the Smith & Wesson. Then he saw the gleam of a gun barrel aimed at him, and a girl's voice spoke:

"Don't try anything. Don't try to call. I have a gun aimed at your heart. I wouldn't hesitate to shoot."

He recovered himself enough to laugh, but not enough to put his heart behind it. "I'll wager you wouldn't, girl. And what do I have that you could want?"

"That thing in your hand."

"This?"

"Yes. The girdle. I'll take it."

Her words hit him like a blow between the eyes. He'd been a fool. His mind had been on the girdles he'd seen pictured in catalogs, but this Indian belt could be a girdle too.

"Give it to me!" she hissed.

"Why, sure, girl." He turned with it, holding it at arm's length, hoping she would step forward to take it. She wasn't tempted. She stood crouched forward, intent, like a spring drawn and triggered.

"Bring it here!"

He moved slowly, and with a change of position he had a better view of her.

She was a slim girl, no more than an inch or so over five feet. She had small, excellently cut features. No Indian blood. Her skin, for that country, was very light. She was dressed in high moccasins. White wool sox folded down below the knees gave her calves a stocky appearance. She wore a buckskin skirt and jacket. On her head was a mackinaw wool cap. Her dark hair had been plaited and wrapped in a coil, but it was too luxuriant to remain hidden, and the cap gave the appearance of perching atop of it. Her eyes might have been blue, but in the half-light they seemed black.

She was excited and fighting to keep the excitement down. Ryan could tell that by her rapid breathing, by the way she kept biting down on her lip.

"Girl," he said, "you're welcome to the thing. But tell me, what are you doing, a girl like you, traveling with the kind you are? What would a young girl like you be doing with robbery and murder?"

She cried in sudden, angry defense, "I have nothing to do with murder!"

"Then you wouldn't pull the trigger?"

"Toss it here!"

The gun was clenched too tightly, her finger too hard on the trigger. He didn't want to push his luck.

"All right, catch it."

He tossed the rolled-up squaw girdle, intentionally a trifle to her right. She might try to reach and catch it, and in that case the gun might be turned for a second, giving him his chance. She didn't move. It struck the ground behind her, a yard or more to her right.

She did not change hands with the gun. She didn't try to bend and reach around with her left. She backed, with the gun still aimed, came around it until it was in front of her, then she crouched and picked it up.

He said, "It's a small thing, the girdle, but still it's robbery at gunpoint. There is nothing for me to do now except get the United States marshal and run you down."

She laughed at him and tossed her head back. "You're not scaring me! What United States marshal would hunt down a girl for taking such a thing?"

It was true. He'd be laughed out of Alaska.

She backed around until she was on the river side. The malamute had stopped barking, and now he started again. There was a gate to the dog pens, held on the outside by a prop-pole. With a heel he felt the prop-pole behind him, and was tempted to drop the gate and let the dog loose on her. The animal, savage as he sounded, wouldn't actually attack her, but he'd get her turned away with the gun.

Ryan hesitated, and took his foot away. Capturing her would do no good. He couldn't keep her prisoner, he couldn't turn her over to the law.

She shouted to be heard over the dog frenzy. "Don't move!

I can see you all the way from the river. I'll shoot if you try to follow me."

She moved backward, over hummocky moss and stones. A canoe had been pulled in to shore among some flooded willows. At fifty yeards, she turned, and watching back across her shoulder, ran to it. Ryan could have drawn, and with the .38, blasted the canoe bottom out.

Now, thinking clearly for the first time in days, he knew it would do him no good to get the girdle back. He had no idea what value it had. It would be better to let her have it, and follow her. That would be the tough part, following her, not letting her get away along those trackless rivers of the North.

He watched her slide the canoe from the willows, leap in, and crouching, drive the paddle with sharp strength and skill that sent the craft, light as bubble, into the current, holding a level course across and downstream.

He ran to the trading house. Swede Nels, beating the table with his fists, was bellowing out another ballad.

Ryan threw his duffle together and was outside in a quarter-minute. The canoe was a shadow strip near the far bank. He launched his own canoe, then, not wanting her to know she was being followed, he waited for what seemed to be a long time as she approached the downstream bend.

III

For the first few miles it was quite dark, with a few stars out, then the sun edged upward, spreading a rose-colored dawn over the water. The girl was far ahead. Driftlogs made it impossible to spot her canoe, but occasionally his eyes caught the sun-flash of her paddle.

He kept catching brief glimpses of her until it was noon, and he'd passed the mouth of the Hsluika, a swift, treacherous stream flowing down from the hill country to the north.

Beaching his canoe, he climbed a promontory and looked

both ways along miles of river flowing between great, barren banks. To the south, the country rolled away in vast undulations toward the Ahklun Mountains, to the north lay the sharply dissected pine and rock country of Porcupine Ridge and the Stormwinds.

No sign of the canoe. Thought that she had pulled up to rest along one of the cottonwood-studded banks made him wait, rolling and smoking one cigarette after another, fighting down a natural impatience.

No sign of her. She had turned off at the Hsluika.

Ryan was a good man with a canoe, taller than he looked, with a strength that gave him a long-reaching power on the paddle, but still the booming stream repeatedly fought him to a standstill. He was forced to use a pikepole; he went ahead with the babiche line, towing it past riffles and rapids, wading waist deep in the icy flood.

Through wet-slick moccasins the rocks of the river bruised his feet. His body ached from the cold water. He kept driving on and on, expecting her around each sharp turn of the canyon walls, but she was never there. At last, with the sun at the jagged horizon, he fell face down among the rocks on shore and rested.

He was protected from the wind that blew a chilling blast on his wet clothes, but after an hour he was forced to get up and rub circulation into his muscles. He ate half of the smoked salmon he'd brought along, put the rest away for next day, and went on.

He kept cursing through his teeth. He was a fool. He should turn back. The girl had tricked him. No girl could battle this Hsluika and keep ahead of him. She'd hidden on shore, watched him go past, and now she was gone, swallowed by the vastness of the North.

He pulled ashore, climbed a steep shoulder of rock from which he could see stretches of the river for several miles.

He glimpsed it there, the canoe, riding with corklike buoyancy, while the girl, maneuvering it this way and that, utilized every crosscurrent to move upstream, skirting crags by the merest breadth, finding clearance along shore where Ryan, with his greater weight, would force a canoe down and rip its bottom out.

Tired as he was, he laughed and shook his head. By the great gods of the North, how she could handle a canoe!

Darkness in the canyon made him stop. He built a fire, dried himself, and slept for a couple of hours.

He ate. He had enough food left for one meal. Wind carried an odor of woodsmoke. Two hours later he found the drenched embers of a fire under a sheltering bank. He placed his hand on them. The charcoal was cold, the rocks beneath barely warm. She'd been gone more than an hour.

He no longer kept track of time. He fought the river until fatigue drugged him. He fell on the bank to rest, and then fought it some more. It came night, he ate the last of his food. His blanket was watersoaked. He sat between a fire and the reflecting face of a cliff, dozing, jerking awake to listen to the close howling of wolves.

At midmorning, in the narrowing canyon, he found a series of steplike waterfalls blocking his way.

There again he saw the blackened embers of the fire. He looked at them with fatigue-dulled eyes, and suddenly jerked erect as he saw a thin veil of steam rising from them. They had been drenched only a few minutes before.

He crouched with misty cold spray of the cascades drifting over him and looked around. She'd seen him approaching. She might be waiting behind rocks or scrub spruce just above, gun ready.

No sign of her canoe. She'd cached it downstream, and come on afoot.

There was a portage trail along cliffs and rock banks to the right. A steep trail, a switchback trail, a mountain goat trail.

Working swiftly, he made a wolf pack of rifle, ammunition,

blanket, and extra clothing. It seemed like nothing after portaging the canoe.

He climbed. The footpath made a series of close switchbacks until it gained an elevation somewhat higher than the crest of the cataracts, then it followed a contour of the side. It still wasn't an easy trail. A man had to watch for footing, steplike up and down, often with footholds barely wider than his outspread hand, with the river vertically below, churning itself to a white froth.

A bullet pinged against rock and screamed away with a clap of explosion following it.

Instinctively he went to one knee. He found partial protection behind a bulge of stone. His hand went over his shoulder, pulling the rifle free of his pack.

Two hundred yards away, beyond a jagged rock shoulder, a puff of powder smoke had appeared.

There was a second squirt of smoke. The bullet hit an instant later. Above him, so close it showered him with stinging bits of rock and left an odor like burned sulfur.

He tossed the rifle to his shoulder, aimed high of her position, pulled the trigger. It was a .35 Winchester, a moose gun, a grizzly gun. Its 250-grain slug kicked a shower of rock and spruce litter about three feet above her head. It made her flinch so her third shot was far wide.

He fired once more, aiming at the same spot, then he lunged to his feet, was exposed for three perilous steps along the cliff, and with a leaping dive, found cover in a narrow crevice filled with twisted spruce roots and wedged-in slide rock.

He half stood, half lay on his side, boots anchored, and got his breath. There was just room enough in the crevice to hide him. He could feel both its walls when he breathed. Bullets screamed down, struck repeatedly within a foot of his head, showering him with stone as they glanced away.

He laughed. "Ryan," he said, "what a woman you picked!"

He rolled a cigarette of sodden paper, with sodden tobacco. The cover of his match can had worked loose, and the matches were crumbly from dampness.

He cursed, tore the cigarette open, chewed the tobacco like snooce beneath his lip.

The shooting stopped, but still he didn't show himself. Carefully, feeling for each foothold, he climbed, using the crevice for protection until he reached the fringe of spruce timber high on the mountain side of the canyon.

He glimpsed her then, a mile away, traveling swiftly through the big timber of the bottom.

Ryan stayed with the high country and kept her in sight, watching her leave false trail, double back, hunt the rocky going, and leave false trail again.

Yes, Ryan, there was a *woman*. Clever as a cross fox.

She left the valley, crossed the narrow ridge of Hsluika Divide.

Beyond Hsluika a wild pattern of gulches fanned into muskeg which still held the frost of winter a few inches beneath the surface.

He bound the driftwood trunks of cottonwoods together and crossed a currentless stream. Here again was hill country covered by jacktimber.

He caught an odor of woodsmoke. Trails laced the hillsides. The benches and bottoms were pockmarked by old placer diggings.

These, he knew, were the old Mucker diggings, discovered back in 1902 by men moving through Alaska from the Klondike diggings. Now Mucker was an outlaw town, reputedly the home of half the sluice robbers and fur theives of the Yukon.

From high along a ridge he looked down on the town.

It had once boasted more than a hundred houses, but now all except seventeen or eighteen lay in ruins, or had disappeared with only their sill logs to show where they had stood. One, a long, narrow building, had the appearance of a trading post. There was a creek which joined a river about two miles below town. It was the same river he'd crossed earlier that day, only larger now, swifter. At one time there'd been another settlement there, but now all that remained was a ramshackle boathouse. The only movement he saw was a man over there, puttering around an upended canoe.

Twilight settled as he descended, hunting concealment among the bench diggings. He stopped behind a dog shed about fifty steps from the long, log building.

The odor of food struck his nostrils, and left him momentarily weak.

He dropped his pack and rifle. Malamutes were barking at him, but he paid no attention. He crossed to the house, stopped outside, listened. Men's voices came from the deep interior.

Candlelight shone amber through some parchment windows. He started around to listen, but a man was coming, and he quickly concealed himself in the shadow of a storm shed that was built against the back door.

The man was familiar. Bill Battles!

Hatred made him start forward, but he checked himself. Now wasn't the time.

Battles went past so close Ryan could smell the tobacco smoke that clung to his clothes, and disappeared inside the house.

Ryan waited. He was sure Battles had gone on to the distant, lighted room. Through the open storm-shed door he could dimly see a kitchen, the teeth of ruddy light glowing through the open draft of a cookstove.

He walked in. He could hear Battles's voice, and her voice. He knew she'd come there, but it made him curse anyway. She was so young and pretty—he didn't like the thought of her coming to Battles.

He wolfed some left-over pancakes. A big, iron pot of squaw mulligan bubbled on the stove. He dipped some in a tin plate, ate, spearing huge chunks of caribou with his hunting knife.

With the edge off his hunger, he paid attention to the voices.

Battles seemed to be in high humor, saying, "I'd liked to have seen his ugly Irish face when you took it."

He could hear the whisky-hoarse voice of Shorty, and the girl was laughing. She seemed to be slightly hysterical. Hunger and fatigue had left her that way.

"Len," Battles said. "You'd better have a little more to eat. You wait. I'll get it for you."

That was her name, *Len*.

Ryan put his dipper of stew aside and stood with his shoulders high, his fists doubled. It would be a pleasure to smash Battles's teeth down his throat when he walked through the door. Then reluctantly he decided to stay quiet. There was no use of kicking things over now just when he was on the verge of learning what he wanted to know.

He hunkered behind the table as Battles walked in. The man was so close he could have thrust a leg beneath the table and touched him. His back was turned. He took a lid off the stove for illumination. Firelight struck him strongly, turning his face to yellowish copper, bringing out its hard lines, the long jaw, the small mouth.

He filled a dish and, without once looking toward Ryan, went out, leaving the damp wool and tobacco odor of his clothes behind.

It went against Ryan's nature to hide. He stood up, cursing him, stabbing chunks of meat with his hunting knife, carrying them to his mouth. Finished, he listened.

Shorty said something about beadwork, and he knew they were examining the girdle. He stood close to the door, but only stray groups of words reached him.

He could hear from the intervening room, but it was too light, and it offered no place for concealment. He considered going outside, listening with an ear to the parchment window, but he gave that up, too.

His roving eyes fell on a four-rung, pole ladder that had been nailed to the kitchen's inner wall. It led to a small loft between the rafters and the roof poles.

He climbed, crawled over some bundled, mildewed hides, and stopped on one knee to get dust and cobwebs out of his mouth and nasal passages.

There wasn't room for a man to stand upright. Even on one knee, his head was bent against the ceiling. It was so warm that sweat rolled off him. Six poles had been laid side by side down the middle, across the rafters. Heavy, gray building paper had been tacked on the undersides of the rafters to form a ceiling, but it had been punctured here and there, and shafts of light from the candle gave a fair illumination.

He edged forward, stopping when the voices lowered, starting again when they were raised, or when someone laughed. It had been a long time since the footpoles had supported anyone. One of them settled with a slight thud. He remained very still. The voices had stopped. Dust rose in a cloud. He wanted to sneeze and cough. He set his teeth, held his breath. Tears streamed from his eyes. They were talking again now.

For the moment he gave up trying to get closer. He lay on his stomach and listened.

The girl had called someone "Uncle Mal." It was Shorty's whisky-hoarse voice that answered her. He should have guessed before that they were related. They had the same broad foreheads, the same sharply cut features.

"He'd want it that way," Shorty was saying. "You can't worry about such things. When you fight a wolf's fight, you have to use a wolf's weapons. Anyhow, nothing will come of it. We'll register this as newly mined gold, and who is there to prove that it isn't?"

Battles laughed, saying, "Well, we're going to dig it out of the ground. Isn't that mining it?"

She said, "You sound as though we had it already."

"We're closer than you think." There was a pause. Battles had looked at his watch. Ryan could hear the snap as he closed the case. "It's been better than an hour. That breed should have been here ten minutes ago."

She asked, "Where was he?"

"At the Siwash camp. Drunk again."

"Where do they get the liquor to stay drunk all the time?"

"Make it out of the spuds old Hakteel raised."

Shorty said, "I could use a few drops myself."

"Uncle!"

He cried, "Damn it, quit ragging me! Who are you to be bossing me around?" She didn't answer, so he said, "Anyhow, I'm only taking a drop. I said I was cutting down, and I am. A man can't just cut himself off like that."

Ryan could hear the squeak of a cork, the sound of little movements. Several minutes passed. Finally Battles said:

"I think I could decipher this myself if I had the time." He was evidently examining the girdle. Ryan wanted to creep a trifle further but he didn't. He lay still. "You see that, Len? That's the Siwash figure for *nas-gin-ax-gan*—three men. And those marks indicate the time of day. That's *ga-gan* or the sun, those indicate the length of shadows, and that the day of the year. I've decided that's how the old squaw established her direction to the cache—through sunset on a certain day of the year."

She said, "The day the gold was buried?"

"I suppose."

"What day was it? I mean, what time of year?"

"Late July, I'd imagine, or August. That's just a guess, but their placer muck wouldn't thaw up in Circle until mid-June, and it would take them anyhow three weeks to sluice it and clean up. Then they'd have to paddle all this distance down the Yukon. Don't worry, Len. We'll figure this out." Something told Ryan that he'd laid his hand on the girl's arm. "Sure. We'll have it out of the ground and be on our way to Seattle before snow flies. Seattle, Len! I'm going to enjoy showing you that town. Then San Francisco, Los Angeles, maybe the East Coast. There's no limit what we can do with that kind of money!"

The pieces all fit. According to the most commonly told story, the four prospectors had been attacked near the headwaters of Stormwind Creek. Three had been killed while a fourth escaped, wounded, to a Siwash village. Ryan could put the rest together. A squaw had hidden the wounded man from his pursuers, and he'd died there after giving her the location of the cache. Squaw-fashion, this information had been worked in the bead pattern of the girdle.

And finally Dave had got hold of it! He grinned and thought, The old philanderer! He'd heard many tales dating to Dave's younger days telling of his prowess among the squaws.

He lay, listened to them talk of small things, move impatiently, walk repeatedly to the door to watch for the breed's arrival.

"There he is now," Battles said.

Two men in moccasins, by the sound. Someone spoke a low word or two in an Indian tongue. They walked through, and Battles spoke, calling them "Steve" and "Hakteel."

"Ha, yes!" the one called Steve cried out. "Here, let me look at it. Yes, that is it. I have seen it hanging on the medicine stick in my mother's wickiup ten hundred times, and she would never let me touch it, I didn't know why. This is it, then. See, Hakteel? What you think of beadwork? Ol' mama damn good, no?"

There was quiet. Evidently Hakteel had the girdle and was trying to decipher it.

"*Ked-jin-qua,*" he said over a couple of times.

Battles asked, "What does he mean?"

"A hundred," the breed answered.

"A hundred what?"

Hakteel muttered, "No savvy. Very hard savvy. You give drink whisky maybe Hakteel savvy."

Battles laughed, said, "I should break your neck," but there was a squeak of the cork, and Hakteel's cough and inhalation after the drink.

"You see? Sharp mountain. You know sharp mountain?"

"Which direction from Stormwind?"

"Like so. Look. Like so."

Ryan could tell nothing from the conversation. He rose on hands and knees, slid forward little by little. There was a tear in the building paper about four feet distant. Finally he reached it, bent his head far down between the rafters, and he could see them below. They were hunched over the table: Hakteel, an old, ragged Siwash, pointing to some feature of the beadwork with a fingernail that looked white as a bit of clam shell on the end of his filthy, black finger; Steve, a tall, lean half-breed of thirty with a deeply scarred right cheek and little pewter rings in his ears; Battles on the other side of the table with Shorty trying to see over his shoulder. He couldn't see the girl.

They kept talking, with Hakteel explaining things in the Tlingit jargon.

Suddenly he noticed that Shorty was looking directly up at him.

He checked the impulse to draw back. He remained as he was, not making the slightest move. It seemed that more than a minute passed, then Shorty turned suddenly and rubbed his forehead as though it pained him.

Ryan slid back. He didn't want to be cornered there. From below, he could hear Battles coughing. He realized that his movement had started dust to sifting through the air.

"What the hell?" wheezed Battles.

Steve said, "You need a drink. All of us need a drink. How about it, Shorty, you need a drink?"

Ryan stood in a crouch, climbed over the bundles of pelts, located the top rung of the ladder, descended to the kitchen.

He glanced around. The kitchen seemed to be empty. He moved past the table with long strides, through the storm shed, and took a deep breath of the cold, outside air.

"Don't move!" said the girl's voice behind him.

IV

He stood stiffly erect. By tilting his head back slightly, he was able to see her moving from shadow at the rear of the shed. Night twilight, coming through the slight mist, gleamed on the gun in her hand.

"So you got here!" she said.

He managed to laugh. "You were the clever one with all that backtrailing, but I had a balcony seat to it all."

"What do you mean?"

"I was at timberline on the ridge, watching every step you took."

"Maybe you were too clever!"

"Now, what do you mean by that?" He looked at the gun. "Oh, I see. You mean your friends will kill me like they did poor Dave Carson."

He remembered her sharp reaction to the charge of murder at Baker. It had a similar effect now.

"We never killed him."

"Oh, but you did. They did."

"What proof do you have?"

"His body showed up drowned in the river below Three Pillars. Drowned with hobnails on. Dave would never use hobs in a canoe."

Her lips curled. "What proof is that?"

"They killed him, girl. It's true as I'm standing here, they killed him. Then they came for me. They were after the girdle. They were waiting in the dark at my room in Blind

Tom's Hotel. Look at my face. See the marks on it. See where Battles beat me while that man they call Shorty held a gun in my back."

"You're lying!"

"No, I am not lying. Look me in the eye and say what kind of men you have joined up with."

Her teeth were clenched. She was listening. Men were talking. Unfamiliar voices coming toward the front of the house. Others in that outlaw valley were probably in on the plot. And there was another sound—a man coming heavily through the house.

With a tightening of his muscles, Ryan realized it was Battles.

"Get back!" she whispered.

He moved into the shadow, but not so far but what he could see Battles in the door. Battles hesitated and said:

"Oh, it's you, Len. I thought I heard something. Why the gun?"

"You surprised me." She put it away.

"This thing's got you jumpy. There's nothing to worry about now. Nobody would come here. Not even a fool like Ryan. You better go back to the cabin and get some rest."

"All right."

"I'll see you later," he said, and turned away.

She called to him, "Bill, will you tell Uncle Mal to come right over? I want to talk with him."

"I'll keep him away from the bottle if that's—"

"Send him over."

She'd drawn the gun again, and Ryan laughed at her. "You're being foolish. There was nothing to stop me drawing on you a moment ago."

She stood with it aimed for a few seconds, then with a nervous movement she stabbed it back in the holster.

"All right. Maybe you want to come to the cabin with me. Maybe you want to accuse him of it face to face."

"Sure. We'll do it any way you like. And we'll get the truth of it, and what then?"

She walked beside him without answering. He knew that she hadn't decided herself.

The cabin was dark save for a slight glow that came from a low-burned fire in the stove.

They went in together, she closed the door. He could hear her moving around, blanketing a window. Then she lighted a candle from the stove.

It had been twilight when he faced her before, this was his first good look at her.

She seemed even prettier. Smaller. Her hair, escaping the cap, fell into thick coils over her shoulders. Candlelight raised a play of color from the strands. It was dark brown but not black. Her eyes were blue, unusually dark, a midnight shade. Excitement had brought a slight flush to her cheeks. Her lips were parted. She kept touching her tongue to them, biting her lower lip with her small, white teeth. Her buckskin skirt was cinched more tightly; it revealed her slim waist, accentuated the soft curves of her body.

She said, "We might as well sit down. He might not even come. He hates me because of the liquor. He ought to know I do it for his own good."

"We drinking men are that way," Ryan said cheerfully, and grinned, showing his two gold teeth. He spoke her name, "Len? Is that it?"

"You were up there eaves-dropping?"

He looked at the dust-coated front of his mackinaw and pants. "I'm in no condition to deny it."

"What did you hear?"

"I heard that your name was Len. Len what?"

"Len Darrel."

It surprised him that she'd answered. "I've heard of no white girl being at Mucker. Where did you come from?"

"Don't try to find out any more. It'll do you no good."

A man's boots thudded the planks outside and she got quickly to her feet.

"Uncle Mal?"

"Yes."

"Come in."

He opened the door, came in, started to close it behind him. Then he saw Ryan. He blinked a few times. He'd had too much to drink; he'd had too much to drink every day for months, and it had deadened his reflexes.

"Close the door!" she said sharply.

Ryan knew by the dart of the man's eyes that he was afraid of the girl.

He said, "You, Ryan! What the hell are you—" He checked himself. Ryan guessed why. He didn't want Len to know they'd ever met.

She said, "How'd you happen to know who he was?"

"I guessed. After you told about him chasing you—"

"And after all that you thought it would be natural he'd be here in the cabin with me? Tell me the truth! You met before?" She waited for him to answer. "Did you? Did you meet him before?"

He seemed to be baffled. He weaved his head from side to side.

She said, "You waited in the hotel room at Moyukuk and tortured him."

He kept shaking his head. He was afraid of the girl. Ryan had seen fear like his in the eyes of a trapped wolf. A fear mixed with hatred.

She cried, "How did the old prospector die? You went to Porcupine and followed him down to the rapids, didn't you? You found him camped there. You killed him."

"No! Damn it, quit shouting at me. I ain't going to take it any longer—"

She reached and grabbed a coiled dog whip from a peg on the wall. He started back as the lash snaked across the room and came to a stop with a crack like a rifle shot.

He tossed both hands up. There was a stool back of his legs. It tripped him. He sprawled to the floor, hands in front of his face.

"Lie to me?" She was a master with the lash. It cracked above his head so closely it riffled his hair. It terrified him without striking him.

He whimpered, "I'll tell you the truth. Yes, we waited for him in the hotel room. Battles and me. It wasn't my doing, though. It was Battles. I couldn't—"

"How about the prospector?"

He crawled off, shaking his head, got halfway to his feet, back braced against the log wall. He twisted aside as the lash came once more, powdering a bit of mud chinking near his cheek.

"We followed him down to the rapids. He was camped there. Battles said we'd talk to him. Them was his words. I didn't know what he had on his mind. I didn't know he intended to scorch it out of him."

"You mean you tortured him?"

"He was going to. Battles. He was going to make him tell where the girdle was. *He can make it easy or tough on himself,* those were Battles's words. Listen, Len, I tried to get him not to. I said it wasn't like a white man to treat another white man like that. Battles threatened to serve me the same way. So I sneaked around and cut him loose. But it was a mistake. Carson made a run for it and Battles hit him with a pikepole. We tried to bring him to, but it wasn't any use, so we put him in his canoe and turned him loose in the rapids. We didn't think he'd be found. Anyhow we didn't think they'd guess but what he got swamped trying the shoot the rapids."

She looked at her uncle as though she hated him. With her lips drawn to a tight line she said, "You bushwhacker!"

"It wasn't my fault." The experience had left him so weak and shaky he could barely stand. "I got to have a drink."

She turned her back, and he found the whisky bottle, took a huge drink, and stood shuddering like a man getting chill out of his body. He kept looking at her. His weren't the eyes of a whipped dog. They were the eyes of a whipped wolf, filled with craftiness and hatred.

He whispered, "Don't let Battles know I told you. He'd kill me, Len. He'd—"

"I won't tell him."

She hung the dog whip back on its peg. She drew her revolver, a .32 Colt, put it back again. She opened a drawer, got out a box of fifty cartridges, dropped them in her jacket pocket.

Her uncle kept looking back and forth between her and Ryan. "What are you going to do?"

"I don't know." She motioned, indicating the other room of the cabin—a bedroom, evidently her own. "Stay in there."

He went in and closed the door. Ryan could hear the creak of a bunk as he lay down.

She said, "All right!" to Ryan, and he followed her outside.

She had stopped him with a press of her shoulder, and he stood looking down at her. It gave him a strange, almost giddy feeling to have her so close. Her shoulder, under the buckskin, seemed to be very frail and soft. He could feel the small movement of her body.

She said, looking up at him, "The girdle is mine, you know!"

"Tell me about it."

"My father bought it. From that half-breed."

"From Steve?"

"Yes. His mother made it. It was a guide to lead him to the Stormwind Cache. But probably you knew all that."

"I'm finding things out. How did she know about the cache?"

"There was one survivor. His name was Regan or Rogan. He crawled there, to Chatna village, and she hid him. He remained there for several years, a cripple, sick most of the time. Finally he died, but he told how to find the cache, and she wove it into the girdle intending to give the secret to their son."

"She had a son by Rogan?"

"That half-breed is their son. Steve."

"Well, what happened? What stopped him from getting it?"

"He was a troublemaker. They drove him away from the village when he was only twelve or thirteen. He wandered the gold camps. He was in jail for robbery at Sitka, and he killed another half-breed at Nome. He didn't know about the treasure until after his mother died and old Hakteel told him. At that time he was at Pavel Mission where my father was a fur trader. He owed my father better than seven hundred dollars. One day Battles and my uncle came around and talked my father into buying a two-thirds interest on the girdle for that seven hundred and a thousand besides.

"That was last autumn. My dad was sick. He'd been sick off and on for years. He signed his interest in the girdle over to me before he died. I didn't know which way to turn. I knew I coudln't run down the cache by myself. So my uncle and Battles came with me on shares. I guess you know the rest. When we reached Chatna village the girdle was gone. He'd taken it. Your partner."

"There's one thing you've forgotten. She never did give it to her son. Maybe she did give it to Dave."

"You have no proof of that! She made it for her—"

"Girl!" He took her by the shoulders and lifted her toes off the ground while turning her so she faced him. "There's no point in us arguing about it. The point is that neither of us has the girdle. It's in the hands of a killer, as you know. Let's face the real fact. According to the law of the North it belongs to nobody and everybody. The treasure belongs to the one who finds it."

She didn't try to escape from his grasp. She seemed to be glad he was there. She was tired of fighting the lone fight. She needed someone to lean against. Ryan liked to think that. He liked the press of her young body against him, he liked the slight, sliding movements of her smooth skin under the buckskin blouse as she breathed.

Finally, with a firm shove of her hands, she pushed away. "We can't delay. I don't know what my uncle will do. If we get the thing, we'll have to get it now.

"Sure, girl."

He drew his .38, broke it, checked on the loads, snapped it shut again. Two hundred yards away, distorted by the night mist, he could see the glowing, parchment windows of the long, log house.

"I'll go down and get it, girl."

"No. You wouldn't have a chance. Dunhill and Williams are probably there. Both of them are dangerous. Dunhill killed a man once over at Shaktolik."

He was reluctant, unconvinced. "How do you intend to get it?"

She smiled a trifle and said, "I got it from you after Battles failed."

They walked together, and stopped at the rear of the house. A mutter of voices came from inside. They could hear Battles and the loud, obscene bellowing laugh of Steve.

She said, "Nulato Bob is there too."

"Who's he?"

"A quarter-breed. A boat builder." She smiled up at him and whispered, "He built that canoe you couldn't catch." Then, moving inside the storm shed, "You'll wait there?"

"For how long? There's less than an hour of darkness left."

"If I'm that long, go back to the house. Keep an eye on uncle. See to it he stays there."

Her uncle had a gun. Ryan wondered what he'd do if the man decided to use it. He didn't want to kill him—not her uncle.

He rolled a cigarette of damp paper and tobacco, felt by habit for his match can. The matches were crumbly and he didn't dare light one anyway. He dry smoked and waited.

V

The night was very quiet. Malamutes kept moving around inside the wire pens, but they were used to his scent now, and they didn't create a commotion. From a great distance across the benches, someone was playing a concertina.

The tune momentarily reminded him of Nels Jonsrud's song, and he sang the words under his breath.

> *"Yah, yah, vat skal ve ha?*
> *Olga on a buggyride, yah, yah, yah."*

Len! There was a girl for a buggyride.

He kept hearing their voices from inside. Len only had a few words to say. Usually it was Battles or the breed. It was especially easy to hear the breed. Sometimes whole sentences came through.

There was a slight sound from the night behind him, and Ryan spun, whipping the gun out with a reflex movement of his hand.

He could see no one. It had been a packrat, a night bird, or just his over-taut nerves. He was too much on edge. He'd traveled too long without sleep.

He put the gun away. Then he heard it again. This time he had no doubt. It had been a man, the light whisper of moccasins across the ground.

He circled the building. He had a glimpse of someone just disappearing around the front corner. It was her uncle.

He ran, covering the distance with long, silent strides. The man wasn't there. He'd already gone through the front door.

He felt slightly sick. He wondered what the man had on his mind. He hated and feared his niece, but with Battles there he'd fear her no longer.

He was undecided. He stood by the door, listened. There was light around it. No one in that front room. He pulled the babiche latchstring, lifted the door to keep it from scraping, opened it three or four inches.

Now he could hear them, Shorty, Battles and the girl. Their voices were upraised. The breed shouted something, and the girl cried, "Stand back!"

There was a scramble, a crash of overturning furniture, and the light went out.

Ryan ran through the front room, found a second door, went through it.

The struggle was all around him. A shot laced the blackness with flaming powder. The girl screamed. He knew it was she who had fired, that someone was trying to hold her.

The gun crashed again, again.

"Len!" he cried. "Len!"

A gun exploded in his face. It left him deaf. He'd lost his sense of direction. He resisted the impulse to fire. He kept going, trod over someone who was just getting to his feet.

He caught the scent of sweat and Indian-tanned buckskin. The man grappled with him, and Ryan smashed him down.

He kept going, saying, "Len! Where are you, Len?"

She hadn't answered him. She was no longer there. She'd had a gun; she'd shot her way out. She'd be looking for him at the rear door. He was a fool. He should have stayed there like he'd agreed.

Men were in front of him. He heard the breed shout, "It's him! It's the Irishman."

He charged, swinging the gun, hurling men from his way. He found the door. He knew his way now. There was an intervening room, then the kitchen.

Men were on his heels. He flung the kitchen door shut, grabbed the table, hurled it agianst the door. It stopped them for a couple of seconds. The stove was there, at his right. He overturned it. It smashed down across the table, spilling fire. It put them in retreat.

Outside, he stopped. "Len!"

She didn't answer him. He skirted the storm shed, shouting, "Len, Len! Where are you?"

A short, heavyset man was on the run around the house. He drew up, bellowed, "There he is!" and lifting the carbine rifle in his hands, fired.

Ryan had pivoted, dived to one side. He felt the wind-whip of lead past his shoulder. His .38 answered in the same fraction of time. The bullet hit. It smashed the heavyset man backward. He dropped his rifle. He reeled for three steps with both arms wrapped around his middle, then he caught himself and took a step forward over crumpling knees and fell face forward to the ground.

Ryan saw it in a glance as he returned gunfire from another direction. He kept firing, moving along in the shadow of the pole eave. His gun clicked empty.

He ran across open ground with bullets from two directions churning the dirt back of his heels, reached the placer trench, dived face foremost into its protection.

He reloaded the gun, untangled himself from brush, moved in a direction that would bring him closer to the dog pens.

His rifle was back there. He wanted to get it.

Men were coming around in two directions, trying to pin him down, but the .38 reached out well, and none of them risked suicide by getting close.

The house was in flames now. Light from the fire, and light from approaching sunrise, made them still more wary.

No bullet had been close for five minutes now. Ryan risked showing himself. He walked to the rear of the dog sheds, found his bedroll and rifle.

He cupped his hands and called, "Len!" knowing he'd get no answer.

He'd seen nothing of her. Heard nothing of her since those shots in the house.

Flames were rolling both ways through the house now, and

a thought occured to him that made him sick. She wasn't in there. She'd gotten out. He kept telling himself that she'd gotten out.

The fight had left him groggy. He didn't know which way to turn. It was quite light now. The rising sun made a rusty yellow flare on the horizon. He walked across to her cabin.

No one was there. His eyes roved the town. Everything seemed to be peaceful. Smoke rose from a couple of cabin chimneys.

He started toward the nearest house. He should have expected to be met with gunfire. He didn't. The night just past seemed like a bad dream.

He could see a man, crouched over, watching his approach through an open window. When he reached the door, the man had moved back and picked up a gun.

"Put it down," Ryan said. "I have no fight with you."

He walked in and sat down. The man's squaw was frying pancakes. Ryan helped himself to a plateful and started to eat.

The man, a short, dirty, middle-aged fellow, laughed and put the rifle down. "You sure got your guts."

He asked around a mouth filled with pancakes, "Where'd he go? Battles?"

"How in hell would I know? I don't keep track of Battles."

"Where's the girl."

"I don't keep track of her, neither." He looked over at his ugly Siwash squaw. "Not that I'd mind the job."

"You might as well tell me."

"Or what?" He picked up the gun again. "You got some ideas of getting rough?"

"I seen enough rough stuff for one day."

"You in on all that shooting?"

"I was sort of on the edge of it."

"You the one that killed Dunhill?"

"I don't know. How many were killed?" He started to rise. "Was there a body inside the house?"

"Just Shorty's." He laughed. "Shot in the back, so you see what way he was headed."

Ryan was unable to get more information from him. He decided that Battles had left the camp. He'd left during the fight and taken the girl with him.

The girl had mentioned Nulato Bob, the boat builder. He walked to the sagging riverhouse where a single skin oomiyak was tied. He could remember looking down from the heights and seeing a canoe there the evening before.

A broad, very bowlegged Siwash half-breed was inside the cavelike living quarters, peering at him.

"Where's Battles?"

The man didn't answer.

Ryan went inside, followed him as he backed across the room. He shouted, "Where's Battles?"

"No savvy."

"You savvy all right. Where's Battles and the girl?"

The breed shook his head violently and kept repeating, "No savvy." He backed up until a table stopped him. He tried to get around it. Ryan's right hand shot out, grabbing him by his grease-blackened buckskin shirt.

Ryan jerked him back and forth until his hat flew off and his long hair strung across his face. His mouth was open and spittle ran from the corners.

"Talk! You savvy all right. Where are they? Talk! Talk!"

"Sure. Me savvy now. Me savvy good."

"They took the canoe?"

"Yes."

"Where'd they go?"

"Downriver. I don't know. They don't tell me. They—"

"Who was with them? Battles, the girl, and who else?"

"Just half-breed. Just Steve. Just three."

Ryan bent his spine over the table until he gasped, and then he bent it a little more. "You know what I'll do if you're lying? I'll come back here and break you in half."

"No, I talk true!" he gasped. "I talk true as hell!"

VI

He had no choice but to take the oomiyak.

The oomiyak was made of skin stretched over a birch frame. Made to carry as many as five men, it was buoyant, but cumbersome.

The current took him swiftly, he turned a bend, and left the town behind. The placer diggings played out. He was in a wilderness of scabby hills and jackpine.

A large stream flowed in from the west. It doubled the river's volume, but its width narrowed. It ran deep and swift between walls of rusty black basalt.

This was the Ophir River. Ever since coming to the country he'd heard white-water men talking about the Ophir, naming its course from Mucker Hill to Yukon Flats the swiftest fifty miles in the North. Certain names came back to him—the Tom Hall Chutes, Big Six Rapids, and Hell's Skidway. Lots of canoe men bragged that they'd shot the Hell's Skidway, but it was something a man did only once, to prove himself, like a Cree lad winning his eagle feather.

The sun rose hot on his back. An hour passed, and the current had carried him far downstream.

The valley narrowed. Ahead of him the stream was pinched down to a third of its former width. He kept the oomiyak in midstream and took the plunge without incident. Below were choppy rapids with the stream cut into many channels.

He rode between sheer-sided islands of stone; boat-shaped islands with gnarled little pine trees growing on their tops. The channel was so narrow he could have reached his canoe paddle and touched the stone on either side.

There was a pocket among the hills with gulches fanning out in all directions. The bottoms were filled with cottonwoods. A cow moose waded and stopped to look at him.

He took a wide sweep of the river, noticed a canoe-float toward the right bank, a tiny cabin on the rock bank beyond.

He kept going with the current pulling his oomiyak faster and faster. He spotted a portage trail along the basaltic bluffs to his right. Too late he realized that he'd stumbled into the headwaters of Hell's Skidway.

The river was quiet. Its current made glassy swells, dipped and swelled again. It slid at a half-mile-a-minute rate along the smooth-worn bottom. Ahead, through rising mist, he could hear the deep boom of water torn to froth by crags and waterfall.

He felt a slight lurch as the boat speeded. It was still smooth. Looking at the water, he had the impression of standing still. It was only on glancing at the canyon walls that he realized how swiftly the current was carrying him.

Spray met him with a sudden wave. The boat lurched and creaked. For blind seconds it seemed that the craft had crumpled under the impact of crosscurrents. Then, through spray, he saw the prow still at the correct angle, sinking, dipping water, rising, dipping again.

He battled to keep it lined with the current. A crag split the channel ahead. To his left lay the broader half of the river, apparently without obstruction. To his right it was funnelled down through a narrow chute.

He fought to swing away from the chute. For a few seconds he seemed to be winning, but a swerve of the current seized the craft, and all his paddling had been futile.

He didn't struggle further. He sat back knowing the river would do what it wanted with him. Its power was too vast.

For a quarter-minute—a quarter-mile—vertical rock walls closed the channel in. He burst in the clear. He saw then that the channel he'd fought to attain was cut to churning froth by a thousand crags that rose from the bottom. They would have swamped the oomiyak, cutting it to ribbons, but luck, in spite of all his efforts, had guided him the way of safety.

There was still a long stretch of rapids ahead, but he was able to maneuver them, and he saw on shore the lower terminus of the portage trail.

He looked for Battles and the girl. No sign of them. He wondered if they, too, had shot the rapids. If not, if they'd taken the portage, he'd been able to obliterate the hour's head start they had from Mucker.

He crossed choppy water, cleared a gravelly point, shot more rapids. They seemed like nothing after Hell's Skidway.

A bullet tore splinters from the front gunwale and whipped past his shoulder. The crack and echo of a high-power rifle smacked down close atop it.

He instinctively went to the bottom of the oomiyak. The craft had shipped six inches of water, and his rifle was somewhere under the surface. He groped, found it, poured water from the barrel.

They were ahead of him less than three hundred yards. Two men, a canoe. It made him go gutless and sick. For a second he feared she had died in the fire; that the men back in Mucker had lied to him. Then he saw her, seated on the bottom, lying back, evidently with elbows bound to the canoe's center seat.

A second bullet shot up a spurt of water a couple yards to his right.

Battles was in the prow, firing at him. The tall breed was in the stern, maneuvering the canoe.

He dropped the gun. He cursed them for hiding behind a woman.

He had no chance in an open chase. They'd kill him without his daring to fire a shot back. His only chance was to get out of range, and follow them until luck gave him an opening.

He swung the oomiyak toward shore. The third bullet skipped water and tore a hole through both sides at the waterline. Battles was firing as fast as he could lever the rifle. The river geysered through from a dozen places. Ryan could feel the craft lose buoyancy. Crouched in the bottom, water rolled midway of his thighs. The craft listed slowly. He tried desperately to compensate with his own weight, but it kept going, water gurgling over the side, and capsized.

He was over his head in the stream. He was being carried with the gray white river all around him. He lost all sense of direction, of up and down. Then, without knowing how it happened, he was on his feet, balanced against the current, wading waist-deep over the rock-slippery bottom toward shore.

He rested and coughed water from his lungs. There was no longer any sign of the canoe.

He felt for his gun. The holster was empty. He was unarmed except for the hunting knife at his belt.

He walked for hours, following the shore where he could, leaving it when the river passed through canyon walls, returning, watching for the canoe. The sun grew hot and dried his clothes; it sank and a cold wind sprang up. The hills played out, the river meandered off into the Yukon flats.

This was barren country, muskeg country, cottonwood and brush country. He climbed a tree, saw the river tracings for miles until it bent westward to join the mighty Yukon, but no canoe.

In half a mile he was startled by a voice from willows near the water's edge. It was Steve, the half breed.

"Ryan, you come. Good Injun hurt bad."

He stopped, drew his hunting knife. The thought of ambush was in his mind but he dismissed it. The breed was no more than fifty steps away, short enough range for any ambush.

"What are you doing here?"

"Hurt—bad. Bullet, you savvy?"

"Where's Battles and the girl?"

Steve cursed until his voice played out, naming Battles every vile word in English and the coastal jargons. He was still cursing when Ryan worked through the tangle of brush and found him.

He was lying on his back, his shirt was open to the waist, a bloody bandage was twisted around his chest.

"Who got you? Battles?"

"Stray bullet. Cabin. I don't know. He shoot Shorty by mistake, maybe me, too. I think—just scratch. You savvy?" He had to lie still to get the strength to go on. "So, I come with them. But all the time in canoe it bleed. I ask for rest, *no you carry the long portage.* I ask for sleep in bottom of canoe, *no you swing the paddle.* Pretty soon I think I die. He kick me overboard. He think I drown." Steve showed his long, yellowish teeth in a grin. "But I die hard, you savvy?"

"How long you been here?"

"I don't know. Maybe he get to beeg river already, maybe not."

"You got a gun?"

"Just knife. You want to kill heem, take knife?"

"I already got a knife."

Ryan took time to look at the wound. The bullet had gone through, breaking some ribs. Perhaps it had nicked a lung.

"Cough any blood?"

"Leetle."

He bandaged it, using dry moss on the wound openings. Then he stood and said, "I'll come back."

Steve struggled to sit up, "Never. He keel you. He—"

"I die hard, too. I'll come back."

He ran now, forgetting the fatigue that had steadily deadened his muscles. He ran for a mile, walked a hundred yards, ran again. A high-water creek lay in front of him. He waded it, moccasins deep in the mucky bottom, water to his armpits. He kept going across tundra and muskeg, through brush and cottonwood.

He cut across a wide bend of the river, and was reapproaching its cutbank shore, when a girl's scream shattered the evening quiet.

Len! He heard a muttered, guttural word from Battles, a thud and crash like a sudden, brief struggle.

He'd gone to one knee in the cover of scab brush, now he edged on, found better concealment in brush saplings.

He wasn't certain which direction the sounds had came from. The river was only thirty or forty steps away, and the distance had been greater than that. He moved swiftly, skirting the brush, for a hundred yards. Ahead of him lay a high-water channel as yet not reached by spring flood, filled with a low growth of saplings and brush.

He glimpsed a flash of scarlet—the canoe. There was movement, a muffled, gasping cry from the girl.

A gun exploded as he took his first step down the bank.

It came from point-blank range. The bullet hit him. It spun him off his feet. He felt no pain. He seemed to be floating. Shock left a high, ringing sound in his ears.

The bullet had turned him halfway around. He fell headfirst down the slope, slid with his left arm outflung, was stopped by a dense tangle of rose thorns.

The thorns hid him momentarily and saved his life.

Battles fired blind through the brush. The slug tore damp earth by Ryan's head.

Acting on instinct, he rolled to his feet, dived headlong through the bushes, and Battles was right below.

Battles tried to lever a third cartridge into his rifle, to bring the muzzle around. Ryan thrust the barrel high. The hunting knife was in his right hand. He swung it in a terrific horizontal arc.

Battles, staggering back, escaped the knife. Its point, grabbing his mackinaw, twisted over and flew from Ryan's hand.

Ryan had recovered somewhat from shock. He knew better than to bend over for the knife. He continued his charge, trying to keep the big man off balance.

Battles got a foothold and pivoted. With a swing of his body he pulled the rifle free. He stood at his full height, feet set wide, the gun gripped in both hands and drove its steel-shod butt down toward Ryan's skull.

It would have crushed his skull like a dry mushroom. He

saw Ryan drop and thought that had happened. He laughed with a wild shout and cried, "So you caught me—for *this!*"

With the word *this* he drove the gun butt again, but Ryan had taken the first blow glancing off his neck and shoulder, and as the second came, he grappled with arms around Battles's thick thighs.

The second blow missed. He carried Battles staggering backward. He got his footing. He stood, lifting the big man in his arms. Battles tried to use the gun and failed. He let it fall, and swung his fists. Ryan carried him, running, and fell with him, flinging him head foremost to the sharp rocks at the edge of the river.

Battles picked himself up. The saw edge of a rock had sliced his right ear until it hung by a ribbon down the side of his neck.

The fall had left Battles groggy. He felt for his ear, knew what had happened. It infuriated him. He charged and was met by a left and right. He went down like one hit by a sledge.

He got up. He took another left and right. His head rolled. His loose jaw sagged, his eyes stared without seeing. He went down again and again. He ended on his face in knee-deep water.

Ryan watched the milky river roll over him for a few seconds and started forward to pull him out, but the big man had a brute's endurance. He got to his feet with a dripping, rectangular chunk of rock in his hands. He tried to lift it, drive it down on Ryan's skull, but his feet slipped from under him. The rock tangled itself inside the front of his shirt. He got up. Its weight carried him off balance. He was waist-deep. He fell, got up. The stone was no longer there, but the river current and its slick rock and mud baffled him. He floundered deep, lashing the water to a froth as the under-tow grabbed him.

He was gone, and the river was very quiet. A big stream, a

deep stream, flowing between muskeg banks to Yukon, to
Norton Sound, to the Bering Sea.

Ryan noticed that the left arm of his mackinaw was heavy
from blood. He climbed the bank and saw Len, fighting
herself free from some babiche thongs that held her wrists
to a cottonwood sapling. A strip of cloth had been wound
tightly around her mouth as a gag.

He found his knife on the ground, cut her free.

"You're wounded," were the first words she said. "Take off
your mackinaw."

He didn't seem to hear. He took her by the arms, just
below her shoulders, helped her to stand.

"Len! I never thought I'd see you again."

"Take off your mackinaw." She got free of him, grabbed
the front of his mackinaw, pulled it open. "Now lie down
before you bleed to death."

He watched her cut the sleeve of his shirt off, revealing the
bullet wound, and work swiftly staunching the flow of blood.

"It missed the vein by half an inch. You were lucky."

"That's the luck of the Ryans. Never good judgment, but
just plain luck that always carried the Ryans through."

"You weren't lucky about one thing."

"What's that, girl?"

She tilted her head at the river. "He had the girdle."

He'd almost forgotten about the girdle. "I'm shedding no
tears, girl. I was rich once, and I want no part of it again. It
was by the merest good fortune that I lived through it.
Champagne! How my stomach grows ill at first thought of
the stuff."

She had finished with the bandage. He noticed that quite
by accident his hand rested on hers. He took her hand, and
gripped it quite hard. She made no effort to free herself.
Seated on the ground, she smiled and waited, her dark eyes
watching him, her lips slightly parted.